Bangkok Changes

An NJA Club Novel

Book Four

Stephen Shaiken

Crosswinds Press

Published by Crosswinds Press

Visit Stephen Shaiken's website at www.stephenshaiken.com
Sign up for his e-mail newsletter: Click here to receive Stephen's newsletters
Follow Stephen Shaiken on Twitter: https://twitter.com/StephenShaiken

First Edition: February 2023
ISBN: 978-1-7321474-9-2

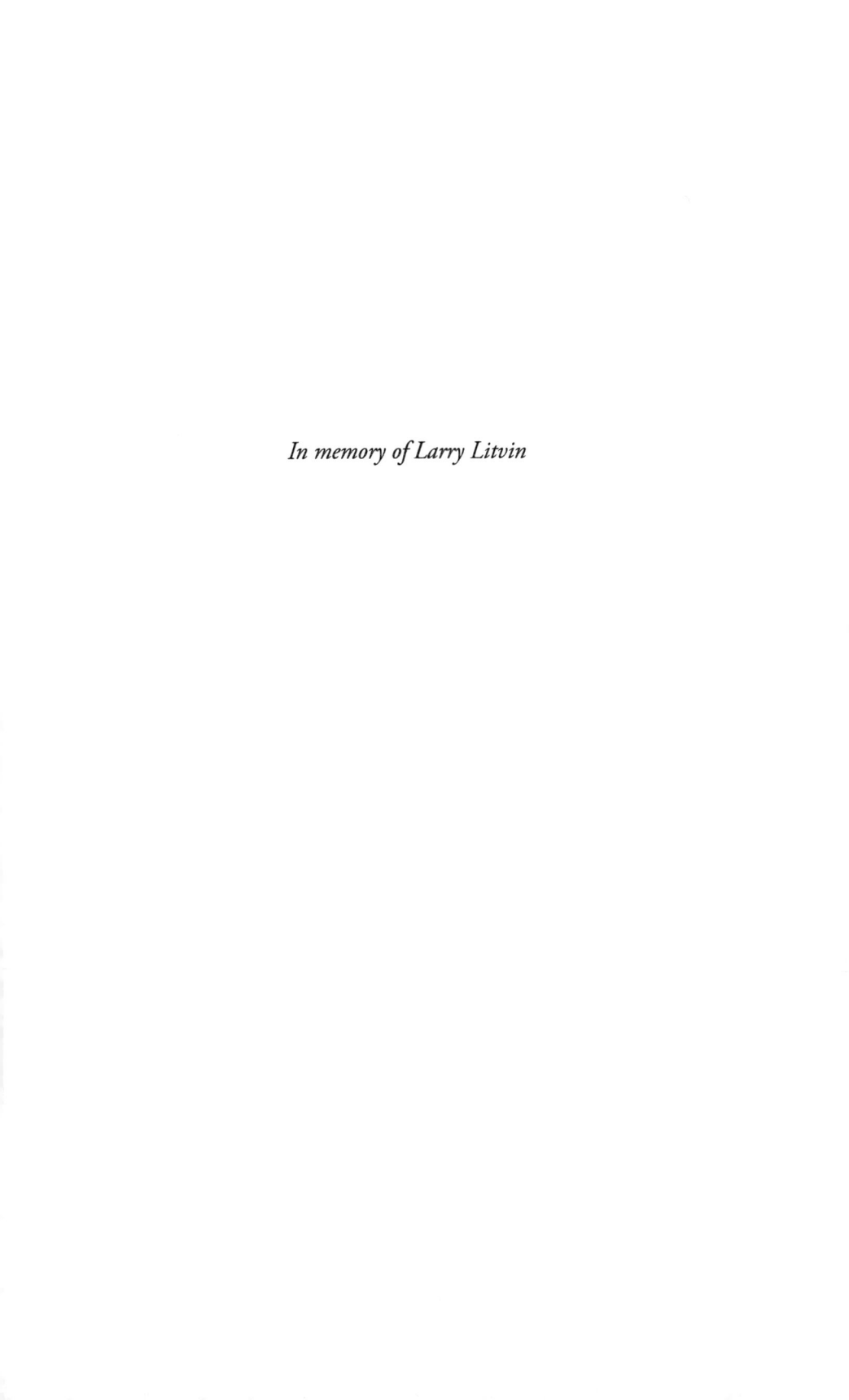

In memory of Larry Litvin

Contents

ONE

Sleepy Joe and the General lounged comfortably in the rear of the General's black Mercedes Benz GLS 450 as the skyline of Bangkok reflected the afternoon sun. The 2019 model was the largest SUV Mercedes ever offered, and the General intended to keep it running as long as possible. Bank, his driver and bodyguard, and Ang, the second bodyguard, sat in the captains' seats in front. The front and rear were separated by clear, bulletproof glass. When the General wished to speak to Bank or Ang, he used an intercom system, which also allowed him to listen in on the front but not the reverse.

The General wore a gray, tropical-weight wool suit ordered online from Brooks Brothers, the veritable American clothier. His good friend, Glenn Murray Cohen, recommended the style, and in the General's opinion, Glenn, once a successful criminal lawyer in San Francisco, knew everything there was to know about suits.

"It's a steal at half price," Glenn advised. "Have your tailor send your measurements, and if it needs any adjustment, it can be done here."

Sleepy Joe wore a Grateful Dead t-shirt and a pair of Levi's jeans beginning to shred at the knees. Glenn, his very best friend, often pleaded with him to throw out such clothing and buy nice new shirts and pants in bargain-basement Bangkok. Sleepy Joe declined the advice.

"Those men walking three abreast have been up to no good," the General said as the SUV crawled along in afternoon traffic. It slowed almost to a stop when they were a few meters behind three large men walking along busy Sukhumvit Road, in the heart of the tourist-centric Green Belt area of Bangkok. The government had gradually released the city from the COVID-mandate lockdown; first there was limited dining and entertainment, but everything was now open, and masks were voluntary as of the week before, though most Thais continued to wear them in public. People could once again roam the streets at will, shop with no abandon, and dine in those restaurants that survived a year and a half of graveyard-like existence. Thais and *farangs* alike were no longer limited to take-out or delivery, and could buy street food, visit friends, dine in restaurants, see their doctors and dentists, get haircuts, massages, manicures, and pedicures. Foreigners could now enter Thailand simply by showing proof of vaccination; gone were the days of quarantine, testing and reporting results.

People once again saw each other's faces. They removed their voluntary masks when eating, singing, chanting, exercising, and for the most part, in cinemas, comedy clubs and music venues. The famous Thai smiles were again on display, though Sleepy Joe claimed they were less in number and not as wide as before the pandemic. He and Glenn had discussed this the day before and concluded that once tourists returned with their money, the economy would improve, and the smiles would stretch out as before.

The SUV slowed as much as possible when it was to the left of the men on the sidewalk, only a meter or so from the curb. The General explained his interest in them to Sleepy Joe.

"They're probably on their way to threaten some bar or restaurant owner. Force him to buy their booze. Thais, farangs, they go after anyone. I'm pretty sure they killed a bar owner in Thong Lor who told them to get out of his place. I hear there are witnesses, but so far no arrests. Not enough evidence for the police to arrest anyone, but more than enough for us to put an end to this."

This is Thailand, Joe thought. *Maybe the dead man wasn't paying the cops either.*

"There is more," the General said. "They had the nerve to approach Wang," referring to the owner and cook at the NJA Club, the favorite haunt of the General, Joe and Glenn. "Followed him when he was leaving one night. He could have killed all three of them, I'm sure, even at his age. He was the best soldier I ever commanded. Instead, he told them to inform whoever sent them that he and his club are protected by me. This message didn't get through to them because they called him at home to remind him they were expecting an answer. He hung up and dialed me. We got a picture of them from a surveillance camera they didn't know about in one of the places they tried to force into becoming a customer. Wang identified them, so we know we're following the right people. I am sending you out to give them a warning for whoever hired them, and it's the only one they get. I'm not relying on the police. They'd probably rely on me to fix it anyway."

"What's the warning I am to give?" Sleepy Joe asked.

"Leave town. In fact, leave the country. Let their bosses find some other place to be big men."

"Just a warning, General?" Sleepy Joe asked. "Nothing more?"

The General thought for a moment. He knew these thugs would not shed much light on who was behind the scheme. The General knew criminal organizations had many layers between the top and the bottom. This had the aura of a foreign gang, and the few people with whom he consulted - his friend Oliver, the information maven; the Lieutenant, his best contact within the police; and his connections in military intelligence - were using their resources to figure out exactly who was behind the scheme. He already had his contacts in all branches of law enforcement looking for any foreign mobster entering Thailand in the last six months. Oliver told the General not to be too optimistic; organized crime the world over had ways of hiding who they were, starting with passports in different names. The General didn't care about passport fraud. Right now, all the General wanted was for Joe to scare these men away and have them pass the message to their higher-ups. Perhaps nothing more would be necessary

"As always, Joe, you have the discretion to respond as the situation requires. You didn't spend all that time as a soldier with the Australian Special Forces and not learn how to handle yourself when things get rough. That's why I pay you. I hope there is no need for violence by either side. Get out, follow them, get their attention when they can't get away from you, and deliver the message. Hopefully, when you tell them you're speaking for me, and I'm angry they didn't listen to Wang, which will end the problem. Even fools can be educated about the General."

"They might come to know and still remain fools," Sleepy Joe replied as the SUV came to a halt twenty meters behind the three men. Sleepy Joe opened the door closest to the curb and left the SUV without a word.

Quicker I get this done, quicker I can get stoned, he thought.

The big men strolled along Sukhumvit Road three abreast, taking up most of the sidewalk. Pedestrians, Thai and farang, stepped aside to let them pass. When the big Thai man on the left of the trio bumped against a table laden with sunglasses, a rack fell over and clattered to the ground. The middle-aged Thai woman standing behind the table came forward and yelled out in English, assuming a foreigner had accidentally bumped the table. She held several pairs of broken sunglasses.

"You wait. Anything broke, you pay!"

The big man laughed and screamed a reply in Thai. The woman stepped back when she saw him. He stopped in front of a pile of unbroken sunglasses and stomped on them. Sleepy Joe heard the breaking of plastic. He heard the big Thai man say something in their language to the woman. She looked down, went back behind the table and remained silent.

"What did he say?" Sleepy Joe asked a young Thai woman with her older farang boyfriend standing to his side.

"He told her to shut up or she will also be broken," the young woman said with anger in her voice. Sleepy Joe felt heat rising inside himself, which happened when he was angry.

~

Sleepy Joe made no attempt to conceal himself from the men. He maintained a distance of only ten feet behind them, scurrying past pedestrians, pushing them aside if they obstructed his path. One of the farang tourists Joe banged into yelled at him, and the three men he was following turned to see the ruckus. One spoke to Sleepy Joe. He looked Asian, but not Thai.

"I saw you get out of a car a few minutes ago, right where we were walking. Why are you following us?" His English was grammatically correct, delivered in a strangely familiar accent.

Sleepy Joe smiled at the big man but said nothing. *I didn't see anyone turning around when I left the car,* he thought. *Do they have watchers on the street or eyes in the back of their heads?*

"Maybe he doesn't speak English," the big Asian man of unknown origin said to his equally large companions.

"Or maybe he burned out his brain with drugs," the huge white man muttered in English. The accent was Russian, no doubt. Russians could often speak English but almost never spoke Thai. His short-sleeved black shirt was pulled tightly over his muscular chest and biceps.

"Perhaps he'll understand this," the big non-Thai Asian replied. He pointed a finger at himself, then at Sleepy Joe, shook his head, and ran his finger across his throat.

Sleepy Joe kept smiling and said nothing. He knew he had seen people like this man but couldn't recall where.

"You got it right," the Russian said. "Looks like one more burnt-out old hippie who landed in Bangkok and never figured out how to leave."

His two companions nodded. The white man pulled a red hundred baht note from his pocket and threw it on the ground at Sleepy Joe's feet.

"Go buy yourself a decent meal, or a fix," he said. "Now you can stop following us." The three men turned their backs on Sleepy Joe and walked on, laughing at the poor muddled fool behind them.

~

The three men had their backs pressed against the wall of a building as they stared down Sleepy Joe, who had followed them off Sukhumvit Road, onto a side soi, then into this blind alley dead end at the rear of a large office building. Joe turned his head ever so slightly as he gauged the situation.

"You were warned to mind your own business," said the big Asian man with the familiar accent. Barely two minutes had passed since Joe left the General's SUV.

Joe then remembered why he recognized the Asian man's accent. The man's features, size, and the way he spoke English made clear he was one of many behemoth immigrants to his homeland from countries his mate Oliver referred to as "those lazy Pacific nations sucking money out of Australia." *Samoan or Tongan,* Joe thought. Joe met many of these island people when in Australia. *Now that I see him, pretty sure he's a Samoan. Big and fat enough. I'm not prejudiced like I was back then. Being best friends with an American liberal like Glenn softened me up. Maybe not towards this one,* he thought.

Joe made the ugly looking Russian as the trio's leader by the glances he threw the other two. *Wonder what a Russian gangster like this is doing away from Pattaya?* There were a handful of them in Bangkok, and Sleepy Joe and the General thought they knew them all. This one was a stranger.

The large Thai who terrorized the sunglass lady faced Joe with a menacing look but said nothing and didn't move a muscle. Joe decided he was there because he spoke the language and knew his way around the city. Sleepy Joe recognized in him a man right at home in a back alley brawl.

Farang tough guy backed up by some local muscle, Sleepy Joe calculated. *All the same to me.*

"Are you trying to intimidate me?" Joe asked. The three men exchanged glances.

"So, you know how to speak, and in English," the Russian said.

"Answer my question," Sleepy Joe replied.

"That depends. You were told to stop following us. Perhaps you didn't understand, since you didn't stop. You're not a very good tail because we made you right away."

Sleepy Joe moved within three feet of the men and stared at the Russian.

"Maybe I didn't care if you made me. Maybe I'm thinking if there's trouble, none of you are going to be around to tell anyone about this little meeting."

The Russian laughed.

"Even if your dream came true, you wouldn't live long enough to tell anyone," he said. "If you don't have the good sense to fear us, you should certainly fear our employers."

"So, you mean I'm dealing with the hired help?" Sleepy Joe asked. "The kind of people who are easily replaced and won't be missed by anyone?"

"Right now, the only thing missing is the point you're not getting," the big Russian said. "Hopefully, I can make you understand, and you can pass it on. Our employers are businessmen with no interest in fighting anyone. We are merely salesmen who offer their liquor to potential buyers. Perhaps our sales pitches are sometimes aggressive, as you'll find in every business, but we offer good prices. I have no idea why you or whoever sent you cares about this, but whatever their reason, it's time to stop. I offer you one last chance to turn around and go back to your superiors and let them know that allowing you to leave us alive is an act of grace."

"And assuming I say no?" Sleepy Joe asked.

The big Russian shook his head, and then, as if choreographed, the other two did the same.

"In that case, we'd have to kill you right here and now," the Russian replied. "Which is a shame, because despite your lack of professionalism, I admire your pluck, and killing a little man like you is like shooting fish in a barrel."

Interesting that he knows an American slang term, Joe thought. *I learned it from Glenn.*

"Are you guys serious?" Sleepy Joe asked. "Threatening me with only three of you? Maybe you ought to take my warning seriously," he said. Without waiting for the three men to agree, Joe kept talking.

"I wasn't following you in secret. I was sent to warn you to stop shaking down bars and restaurants to buy your booze. This is a one-off, no more warnings. Every place in town has its own supplier, including the NJA Club. Bangkok's just getting back on its feet and doesn't need guys like you destroying long time businesses. The NJA Club is a favorite of the General and I work for him. If you don't know of him, you need a new line of work. Stop trying to make Wang or anyone else buy your booze. Don't even come by the NJA Club for a drink; just stay away. In fact, tell your bosses to stay away from this city and this country. You won't be able to threaten your way to success for them like you have in the past. The General can have you killed any time he wants. Consider it an act of mercy that he did not ask me to do that today. As for whoever was dumb enough to hire you three, if they are not Thai, I really urge you tell them to leave the country. If they are Thai, they'll know not to anger the General. I've delivered his warning and it's the only one you get."

The Russian spit on the ground.

"Tell this General to take his mercy and shove it up his ass," the Russian said.

Sleepy Joe took a step closer. The top of his head barely reached the Russian's shoulders, and he didn't stack up much better against the Samoan or Thai.

"For a Russian who speaks English so well, that remark is beneath you," Joe said.

"I told you the General didn't ask me to kill you," Joe continued. "He never said I couldn't kill you if I wanted. Like you killed that poor guy who wouldn't buy from you. Or like your flunky might have killed that poor lady trying to make a living selling sunglasses. Do you have any idea how long she was unable to sell anything because we were locked down? That's why I'm adding a new requirement not given by the General. It's coming directly from me. You three never again bother a decent working person in Bangkok, for anyone, anytime."

The Russian began to laugh and turned his head slightly to his right. Joe saw in the Pacific Islander's eyes an understanding he was to join the Russian and attack Joe. Their one-second exchange of glances was enough time for Sleepy Joe's foot to strike the left side of the

Russian's head and drive it into the brick wall. His skull hit the wall with a sound Joe loved, somewhere between a crack and a crunch. Joe pivoted towards the Pacific Islander in the middle as the big man lunged right at him. Joe interlaced his fingers, palm facing the big Samoan, and shoved it into his neck, pushing back forcefully until he heard the snap, another favorite sound. The Pacific Islander slumped to the ground.

The large muscular Thai, the last one standing, reached into his waistband and withdrew a knife from a scabbard hidden by the shirt overlapping his waist. He pointed it out towards the Australian. The blade was at least six inches, and the sharp edge was up.

He knows how to use a knife, Sleepy Joe thought as the big man moved towards him slowly, a few centimeters at a time.

Been trained to cut upward. He heard the voice of his own military trainer, the sergeant who turned him from a lazy bum into a member of the Australian Special Forces.

If a knife is pointed at you, stay far enough away from the attacker to avoid contact with the blade but close enough to use your feet. You have to find that sweet spot where you can kick the wrist or hand and drive the knife into them.

When the tip of the blade was less than a foot from his chest, Sleepy Joe swung his left leg shoulder-high and forward, striking the right wrist of the big Thai. The force of the kick turned the wrist so the blade pointed at the Thai's throat and drove it forward and into the soft flesh of the neck. Blood started to seep from the cut and the man gurgled like a fish out of water. The Thai instinctively put his other hand on the hilt and started to pull the knife out.

"Don't do that, it'll make you bleed out faster," Joe said. "Throw me your cell phone and I'll call an ambulance. You have a chance of surviving if they get here fast enough." The man kept slumping downward. When his butt hit the ground the Australian shook his head,

"Too late, Well, I tried."

The Russian had fallen face forward on the ground. Blood poured from the back of his head. The Australian rolled him over with a foot. The Russian's eyes were as wide open as his mouth, as if he were trying to say something at the moment of death. The Thai sat propped against the wall, the front of his body soaked in bright red blood. The handle of the knife protruded from his neck. It propped up his head and kept it from falling onto the bloody chest. There was no need to check on the Pacific Islander; the snap announced his demise. He lay on the ground with his head at an impossible angle.

Joe saw that blood had gotten onto his sneakers. The light gray canvas was splotched with raisin-sized spots of red. He glanced at the dead Russian's feet, encased in a pair of expensive Italian loafers. Not footwear exactly in conformity with Joe's worn jeans and a rumpled t shirt, but better than a bloody calling card leaving footprints as he walked away. He took off his sneakers, then slipped the loafers off the dead Russian and stepped into them. They were a little loose. He saw the Russians' socks were thick cotton. He slipped out of the loafers, pulled the Russian's socks over his own, and stepped back into the dead man's shoes. *A little loose, but they'll do. I bet these shoes impress Glenn.* Then he turned back.

I forgot to check for weapons. The General pays well for any weapons that can't be traced back to him. He frisked each body and found a Glock in the Russian's waistband and a .365 strapped to the Pacific Islander's ankle. The poor Thai had been armed only with the knife that killed him. The General would give him a bonus of ten thousand baht for the Glock and half that for the smaller gun.

When he was going through the Russian's pants pockets, he felt a wad of what he suspected were baht notes. He pulled it out and thumbed through the notes. They were all the thousand baht denomination, at least fifty of them. *Walking around money for a Russian gangster in Thailand,* Sleepy Joe thought disdainfully. He stuffed the wad into the right front pocket of his jeans – he deserved his own walking around money.

There was a storm drain twenty meters away. The clouds above told Joe it would soon rain and anything in that drain would be swept away. He dropped the sneakers through the drain slot at the curb.

Not a bad tip, he told himself as he walked away in his fancy new shoes.

When Sleepy Joe reached Sukhumvit Road, he turned toward where he had been dropped off by the General. He stopped in front of the sunglass lady's table. She sat behind her display of remaining sellable goods, a sad look on her face. Joe saw a pile of broken glasses at her feet.

Joe studied the rack of glasses for a few seconds and then grabbed one, a pair of oversized sunglasses so dark one's eyes could not be seen when wearing them.

"*Tao rai?*" he asked the woman, using two of the handful of Thai words he knew.

"Two hundred baht," she answered in English.

Joe nodded in approval and reached into his pocket for the money he'd taken from the Russian.

"Keep the change," he said, dropping the wad on her table and then walking away.

Ten minutes later, Joe reached the nearest BTS station and rode the Skytrain to the Phrom Phong stop nearest the NJA Club, where he made a call.

"I'm on my way over," he said as soon as Glenn answered. "We'll grab a spot of lunch and then we can head to your place for an afternoon of music, movies, and weed. How's that sound, mate?"

"Get over here as fast as you can," Glenn said.

Two

Bangkok unlocked as quickly and unexpectedly as it had locked down. Two years of cocoon-like existence left a trail of shuttered businesses. Essential services were once again available without making a reservation well in advance, but many of Glenn Murray Cohen's favorite music venues and restaurants had disappeared forever. Glenn welcomed the reemergence of the Bangkok he loved for thirteen years before COVID slammed the country like a once-a-century monsoon. *New places will open soon,* he convinced himself.

Thailand kept infections and deaths to a fraction of the West's by strict adherence to masking, social distancing and banning large crowds. Thais willingly vaccinated as soon as they could. Thai reverence for life and a long tradition of unquestionably obeying the government resulted in compliance. People who would have died in the West lived. Despite this rational behavior, the Southeast Asian nation was less capable of withstanding the economic devastation brought by the pandemic. Businesses closed in droves, many never to reopen, as tourists evaporated like the morning dew. Glenn understood that no matter how many silver linings he envisioned, the cloud of COVID would not easily be burned away, and hung over the city like a gauze curtain, filtering out the full light of economic prosperity.

Among the more notable silver linings Glenn found after the year and a half shutdown was the cleanest air he had seen in all his time in Bangkok. His Australian friend, Oliver, reported that the beaches and waters of Koh Phangan and other islands similarly benefitted by the pause, not to mention the marine life. There was almost never a wait at reopened establishments, a plum Glenn hoped to enjoy as long as it lasted. *I'll do my share to help the economy,* he thought with a smile.

In truth, the lockdown never affected Glenn and the other NJA regulars as it did the rest of Bangkok. The Club remained open every single day of the lockdown, if "open" is defined as admission of a select few members, under secure precautions. The General decided these sorts of things, and he wasn't going to surrender his prized redoubt to a microscopic virus.

"I didn't let the commies stop me in the late seventies, and I'm not letting COVID stop me in the two thousand twenties," he explained after the strictest lockdown was announced in the middle of 2021. When the retired military man spoke with Glenn about the war against the guerrillas in the late 1970's, it conjured images of a younger officer running through the forests of Isan with an assault rifle in his arms, looking for any stray communist. Hours after the government declared a nationwide club lockdown, the General called Glenn to inform him the rules wouldn't apply to the NJA Club. Select regulars went around to the back alley and knocked on the rear door with a designated pattern. Wang checked them out on camera and if he recognized the knocker, he'd buzz them in. Otherwise, the NJA Club was just another closed business.

Besides Glenn and the General, the anointed ones included Glenn's best friend Sleepy Joe, and Oliver, Joe's fellow Australian, a large, cocky information-expert. Several of the General's old military friends were granted the privilege of entry as was Edward, a native of Wales and a former tax auditor in the United Kingdom. Glenn could not fathom why Edward was treated so well. Edward rubbed Glenn the wrong way as he considered the Welshman weak and untrustworthy. On more than one occasion, Edward had provided information to people looking to hurt Glenn and his friends. Despite Edward's protestations, Glenn did not believe it was completely unintentional, especially when there was money involved.

"He's of some use to the General or he wouldn't be here," Sleepy Joe opined to Glenn and Oliver one evening at the Club, when the rest of Bangkok was still trapped at home and the General was not present. The government promised the end of the lockdown was coming. A few days before, the General had explained this meant a matter of weeks.

"The Prime Minister is retired military like me," the General said at the time. "I get the inside story."

"Perhaps the General doesn't trust him and wants him close by," Oliver said, explaining the General's inclusion of Edward. "Edward's a huge blabbermouth and hanging around here all these years, he's picked up quite a bit of information that could be very valuable to some really bad people."

"What a recommendation," Glenn said. "Just what I want to hear, that Edward has more information to spill. Let's hope from now on there isn't anyone interested."

Oliver shook his shaved head, atop his large, well-muscled body. Glenn was in awe of the big Australian's physical condition, especially since Oliver was several years older than he and never seemed to exercise. *Have to make sure to get his secret before it's too late.* Then he remembered Oliver had undergone a stomach bypass a few years back, and Glenn wasn't interested in that procedure. *Lucky for me I'm still in pretty good shape for a man of fifty-five.*

"The General does not limit his favors to those he admires," Oliver said. "You don't see him hanging around with Nobel laureates or respected philosophers. If someone is in the General's circle, rest assured he thinks they are of some use to him."

"Edward is of use to the General?" Glenn snorted. "Does the General need a weakling blabbermouth who opens up to anyone who asks with a stare? I'm not on board with that theory."

Oliver laughed.

"If Edward was solely as you described, I'd agree fully," he said. "But Edward ran a rather profitable money laundering operation between Bangkok and Vientiane and was a British tax auditor before that lucrative venture. He only gave it up when the CIA handed him fifty grand and ordered him to stop unless they hire him. Do any of us doubt that our dear General might on occasion have use for someone with such knowledge and skills?"

When neither Sleepy Joe nor Glenn responded, Oliver broke the silence.

"Enough of Edward. Let me buy my mates a drink to celebrate the pending return to normalcy in Bangkok. Assuming that's what we want." He motioned to Ahn, the waitress Wang hired in anticipation of reopening.

The Club always had two waitresses, even during lockdown, but had been managing with one for a while. Kit, who Ahn replaced, left Bangkok three months before to marry an old boyfriend from her village in Isan. Wang would replace her when business picked up. Kit and Glenn were in a relationship he thought was very strong and probably permanent, and her departure came out of the blue, stunning and depressing Glenn. He recognized he was still in the healing phase, and based on being dumped in the past, estimated it would take a full year for the pain to no longer be felt every day.

Three Days After the Unlocking of Bangkok

Glenn, Sleepy Joe and Oliver sat around a table at the NJA Club, waiting for the General. His call to meet was the equivalent of a military order. The last remnants of lockdown were three days before, and anyone who wanted could walk through the front door.

The General entered with Bank, the driver/bodyguard, who pulled up a chair a few feet behind him. The General motioned to the waitress for service.

Ahn took their orders. The new waitress was in her mid-forties, tending towards stocky, neither pretty nor unattractive, her hair still all black and cut short enough to barely reach the bottom of her ears. She was married to a retired Thai Army sergeant who worked as a security guard at a fancy condo in Phrom Phong off soi 31.

"Wang's had it with losing waitresses because of Glenn," the General declared as soon as he was seated. "First Mai runs off to Israel, of all places, because she couldn't land our Jewish friend Glenn, and then Kit, Mai's replacement, runs off to Isan to marry one of her own kind. Wang figures by hiring an older married woman, Glenn won't cause her to leave." He raised his martini glass and called for a toast. Glenn's face turned deeper shades of crimson.

"Lighten up, mate," Oliver said. "The General's only joking with you because he knows you're over the whole mess. At least we hope you are. Let's move on. Why did you call us here, General?"

The General carefully placed his martini glass on a cardboard coaster.

"I don't know if any of you have given much thought to how the beer and liquor wind up in this club or any club for that matter. I can tell you that for beer, Wang gets deliveries from the authorized Singha and Chang distributors, right from the breweries, bottles, and kegs. Someone else brings us bottles of Tiger and Leo as well as Heineken. Wang doesn't sell all that much wine, and what we need we get from the same operation that supplies the big hotels. Wang got a special deal with them. That's why the wine here is always good and not so expensive."

"How did Wang negotiate such a sweetheart deal?" Glenn asked.

"He just mentioned I was a regular here," the General replied. "Now back to business."

"What business?" Glenn asked. "I have no business. I'm retired. No more business visa for me, starting in a few days. I'm switching to a retirement visa. I won't be allowed to work. And even if I wanted to, I wouldn't work with you. It's always dangerous."

"I suppose I could say the same about you, Glenn," the General said, "but I won't. Just let me finish what I have to say and then you can throw your tantrum."

Glenn leaned back in his chair, as a sheepish look made its way across his face. He turned his attention to the General. Oliver and Sleepy Joe also had their eyes riveted on the old officer, their faces showing they expected something important was about to be disclosed.

"Bangkok is open again," the General said. "This time it's for real, fully open, no restrictions, and it's for good. Don't question me on that. My sources, as I have told you, are impeccable. The problem is that along with all the good Thai people and tourists free to come out into the world again, we are going to see the vermin and scum of the world, the parasites who feed off the good people."

"You sound like a communist, my dear General," Oliver said.

The General glared at Oliver, his dark eyes glowing.

"They're parasites too. Right now, I'm talking about a criminal syndicate that came to town just as things started loosening up. They have been trying to force people to buy their booze by offering lower prices than anyone paid before COVID at a time when the old suppliers are struggling to make up for lost income and the problems of getting the booze after the world's been shut down for a while. Wang's suppliers aren't raising rates for the NJA Club and I doubt any other suppliers are either, not if they want business.

"This gang showed up, and they seem to know who owns the places that buy booze, and they know how to find them at home or anywhere else. These new guys are using implied threats of violence to make owners buy from them. They are sending out thugs to do the dirty work. I am fairly certain they killed a bar owner the other day because he told them he wasn't afraid of them and if they ever bothered him again he'd kill them. Poor man was found dead in the doorway of his house. His throat was slit but nothing was taken from him or the house. They've even had the nerve to approach Wang, right here. They even called him again. When he told them he was happy with the supplier he had and that I protected him, they laughed in his face."

Glenn knew nothing of this. His back straightened and tensed when he heard the General say Wang had been approached by the thugs right after telling them one owner was killed.

"So far nothing has happened to Wang or the NJA Club," Glenn said, more to assure himself than the others.

The General frowned.

"The individuals who came to see Wang won't be coming back." Glenn and Oliver turned to Joe, who flashed a goofy smile as he shrugged his shoulders and raised his hands, palms facing his friends. Oliver and Glenn interpreted this as Joe's way of telling them he didn't know any more than they did.

Glenn raised a hand, and the General acknowledged him.

"Maybe it's because I'm not business oriented like you guys, but can someone explain why people who are selling booze at cheaper prices have to use threats of violence to get customers? Seems like it's the old seller who ought to be thinking that way."

"One would think so if they were in the West," the General explained. "But Thais understand what's going on here. If this new gang manages to drive the competition away with their low prices, we all understand that once they have the field to themselves, prices go up and keep going up. Then they use tough guys on the customer who can't or won't pay."

Oliver paused to collect his thoughts and continued.

"I'm assuming the old suppliers, who are thinking business is about to start up again, won't take this very well," Oliver said. "Maybe they will be the first to use force. I understand that legitimate liquor distributors are not known for fighting, but we all know they can buy as many tough guys as they need. They will if it means survival. Owners may not want to ditch their current suppliers but will also be afraid to cross the syndicates who show up with tough guys and guns. They know one of the two sides will end up punishing them. Both sides will have to be armed and ready to fight. The thugs will kill each other, each side will kill owners, and everyone loses. Not what Bangkok needs. Certainly not now."

The General nodded. "Exactly, my friend. What we're looking at is a possible gang war, a violent extortion attempt, and the end of a lot of good businesses just when we need them to come back to life."

"You believe they have already killed a man?" Glenn asked.

"My information leaves no doubt they have murdered one man and would have kept going. The problem we face is that those kinds of men are easily replaceable. We're dealing with a large criminal organization from outside Thailand."

Glenn considered the General's words, *would have kept going.*

I wonder what happened to those men and if Joe was involved despite his apparent denial. Or maybe I don't want to know.

"Who are we talking about?" Glenn asked. "The Chinese?" *Could be one of the triads.* The General shook his head.

"Russians?" Oliver asked.

"They may be used for local muscle in Bangkok, but they don't call any shots," the General replied. "Same goes for any Thais they hire."

"Burmese perhaps?" Glenn asked.

"If it were them," the General said, "I'd grab my old assault rifle and start shooting." The General, like many Thais, showed little warmth towards their various neighbors. He held a special contempt for Myanmar, as Burma had been known officially for years. He once explained to Glenn that it was because the military dictators of Myanmar gave all armies a bad name, but Glenn suspected it was simple bigotry, not tied to any politics.

"Okay, I give up," Oliver said. Glenn nodded in accord.

"I've been given information from our good friend the Lieutenant," the General said, referring to the officer with the Thai Royal Police, who was the cousin of Lek, Glenn's condo concierge and friend. "He's been investigating this for a few weeks, and he's consulted with our national government's experts on all criminal organizations, domestic and foreign. He is confident this fits the way one of them operates."

"Will you please end the suspense and tell us?" Oliver asked.

"The American Mafia," the General said softly, sipping his drink.

THREE

J ohnny Brancini, known to colleagues as "Johnny the Brain," turned off the movie when it reached the final credit. It was the third he'd watched and he still couldn't fall asleep. The flight guide on the seat screen showed another six hours until landing in Bangkok.

Johnny was dubbed "the Brain" because he was the smartest connected guy in Brooklyn. Johnny knew from childhood that most organized crime work required fiery brawn and icy hearts, but rarely called for intellect, making it a scarce commodity in any crime family. When a mob boss spotted a bright young man, he would be groomed for an advisory or strategic planning role and not sent to the streets to do battle with guns and fists. Throughout school, Johnny was an A student in almost every class. His mother periodically reminded him that if he had not been arrested for stealing cars his senior year in high school, he would have gone to Brooklyn College and become the kind of professional whose briefcase does not contain a gun or bribe money.

Johnny looked to his left and watched Tommy Turterello sleep. His broad chest rose and fell like ocean waves. Tommy was the Boss's best persuader, collector and hijacker. He was big, almost six foot three, two hundred thirty pounds, and his face looked like it had been in a collision with a potato masher. Those few not cowed by his looks and size were inevitably persuaded by his fists and feet into handing over payment or a truck loaded with goods.

Tommy's snores were audible from the four rows behind Johnny. *Good thing the Boss made us sit separately and act like we don't know each other. Exactly how it should be done to avoid attention and people eavesdropping. Besides, I don't need constant snoring right next to me.*

Tommy's handle was "The Turtle," and not just because of his last name. Tommy Turterello twice escaped death by gunfire. The first time he was shot point blank in the chest by a rival gang's hitman who got off two .380 caliber rounds before tossing the gun into the first sewer he passed as he melted into the crowd on 14th Street in Manhattan. The bullets were stopped by the big St. Christopher's medal dangling around Tommy's neck, and barely pierced his skin. Aside from a week of mild pain, there was no damage. Tommy thereafter tried to stay at his home base in Brooklyn most of the time, where rivals were less likely to take pot shots at him. He also regularly prayed to and thanked St. Christopher.

The second attempt on the Turtle's life was by an enraged husband Tommy cuckolded. The man, a New York City bus driver, fired a .32 revolver at him, but the bullet struck the three-inch wad of bills Tommy collected earlier as protection payments and secreted in the inside pocket of his leather jacket. Thousands of dollars in currency of were rendered worthless by holes and powder burns, but the Boss valued Tommy more than the cash and was so grateful he survived that no tears were shed over the money. The bus driver disappeared a few days later, never to resurface.

After that, Tommy was the Turtle, protected by a shell.

Tommy may not be the brightest bulb in the lamp, but he's tougher than anyone else and totally loyal to the Boss. In this business, that counts a lot.

The third member of the delegation, Paulie "The Arranger" Arginotti, sat two rows behind Tommy. Paulie was so named for his skills at bribing, compromising or threatening to expose public officials or anyone else who needed to be bought, and every one of them had something they would prefer to keep secret. Paulie was not prone to violence nor expected to use any. His position was "everyone has their price, everyone has their selling point or their breaking point." Paulie's greatness was his ability to bring stubborn people to that point so the Boss's family could operate free from police investigations or the need to bury bodies. Johnny always advised the Boss to use Paulie before using Tommy, advice that was generally followed. "Paulie could sell ice to the Eskimos," the Boss was fond of saying.

It was only a week ago when the Boss first told Johnny he and the other two would be taking a trip to Asia. Bangkok, Thailand, to be precise.

"I'm thinking we need to look for ways to make money any way we can. Business here is drying up as times change, and the law is all over us these days. The further away from the feds and the NYPD, the better we are."

"Yeah, Boss," Johnny had countered. "But Bangkok, Thailand? From what I hear, mostly from wise guys who took vacations there, they already got their own people running girls, also whatever gambling isn't done by their legal lottery, plus drugs, even guns. Not just the locals, also the Chinese, the Burmese, the Vietnamese, the Russians. Is there room for us without getting into a turf war in a place we don't know?"

The Boss reached into the dark wooden humidor atop his desk and withdrew a large cigar, a seven inch Churchill, which he cut at the end with a small scissors and lit before replying.

"Johnny, as usual, you know what you're talking about. That's right, others have grabbed all the Thai drug business, the hooker bars, counterfeit goods, and from what I hear, murder for hire. But that's not what we're going there for, so no toes are being stepped on. Not by us."

Johnny stared at the Boss and moved his head just enough to avoid the cloud of cigar smoke being blown in his direction.

"If there's no room for us in drugs, no hookers, gambling, counterfeit or stolen goods, what the hell are we doing there?"

The Boss rested his cigar in a ceramic ashtray.

"Johnny, we're going to be operating a legitimate business. We're going to be selling booze to any bar or restaurant interested in top shelf booze at the best possible prices. I spoke to some capos from other families, the ones that bring in heroin and pills from Southeast Asia. They tell me when you get away from the girlie bars and the ones owned by the Russians, there's an opening. They might be paying cops to leave them alone, they may pay some gang for protection, but the gangs aren't selling those guys their booze.

"Liquor is gotten from distributors, not gangsters. If those gangs want to keep on shaking them down for protection, that's not our business. Long as the local wise guys stay out of our affairs, we'll stay out of theirs. As long as we stay away from any place already claimed by the Russians, and there ain't all that many, we'll be fine."

Johnny didn't have to ask where the booze would come from. The Boss's family did not deal in drugs, because the Boss knew that carried the greatest risk of bringing the feds down on the family, not to mention the strong possibility of violent opposition from Black and Latin gangs. Legalized gambling killed bookmaking, and neither loansharking nor prostitution brought in the money it once did, at least not in the neighborhoods the Boss controlled. The demise of labor unions and the modernization of the dock processes stripped the family of the once lucrative union and shipyard income. The current big-ticket item was hijacking and selling goods which cost them nothing.

The Boss employed some of the best hijackers and commercial burglars in America, and Tommy the Turtle personally oversaw this operation. Whether robbing a truck or emptying out a store or warehouse in the dead of night, Tommy's men were the best. They were loyal to the end, because if caught, the Boss paid for the best lawyers, took care of their families, and welcomed them back with open arms when they finished their sentence. The Boss appreciated the fact that Tommy personally recruited the teams, all made men, admitted to the Mafia with all the rights and privileges appurtenant thereto. Tommy never mentioned their names to the Boss or brought them anywhere near him, giving the Boss plausible deniability in any investigation.

"I still don't get it. Why do we have to ship the booze across the world to sell it?" Johnny asked. "What's wrong with selling it here, like we've been doing for as long as we could shave. Well, maybe not that long, but close to it."

The Boss picked up his cigar and this time blew the smoke well to Johnny's left.

"That's just it, Johnny. We've reached our maximum, our quota if we want to call it that. We got every bar and restaurant for four square miles and that's it. No one else comes here and we don't go nowhere else. That's how we keep the peace around here. Also means we run out of customers."

"What's the problem?" Johnny said. "We're surviving quite well. If it's not broken, why fix it?"

The Boss took two puffs this time, and it looked to Johnny like he was deep in concentration between them.

"That's just it, Johnny," he replied. "It is broken and it needs fixing." He saw the look of disbelief on his number one man.

"Johnny, things just ain't the same. Not the way it was thirty years ago, not the way it was ten years ago. We ain't the only ones stealing booze and or making people buy ours. Take Brighton Beach, Coney Island. The Russians got them sewed up like we once sewn up that snitch's lips before he disappeared. Forget any Asian place, we don't want to mess with them. If we don't find someplace where we can make more money, we'll get wiped off the board sooner or later by someone bigger, because we're gonna be real small and an easy target."

Johnny knew about the Chinese and Vietnamese gangs. They weren't afraid of anything and were better at fighting and killing than any white men he or the Boss had ever seen.

"Yeah, Boss, but if we're trying to forget Asian places, shouldn't we stay out of Bangkok? You think all the locals who have an interest in the booze will just sit back and let us waltz in like we own the place?"

The Boss put his cigar in the ashtray and pushed it off to the side of his desk. Johnny knew from long experience this signaled he'd had enough for the time being and the room would become temporarily smoke free. The smell of cigar never left the room, floating in the air, clinging to the walls, seeping steadily from every pore of the Boss's corpulent body. Johnny had never smoked and hated the smell of burning tobacco, especially cigars.

I take what I can get, Johnny thought as he half smiled when he saw the cigar shoved aside.

"We're not talking about the Chinese or the Vietnamese," the Boss explained. "The Vietnamese kicked everyone's ass over there and they're kicking everybody's ass over here. They're not pushing booze to bars and restaurants in Thailand, and we're not getting involved in their violent shit or their scamming. I hear the Chinese have their own quiet little markets and stay away from the foreigners and Thais. So long as we all stay out of each other's way over there, we can do our business and they can do theirs.

"From what everybody tells me, the Thais ain't like those two." the Boss continued. "I hear they're real peaceful, Buddhists or Hindus or whatever. I hear they also got Russians, but they work among their own, just like here. I hear the whole country is loaded with bars, restaurants, whorehouses, all the kinds of places that need booze. We hear about gangs over there selling drugs, some running whores, both sexes, loan sharking, but nothing about a booze syndicate or anything like that."

Johnny drew a breath now that the smoke had subsided to almost none.

"Boss, you know I don't drink, just like I don't smoke, but I understand the business side of booze. Maybe we get the stuff for free, but we got to pay the guys who hijack the trucks, the guy who keeps it for us, and the guys who persuade places to buy our booze. We can only charge them so much, because it does us no good if they go out of business or get so pressured they start talking to the cops. So how does it get better for us over on the other side of the world?"

The Boss smiled at Johnny as he reached into a drawer in his desk and took out a bottle of whiskey and a shot glass.

"It gets much better, Johnny," he said just before downing the shot. "You really ought to give this a try," he added. "Once in a while won't kill you."

"Neither will never," Johnny replied. "So how is it better?"

"Booze is very expensive over there," the Boss explained. "I been hearing about it and I did some reading on my own. They got really high taxes on any imported alcoholic drinks. Wine and booze cost twice over there what they cost here. That's why they drink so much of their local stuff, which is more or less cheap rum. Or they drink cheap imitation crap from other Asian countries. The rich folks over there and the foreigners coming for good times are willing to pay higher prices. It's just the opposite of what you think. We can charge more per bottle and the customers can charge more per drink than they could ever get for local stuff and they all see it as getting a great deal."

Johnny thought about what the Boss was saying. It made sense, but he didn't think it could be that easy.

"How are we going to get it over there?" Johnny asked.

"We still got some hooks with longshoreman, those few there still are, and we can get a whole bunch of crates snuck in on cargo ships. They'll handle that for us. We just got to get someone to pick it up at the docks. Ain't that what Paulie does? He's working on it now, talking with people who have been there, trying to figure out how to hire the locals we'll need over there."

"I get that," Johnny said. "But these Thailand places have been getting booze, and the people selling to them might not like some new people taking their business. They can find killers if they have to. We know anyone can find a killer anywhere in this world if you know where to look. Don't we see straight businessmen coming to the Mob when that's the only option they have left? We have no protection over there and it will take a while to figure out who we can trust for help, no reflection on Paulie. I bet those other sellers can get all the muscle they need. So how can this work?"

"Simple," the Boss said. "Since we are paying zip for our booze, we can undercut everyone. I was thinking about offering a really low starting price just to make it easier. If we're getting booze to the places at less than they are paying the current guys, the customers are going to want us without us having to force ourselves. They'll take care of the competition. We're putting money in their pockets, not to mention our own."

Nowhere nearly as dumb as he looks, Johnny thought. *How long is he planning to keep prices low?*

"I'm having a travel agent set you and the other two guys up right now as we speak. Air tickets, hotels, limo waiting at the airport, little bag of cash, some gold. Tommy the Turtle is putting together a crew to grab a rig full of high-end booze. He's got someone on the inside helping him. That's gonna be your first inventory over there. By the time the boat reaches Asia, you guys will be all setup and ready to go to work. Paulie is the Arranger, and I'm sure he'll figure out how to hire some muscle and where to push the booze. You're standing in for me and making any decisions that need to be made as if it were me making them. You'll be leaving in a week, so get your affairs in order, because it's gonna be a good six months at least till we see your face back here."

Johnny understood he was dismissed. He rose and started to turn toward the door but turned back toward the Boss.

"Travel agent, Boss? Who uses them anymore? Everything gets done on the internet these days."

The Boss scowled.

"I ain't got time to go learning no internet," he said. Then he smiled.

"Now beat it. Try and have some fun over there. I hear there's lots of good times to be had."

But I don't see you going over there, Johnny reflected as he left the office.

FOUR

TWO DAYS AFTER JOHNNY'S MEETING WITH THE BOSS

"I really gotta take a piss," Mickey told Bobby as they approached the Metropolitan Avenue exit of the Brooklyn-Queens Expressway, known as "the BQE" to New Yorkers. "It's dark already, we can stop in front of some warehouse and I can take my leak." They were in the largest commercial vehicle allowed on the BQE, a three-axle, ten-tire single-unit truck. The name, phone number, and website of the liquor distributor were painted on the outside.

Bobby Giannelli looked at the clock on the dashboard.

"Okay, but the manager is gonna be real mad if we don't get to Supreme Liquors before it closes."

"Don't worry," Mickey said. "We're no more than a half hour away. What liquor store closes before seven?"

This satisfied Bobby, and he maneuvered into the exit lane and drove towards East Williamsburg, where he knew the industrial area would have plenty of closed businesses offering suitable opportunities for a man to empty his bladder.

"Take a left next block," Micky said. "Great spot there."

"Sounds like you're the expert in pissing," Bobby said.

"Yeah, well I've taken enough of them in my time," Mickey replied. After Bobby turned, Mickey directed him to a large, dark building on the right side of the street. Bobby put the truck in parking gear and Mickey stepped down onto the street from the passenger side. "Jeez," he said as his feet touched the sidewalk. "I'm getting old. Stepping out of one of these guys is a lot tougher than getting out of my Cadillac." Bobby watched Mickey as he walked towards the wall of the building, apparently his designated place to relieve himself.

He ain't much older than me, Bobby thought. *Maybe three, four years, so he can't be more than forty-five or so. If he'd take off thirty pounds and do some exercise, he wouldn't be such a mess. That's what working inside does to a man. Driving this rig and helping to move those liquor crates keeps me from looking like him. Even if he makes more money.*

Mickey almost never rode with the deliveries. He sat on his rather expansive rear end making phone calls to sell booze and collect money owed. Bobby didn't see him as suited for such work, since Mickey was as rough and uneducated as Bobby, and cursed more than any of the longshoreman Bobby grew up around in Red Hook, Brooklyn. *Helps when your brother-in- law owns the business.* The word at work was the owner regretted ever bringing Mickey on board, but he was married to Mickey's sister and there wasn't any way he could fire him and preserve his marriage.

Bobby was checking his cell phone for messages when the passenger door opened. Bobby turned his head, but it wasn't Mickey who sat himself in the seat. Bobby faced a huge, ugly man whose face looked like Robert De Niro's interpretation in *Raging Bull* of Jake La Motta after a bruising fight. He held a large pistol in his hand, though he wouldn't need it to make Bobby comply with whatever he asked.

"Let's not get too worried," the big man growled. "Just get out of this cab and nothing's gonna happen to you. You ought to know that."

Definitely mob, Bobby thought. *The look, the way he talks. It's not like I didn't see any of them growing up in Red Hook. And who else hijacks liquor trucks?*

Bobby did as ordered. He skillfully stepped out the door onto the ground. Another armed man greeted him, this one shorter and thinner than the goon in the truck. Bobby was pushed in front of the truck.

Mickey walked towards them, a third man walking behind him with a gun pointed at his head.

"If I had known this was gonna happen, I would have held it in," he said sheepishly.

"Yeah, well let's just do what they say and we'll be fine," Bobby said. *My grandfather's advice and he knew. He was from Sicily.*

The man behind Mickey put his gun into his rear waistband.

"That's what we like to hear," he said. Then the big man who ordered Bobby from the truck moved in between Bobby and Mickey, gun still in hand but pointed down. There was enough light from the lampposts and truck headlights so that Bobby recognized Tommy Turterello. When Bobby was a teenager, Tommy came around the neighborhood selling televisions, stereos, microwaves, computers, and anything durable that could be stolen from a truck. He'd grown bigger and uglier but no doubt it was the same man.

Be careful around him, Bobby's grandfather warned. *I knew men like that in the old country. There are those who become criminals because it's easy money and then there are those who do it because they like hurting others, Tommy Turterello is a special case who enjoys both.*

"I'm going to have to hurt you just a little bit so it looks real to the cops," Tommy said to Mickey. Tommy said this with a big smile.

"What the hell is going on?" Bobby yelled. "Mickey, are you mixed up in this?"

"You're so scared you're hearing things," Mickey yelled back at Bobby. Tommy and the other armed man looked at Bobby. The other armed man's lips were pursed. Tommy wore the same smile as he turned around and delivered a solid right hook to Mickey's jaw, followed by a left jab to the side of his head. Mickey went down like one of Muhammad Ali's opponents during his glorious run. Then Tommy shot Bobby Giannelli in the face.

Tony, the third member of Tommy's crew was sitting in a Cadillac Eldorado parked across the street when he heard the gunshot. He ran over to Bobby. When he saw the hole Tommy's .45 had put in his face, he lost control.

"Jeez, Tommy, what the hell were you thinking when you shot this guy? Any idea who you just killed? It's Bobby Giannelli. His grandfather and the Boss's grandfather grew up in Sicily and came across together. The Giannellis were always straight people, civilians for sure, but the two old men stayed close till the Boss's grandfather died. When Bobby's grandfather finally went, the Boss insisted on paying for the whole funeral. Boss ain't gonna like this, no way."

"Then Bobby should have known better than to open his mouth," Tommy said. "Besides, the Boss don't gotta know."

"How we gonna keep this secret, Tommy? You don't think Mrs. Giannelli will ask her good friend the Boss to find out what happened to her little Bobby?"

Tommy stood quietly in the street, his gun still dangling from his hand, as he disassembled the facts of the past few minutes and reassembled them with a more favorable outcome.

"Don't worry, Tony. The Boss thinks just like us, that Mickey must have cut the driver in so that he keeps his mouth shut. That's one of the things he's getting ten grand to handle. But he didn't." Tommy pointed his gun at Mickey's head, pressed his body against the asphalt, and shot him in the head. Tony gasped loudly.

"Keep cool, Tony," Tommy ordered. "These ain't the first two bodies you've seen and they won't be the last. I want you to take these two over to Rosselli's Iron Works out by Jamaica Bay, you just put that into Google Maps and it'll get you there. You'll ring a buzzer at the gate. You'll be expected. You'll meet Little Sal, no more stand-up guy than him. When he asks you what you need to do, tell him you need to clean some metal plates. That way he knows you're my guy and just do what he says. Got it?"

The other two members of Tommy's crew were already seated in the truck. The driver waved to Tommy as he pulled away.

"I'll give you a hand loading these two stiffs into the truck," Tommy said when the big rig was out of sight. "At Rosselli's you might need Little Sal to give you a hand. These things get really hard to pick up and move once they get all stiff. Guess why they call them stiffs?" Tommy dropped his cigarette to the asphalt and crushed it with the heel of his shoe. When the bodies were in the Cadillac's trunk and the lid slammed shut, Tommy handed his gun to Tony and told him to take care of it when he got rid of the bodies.

Tommy watched Tony drive away.

I'll walk all the way back to the clubhouse. Can't risk taking a cab or a ride app or getting seen coming in and out of a subway. It's a few miles but I'm strong.

FIVE

A WEEK AFTER BANGKOK REOPENED

Edward moved towards Glenn's table, twisting his pudgy body between tables and chairs. Glenn saw him coming but wasn't quick enough to make a polite exit. Edward took a seat at Glenn's small table. His rumpled and garish Hawaiian shirt contrasted with Glenn's well-tailored tropical GQ look: well-fitting light blue short-sleeved polo shirt and khakis.

"For the first time in quite a while we don't have to sneak around like criminals to enjoy the NJA Club," Edward said. His Welsh accent, delivered in a twangy voice, annoyed Glenn. "Let me buy you a drink to celebrate," Edward continued. "I hope you haven't had your daily limit of one Martini."

"I'll enjoy a vodka martini with the General later today," Glenn replied. "I'm still working on this coffee," he added as he stared into the nearly empty cup.

"I detect a certain degree of hostility in your voice, " Edward said. "I sincerely hope you don't blame me for the end of your unfortunate relationship with our friend Mai."

Glenn's jaw tightened until it tensed to its fullest. Edward had that effect on him.

"I don't blame you at all," Glenn said. *At least not for the breakup,* he thought. *But if you hadn't pushed her to make her moves on me, nothing would have happened, so I guess I do blame you.*

"Good, Glenn," Edward said, "because I feel bad about what happened. Had I known this would be the end result, I would never have suggested Mai make her overtures to you and certainly would not have encouraged you to reciprocate."

Glenn thought for a moment before replying, weighing every word before speaking.

"There's no way you could have known she'd visit her family in Isan as soon as she was allowed to travel, and during that brief time her old high school flame would win a few million baht in the lottery the same week his grandmother dropped dead and left him a few million more plus a house. Mai never came back."

"My assumption is that as a Buddhist, she saw it as her karma and promptly married the man," Edward said, a dour look on his pudgy face. His hair was turning gray faster than Glenn's and reminded Glenn of a late uncle he never liked.

"Whatever it is, you're off the hook," Glenn said. "I don't hold any of it against you. I'm sort of touched that you cared enough to try so hard to get us together." *I'm even more glad that she never came back because it prevented my greatest fear, that the NJA Club would become hostile territory if I had to face her every day.*

"Then it must be you don't like me because I'm gay," Edward said. His eyes locked on Glenn's.

"That's ridiculous and you know it," Glenn said, his voice louder than usual. "I don't trust you, because whenever the wrong people came to this club to find out about me and my friends, it was always you that gave them what they wanted."

Edward's head dropped so far that his chin almost touched his chest.

"I'm not strong like you are Glenn, or like the General, Sleepy Joe or Oliver. Unlike you men, I never sought danger. It always seemed to find me. I didn't think people were inquiring for the wrong reasons. Why would I? You certainly never seemed like the kind of man who attracts trouble."

"I'm not so sure it's fear alone that motivates you," Glenn replied.

"After you told the CIA everything they wanted to know about me and my friends, they handed you fifty thousand dollars and told you not to launder money except when they're paying you to do it. You tried lying to us, but when Sleepy Joe dangled you over the rail on my balcony, you came clean."

Edward raised his head, and an angry look crossed his flushed face.

"That's not fair, Glenn. You know damn well they discovered I was running a money-laundering service up to Laos, where the banks don't comply with America's stupid reporting requirements. In fact, I was running it with that woman Noi you had the hots for. I could have gone to jail, but it didn't happen. They paid me to stop doing it illegally and if they needed me to launder money for them, they would get in touch. If you recall, Noi was being investigated by both the Americans and the Thais – and, if you remember, the charges mysteriously disappeared after I told them what they wanted to know. Sounds like things worked out very well for everyone."

The fool thinks the CIA cut Noi loose because of him. Glenn thought. *The investigations into Noi closed when I agreed to help the CIA kidnap a Russian gangster under American indictment. He doesn't know any of this. That's not Edward's business any more than the money the CIA paid me and my friends.*

"Quit when you're ahead, Edward. I told you why I was angry with you, but it's in the past. I've moved on." *Not really,* he thought, *but the country is reopening and there are better things than Edward to command my attention.*

"And it's time for reopening our relationship," Edward retorted. "May I start off by offering you some free advice on how to legally avoid taxation by the American government?"

"I'm not interested in your money laundering schemes, Edward, and I have no idea why you even think I would be." *He's the last guy I'd trust with my finances.*

"Well, Glenn, I was a tax auditor for Her Majesty for over a quarter century and I did run a rather successful operation over here. I'm not suggesting any illegality or even an impropriety. It seems to me you must be wealthy or at least affluent. You've been living here as long as I have, what is it, fifteen years or more? You haven't been known to work a day over that entire time, except for wasting a little time late and effort on the late and unlamented guitarist, Mr. Phil Funston.

"I'm guessing you were a successful lawyer who retired early and is living off investments in a less expensive nation where the money can last forever if need be. But your country is the only one in the world that taxes people on income earned outside America. I can't help you much with money invested in America, but if you've got anything in banks, stock markets or real estate invested anywhere else, I can help you save on taxes."

Glenn interlaced his fingers, brought them chest level, and leaned back in his chair. He closed his eyes for the briefest moment and then focused them on Edward. The pudgy little Welshman's smooth cheeks contrasted with the deep furrows across his forehead. His eyebrows were bushy and his lips oversized. When he smiled, he flashed rows of yellow teeth. Glenn was constantly amazed that over the years Edward had so many boyfriends, as he couldn't imagine any person finding Edward attractive or pleasant to be with. Then again, Glenn acknowledged he knew nothing about the dynamics of gay relationships, not surprising, as he didn't know very much about his own heterosexual relationships either. His wrecked marriage in America and his string of romantic failures in Thailand evidenced that fact.

"That's okay, Edward," Glenn said, "I've got the same CPA I used back in San Francisco, and taxes are hardly a burden. But thanks for your concern."

Glenn used no CPA and filed no taxes. His money consisted of what he'd grabbed from a murdered drug dealing client to start a new life in Thailand, plus the handsome fees the CIA paid him after twice dragging him into their dangerous exploits. He was assured by his CIA contact, Rodney Snapp, and by his dear friend Oliver the information expert, that Glenn Murray Cohen was off the IRS watchlist for life. *Probably because they don't want to have to explain why they paid me.*

"Just trying to be helpful," Edward said.

"You actually have been," Glenn replied. "Reminding me that now that Bangkok is reopened, I would be wise to take a good look at my assets, maybe rebalance my portfolio, set up a new budget for new times."

"I'd be most happy to assist you," Edward said. His eyes brightened and he showed a thin smile.

"Thanks for the offer, but like I say, I've been using this guy for decades and I have total faith in him."

The brightness and smile faded from Edward's face.

"Well, if ever you need advice or a safe place to store your wealth just call your friend Edward."

"Who else?" Glenn asked.

The "who else" was Oliver. The big Australian with the shaved head was not only Bangkok's greatest information maven and sleuth but was also one of three people who knew that Glenn began his life as an affluent expat with hundreds of thousands of dollars in cash he'd taken from a drug-dealing law client gunned down before his eyes with no witnesses around. His gray-market lawyer friend Charlie set it all up, and that money was in a bank account in the name of a Canadian, William Rawlings, complete with a Canadian passport issued by the appropriate authorities.

The money Glenn received from the CIA for his involuntary assistance against Russians and North Koreans was deposited into William Rawlings's bank, which even managed brokerage accounts for the mysterious Canadian. The CIA, who never mentioned Rawlings and his account, assured Glenn that there would never be any tax inquiries about his money. Oliver, who received a fair share himself for his efforts on behalf of the CIA, assured Glenn their word was good.

"No one except the parties with current knowledge will ever know a thing," he told Glenn for the tenth time when Glenn came to see him about the Rawlings account. Oliver was spending a few weeks in his Bangkok condo before returning to his home on the beautiful island of Koh Phangan. He and Glenn lounged lazily on his big leather couch, an Australian rugby game playing softly on Oliver's huge wall-mounted television. Glenn explained that he too understood that to be the case and wondered whether he still needed the Rawlings bank account.

"I don't know if I mentioned this," Glenn explained, "but I'm not going to need Charlie's quasi-legal immigration consultant anymore. My current visa expires next month, but now that I'm over fifty, I can get a retirement visa. I need to show eight hundred thousand baht in a Thai bank account. No problem for me. I may as well shift the Rawlings money into a Thai bank."

"It's usually not easy for an American to open a Thai bank account," Oliver explained. "You Yanks are subject to that asinine FATCO law that forces you and the foreign banks to report on the accounts. You're too much trouble for them. But unless you've been uncharacteristically unwise with your assets, I'd suspect that the total amount you would deposit is more than enough to make even the FATCO reporting requirements worth their while. I'm not entirely certain that's in your best interests. The taxes would be enormous. Your government has agreed off the record to look the other way when it comes to your past tax indiscretions because they don't ever want to explain any of their dealings with us. If they can grab a piece of your current income in taxation, that's a different story. No one reports anything about Rawlings's account because he's Canadian. So, leave it alone, open a local account in your name with just enough to get the visa, and pay whatever taxes you accrue from that account."

Glenn told Oliver he gave better advice than Edward, and the two men laughed. Glenn picked up the conversation.

"Oliver, you're the only person I've ever told about my assets besides Charlie. I bet you know to the penny what I've got in every account."

"Actually, I don't know at the moment," Oliver said. "Should I want to know, I would just look it up. Finding these things out is my game, as you well know."

Glenn's eyes widened and his lips separated by an inch.

"You've been spying on me? Hacking into my accounts?" he asked in an angry and excited voice.

"Not at all, mate," Oliver said. "Never have and never will without your consent. I said I could if I wanted to, not that I have or will."

"You don't have my consent," Glenn said.

"Then there's nothing to worry about, mate," Oliver responded.

I don't like the smile on his face, Glenn thought.

"Lighten up," Oliver said. "In the world of intelligence and information, we have ethics, unlike you lawyers."

"I'm a former lawyer," Glenn said.

"Well," Oliver replied, "if you had no ethics when you left America, it's highly doubtful you picked any up in Bangkok."

"I vehemently disagree," Glenn said.

"As you wish," Oliver said. "In any event, I am confident you have no past tax worries from the U.S. government and as long as you report and pay taxes on your reportable income from the local account you'll open, you'll never have any. Keep the Rawlings account as long as the passport is good. I recall you telling me about five years ago your man here got it renewed. That means you've got five years left on it. Might as well keep it in case you have occasion to use it. If you needed money that couldn't be traced to you, the Rawlings account does the trick."

"I'll think about it," Glenn said. "I'd like to put all of that behind me and just live openly as Glenn Murray Cohen without the need to think I might someday have to be William Rawlings again."

Oliver reminded Glenn of the past service that a Canadian passport had afforded.

"Remember how a few years back when we wanted to give some North Korean agents the slip, you used that Canuck passport to buy train tickets so in case anyone had access to those ticket sales they'd never know it was us? Never know when we might be in a similar spot. Remember, for a Yank there's no nationality easier to fake than Canadian."

During Glenn's earlier days in Bangkok, when he was keeping the lowest of profiles, all his money was in the Rawlings account. Oliver was correct that Glenn's involvement with the CIA assured him he would never be audited. Fear of the IRS was not what was driving Glenn's feelings.

"I do know when we'll be in a similar spot, ever. I'm through trying to help other people with their problems if it means risking my life. Now that I'm about to officially become a retiree, I ought to act like one."

"The General is retired, and he doesn't get skittish every time there's a little excitement," Oliver said. He then turned his attention to the rugby match.

Glenn allowed Oliver a half minute to hear whatever the sportscasters had to say about the game he didn't understand very well.

"The General retired from the army and started a whole new career as a businessman if we can use the term. I retired as a lawyer and except for a few short and unhappy years managing the late guitarist Mr. Funston, I haven't worked a day and don't intend to ever again."

"If I'm not mistaken, mate, there were three occasions where we might say you were lured out of retirement and got yourself into a spot of danger. It was through you that the rest of us were dragged in and while it was a bit dangerous, the General, Sleepy Joe and I thank you for the income you enabled us to earn. The incredible parts are that the first time you were trying to protect a woman who didn't care at all about you, another time some sleazy friend of yours from America nearly got us all killed. That was definitely work, mate."

Six

Tony drove the Cadillac as if he were taking his driving test. He made certain not to exceed the speed limit by even a mile. He made full stops at every light and stop sign. When on the freeway, he stayed in the center lane and watched his speed. If he had to change lanes, he was sure to signal. Before he could leave the car in the Newark Airport parking, he would first have to ditch the two stiffening bodies in the trunk. If he were stopped for any reason, like if the car was already reported stolen, the cop had the right to check the trunk. *Since this one was taken from a long-term parking lot at JFK a few hours ago, not much chance it's on the hot list,* Tony assured himself.

The car was indeed stolen twenty-five minutes before Tony hopped behind the wheel to meet Tommy in East Williamsburg for the hijacking. The radio was set to the oldies station, and Tony sang along with some of his favorite songs from the decades before he was born. He loved the Four Seasons and Jay and the Americans. Before too long, he saw the lights reflecting off Jamaica Bay and the landing lights on the runways of JFK International Airport. He left the expressway, followed the service road for a mile, then turned onto a narrow strip of road fronting the bay. He kept driving until he came to the end of the road, where a ten-foot fence blocked any further advance. Tony spotted a speaker box on a pole a few feet in front of the fence's gate. He rolled down the Cadillac's window and yelled out that he was here to see Little Sal. A voice distorted by static told him to wait. *Like I got a choice here,* Tony thought.

A few minutes later the gate opened, and through it walked one of the fattest men Tony had ever seen. His massive bulk was clear in the Cadillac's headlights. He stood five-eight, the same as Tony, but unlike Tony, Little Sal was almost as wide as he was tall. His face was a beach ball dripping gobs of fat that puddled around his neck like a collar. He waddled over to the passenger side of the car, opened the door, and to Tony's amazement, quickly squeezed into the seat. Tony noticed Little Sal was wearing a bathrobe over his underwear.

"You caught me just as I was getting ready to have a little nightcap, lie down in bed, and watch something on Netflix," Little Sal said. "But Tommy called and said you were on your way. Always glad to help out Tommy. You know if it wasn't for him, I would have never been able to own this place. He arranged for the old owner to sell me this place real cheap with nothing down. Tommy had his buddy, the guy he calls The Arranger, work out all the details and got me a lawyer to make it all legal and official. I been here ten years now, thanks to Tommy's good heart. I never miss a payment of course. Why would I? It's practically nothing. So whatever Tommy the Turtle wants, Tommy the Turtle gets."

Including getting rid of bodies some way I'm about to learn, Tony thought. Following Tommy's instructions, he told Little Sal he was there to clean some metal. The fat man nodded. He sat squeezed into the passenger seat, but seemingly comfortable, his massive love handles covering the center console. Fortunately, the shifter was on the steering wheel.

"Keep driving straight, and when you come to my house, you turn left and keep going about two hundred. Stop next to the big corrugated steel hut."

Tony drove slowly past mounds of battered and broken vehicles, appliances, and piles of metal so misshapen he couldn't tell what they were. He saw pallets of metal squares and rectangles of all sizes piled ten feet high. Shipping containers lay scattered about. The scene reminded Tony of the apocalyptic films he enjoyed watching.

Tony turned when he saw the medium sized single family home set amidst the landscape of rubble. The porch lights were on. Tony drove a little further and stopped. The two men left the car and walked to the steel hut.

"I didn't realize you lived here," Tony said. "What's it like being out here?" *If you're a watch dog or a five hundred pound slob, maybe it's okay, but normal people living out here in a junkyard?*

"Took some getting used to, but I love it now," the big man replied. "I love waking up to the sunrise, hearing and seeing all kinds of birds most of the year, listening to the wind come through all them reeds and plants along the shores, no other people around to get in my way. I don't feel like driving to get something to eat, hey, these days they come to you. Even out here. I tip 'em real well."

Tony stopped in front of the steel hut. Little Sal opened the door and surprised Tony as he had with the ease of his movement when he left the Cadillac. Tony popped open the trunk and called out to Little Sal, telling him he'd need a hand.

This guy is always carrying around more weight than these two stiffs combined, Tony thought. And he looks like he enjoys doing Tommy a favor.

Little Sal made his way to the Cadillac's trunk. He put one thick leg in front as he took each step, first right, then left. Tony thought it took effort, but Little Sal didn't look like he was having any difficulty. *He travels like an earth moving machine,* Tony thought.

By the time Tony exited the car and walked around the back, Little Sal had pulled both corpses from the trunk and was dragging them to the shed, pulling them both, with an arm of one dead man in each hand. Tony followed him into the corrugated shed. Sal told Tony this was where metal was cleaned when necessary. Tony could hear Little Sal struggling for breath when they were inside and Sal dropped the arms, which hit the floor with a thud.

"Would you flick the switch to the right of the door?" Little Sal asked. When the lights came on, Tony saw that the hut had a bare earthen floor and was empty save for a large vat in the center of the room, about five feet high, ten feet wide and five feet deep. It looked to Tony like an oversized bathtub constructed of some sort of metal.

Little Sal stopped dragging the bodies when he reached into the vat.

"This is hydrochloric acid," he explained. "It's one of the most corrosive chemicals available. It's used to clean metals when they arrive really dirty or when they need to be spotless for electronics or stuff like that. It's so powerful we have to dilute it to one-tenth of its full strength. This is a little stronger. Watch what it does to these two. Can you give me a hand with them?" Tony realized that while Little Sal was able to drag the bodies from the trunk, once they were at ground level, he couldn't bend down far enough to grab them.

Tony didn't like touching dead bodies but long ago accepted that in his line of work it was inevitable. He closed his eyes as he grabbed one arm from each dead man and pulled the bodies up far enough for Little Sal to reach. The big man effortlessly hoisted them to the five-foot high rim level and dropped them in to the vat.

"Watch this," he instructed, and Tony watched as bubbles began forming on the surface, growing in intensity as the bodies quickly sank. In a matter of seconds neither could be seen, and after a half minute, the bubbling disappeared just like the two bodies.

"Dissolved," Little Sal said. "Everything, even shoes and belts. Nobody's ever finding these two."

Tony gazed into the vat and nodded his approval. "I've heard Tommy and the Boss talk about cleaning metal, and I figured that was what was up when Tommy said to tell you that's what we needed, but this is the first time I've seen it. Oh yeah, Tommy always has me take care of a guy that gives a hand when needed." He pulled a wad of bills from his pants pocket and peeled off a few hundreds.

"For your efforts," Tony said. He extended the hand holding the money and Little Sal reached for it. Except he didn't grab the money, and instead wrapped his own ham-sized hand around Tony's hand, squeezing so hard Tony cried out in pain and dropped the hundred dollar bills to the dirt floor. Little Sal moved his free hand to Tony's rear waistband and lifted him, until he was level with the top of the vat. The gun Tommy gave him fell from Tony's waistband to the ground just before he went over the edge and into the acid. Tony's cries ended when he hit the surface and the bubbling began, building in intensity until they were all gone along with any trace of Tony.

Tommy the Turtle knows his crew, that's for sure, Little Sal thought as he heaved the gun into the acid. He had to sweep it into a dustpan with a long handle, and lift it up, as he could not bend. *He said Tony would probably not dump it as told but would keep it and use it for his own purposes. That proved he was planning to double-cross Tommy, which also meant double-crossing the Boss.* Sal picked up the hundred dollar bills with the broom and dustpan method and put the money in the pocket of his robe.

Too bad I didn't have a chance to get the rest of his cash, Little Sal thought as he walked to the Cadillac. He stopped to lock the gate. He liked the oldies played on the radio and he liked the feel of the big Cadillac as he accelerated onto the freeway.

Forty minutes later, he locked up the car at the Newark Airport long term parking lot. He put on a ski mask as he approached the ticket machine and removed it when he was parked. Sal opened the trunk and removed the portable electric wheelchair he'd picked up at the house on his way out. Sal found it inside an old ambulance he bought for scrap and parts, and he was able to get the motor working. He used it to get around his property on those days when his strength was sapped by the heat or the cold or the normal wear and tear of lugging around over four hundred pounds.

He sat in the wheelchair and made his way towards section 107, as Tommy instructed. He kept his head down as far as it would go. He saw Tommy sitting in a green Lincoln Town Car with Jersey plates, so he knew it wasn't Tommy's own car. The car was stopped in front of the shuttle station. He rolled himself over to Tommy, who popped open his trunk so Little Sal could store the chair.

"You did good, Sal, real good. Me and the Boss are real happy."

Little Sal smiled and felt warmth spreading inside his corpulent body.

"After all you done for me, Tommy, this is the least I could do in return. I did just like you said, put on the mask, pulled the black bathrobe so tight my balls were hurting, and kept my head down over here from the car. I didn't see cameras, but if there were any, no way there's a good ID of me. It's not like I'm the only fat guy in America, and sooner or later some poor sucker's gonna wonder how the hell his Caddie got from JFK to Newark."

Tommy reached his right arm across to Little Sal's cheek and gave it a hard pinch.

"Hey, *paisano*, we help each other out, don't you forget that. I need you and you need me. We're like, what-do-you call-it, when two things need each other to live?"

Little Sal screwed his eyes as he concentrated.

"I don't know that word, Tommy, but I know what you mean."

They drove in silence for a minute. Little Sal remembered something that stuck in his mind as a loose end.

"Tommy, you told me there was the two stiffs. I got rid of the stiffs and Tony for you, and I know you did it because you couldn't trust them. What about the other two guys in your crew, the ones that took the truck full of booze? Weren't you supposed to meet them at the drop off point, give them their money before they drop off the rig at some truck stop?"

"I just got back from the truck stop, Little Sal. As for their dough, I'm giving it to you."

"How's that work, Tommy? You're never wrong when it comes to paying your people. Just like everybody else, they're working because they need the money."

"Well, that's just it, Little Sal. They don't need it. They're in the trunk and you're gonna have to do some more metal cleaning tonight before you go to sleep."

Little Sal did exactly as Tommy told him, including another drive to Newark Airport after the two additional bodies were dropped into the acid. Tommy had a man meet Sal at Newark just as before. Sal was driven home and before the man dropped Sal off in front of his house, he handed him an envelope from Tommy.

"It's okay, you can count it if you like," the man said. Little Sal thumbed each bill and counted in his head. There was ten thousand dollars in hundreds.

"Tommy really likes you, Sal," the man said just before he left. "And that's really good, because you saw tonight what happens if he doesn't like you." The man smiled in a way that told Little Sal he'd happily shoot him in the face right then and there were Tommy to ask.

SEVEN

Two weeks after Bangkok reopened and
Tommy hijacked the liquor

I t was one of those rare mornings when Glenn didn't feel like
making his own high-end coffee at home and headed straight to
the NJA Club for breakfast. He and Sleepy Joe stayed up late the
night before, watching old horror movies and smoking one large joint
after another. The coffee at the NJA Club was certainly acceptable, if
not on the level of his home brew, and Wang knew how to cook eggs
easy over and make hash browns as proficiently as any short-order
cook in America.

Ahn the waitress brought Glenn his breakfast. Glenn watched as
she walked back to the kitchen, then pulled his head forward again.
He was glad to have a waitress he liked as a person, but where there
was no physical or emotional attraction. *No more getting involved with
waitresses at the NJA Club.* He was still hurt and confused by Kit
running off to marry another man, trying to figure out how he hadn't
seen it coming. A female voice from behind him interrupted his
thoughts.

"Mr. Glenn Murray Cohen?" Glenn turned around and faced a
farang woman, an attractive blonde Glenn thought to be somewhere
in her mid to upper thirties. Her hair was cut short, just below chin-
level, her skin tinged red, the sign of a new arrival in the land where

the sun shines long and bright and hard. She was a few inches shorter than Glenn's five foot nine. Glenn saw no sign of fat pushing against the gray the pants suit or white blouse that fit perfectly. She set her blue handbag on the table.

"Mind if I join you?" she asked, her blue eyes focused on Glenn.

"And if I said no?" Glenn asked.

"I'd sit here anyway," she replied. When she sat down, Glenn caught the scent of the very same perfume his ex-wife favored. *We've been divorced over fifteen years and I'm not sure I really remember her face anymore, but I remember the smell of her perfume,* Glenn thought ruefully.

"In that case," Glenn asked, "can I get you a coffee and maybe a bite to eat?"

The woman thought for a moment and said she'd take a coffee, black, and toasted wheat bread. Glenn signaled to Ahn, who took the order.

"Maybe now you can tell me who you are, since you already know who I am."

The farang woman reached into the neckline of her blouse and pulled out a badge on the end of a chain. Glenn had seen enough FBI badges in his criminal lawyer days to recognize one. They hadn't changed at all.

"A little out of your jurisdiction, aren't you, Special Agent . . .?"

"O'Halloran," the agent said. "Mary O'Halloran." She reached into her purse and after fumbling for a few seconds pulled out a card which she handed Glenn. He ran a finger over the embossed FBI seal.

"As you know," he said, "fake badges and business cards are a cottage industry around these parts."

Mary O'Halloran smiled.

"I'm well aware of the counterfeiting and fraud that goes on here," she said. "I am FBI after all. But I'm not with those specialized units, important as they are. If you have any doubts about my credentials, ask your friend Oliver. He'll vet and verify me in minutes. Give him a call if you like."

Glenn shook his head.

"No need," he said. "I'll find out who you really are through Oliver or elsewhere and if you're not who you say you are, I'll know that in a New York minute. Until I have some reason to believe otherwise, you are Special Agent O'Halloran, with all the rights and privileges appurtenant thereto." Ahn brought the food and coffee, and the two Americans were silent until she was gone.

"Call me Mary," the agent said. "As for rights and privileges, there aren't a whole lot of them an American agent has over here, as you stated when we began our conversation.

"Which is why I need you," she added.

Glenn struggled to not spit out the coffee he had just sipped. He put down his cup.

"Mary, Special Agent O'Halloran, or anyone you want to be, please be advised I am retired from the law and my brand new visa here absolutely will not permit me to do any kind of work. I'm very sorry to disappoint you, but that's life."

Mary O'Halloran stared at Glenn long enough for him to appreciate the intensity behind her blue eyes and the wiliness behind the white-toothed smile.

"If you think I'm disappointed, Glenn, wait until Freddie Trammel hears you wouldn't help us to get him free."

Glenn froze in his chair, not moving a muscle, not even blinking. He didn't even breathe for ten seconds. He inhaled and exhaled a deep breath but the memory he had inhaled years before stayed with him.

Freddie Trammel. They always do it this way, they get what they want out of you because you care about someone else.

Twenty years before Mary O' Halloran showed up at the NJA Club in Bangkok, Glenn was a journeyman criminal lawyer in San Francisco, on the mid to upper level of his craft. He was respected and well-known enough to own a house in the city and eat in expensive restaurants. His name got around enough for Freddie Trammel's family to know of him.

"You must have really dug into my past to know about Freddie," Glenn said when he recovered his composure. "I haven't spoken to anyone about the case since the day I called his mother to say the California Supreme Court denied our petition and that was effectively the end of the road. A life term for something he didn't do."

"I know," Mary said. She patted Glenn's hand. "We know now he didn't kidnap and rape that young woman, which is why none of his DNA has ever been found on any evidence, no matter how much the tests improve."

Glenn watched her remove her hand from his just before he replied.

"U.S. Supreme Court says even being innocent isn't good enough anymore if it becomes known too late in the game. Talk about exalting form over substance."

Mary patted his hand again before continuing.

"This may come as a surprise to you, Glenn, but a lot of us FBI agents hate the thought of an innocent person sitting in prison. It means somebody in law enforcement screwed up and that poor person is paying the price. And by the way, here's a second surprise for you. We have the guy who really did rape that woman and we have his DNA and two eyewitnesses putting him at the scene."

Glenn bolted forward and gripped the arms of his chair.

"You need my help getting Freddie out of prison and clearing his name? You got it, all the evidence, Special Agent O'Halloran. What do I have to do?"

"First of all, I told you to call me Mary," she said. "Second, I already told you I needed your help, but I didn't say I needed it to free Freddie Trammel. I can have that done with a phone call. The governor will pardon him on the grounds of innocence. It will all be over with the stroke of a pen. He could be home in time for dinner."

"You haven't even told me what you want me to do," Glenn said. "And what kind of an FBI is it that knows someone is innocent but lets them rot in jail unless they can extort another person to do their bidding?"

Mary sipped her coffee and then answered Glenn.

"We'll get to what we want you to do. But you have to understand that the FBI is not keeping Freddie in jail. We're the ones who put together the case for a release and a full pardon based on innocence.

He's getting out with or without your cooperation, though the latter may speed things up by years. You are his attorney of record, and it is our duty to inform you."

"Couldn't you have just sent an email?" Glenn asked.

Mary smiled. Glenn again noticed her facial features and her hair, and this time, even when they were both seated, he observed she was well-built.

"Then I wouldn't have the chance to meet such a handsome and charming man who will be of such great assistance to the United States."

"I'm not breaking any laws or hurting anybody in any way," Glenn said. "And I'm not getting into anything too deep or lasting too long. If what you want fits within those guidelines and gets Freddie out right away, let's hear what it is right now, and I'll decide on the spot."

"You drive a hard bargain," Mary said. "Sit tight and let me explain."

Mary told Glenn almost exactly what the General had said about the Mafia coming from America to force liquor on local businesses in a switch and bait scheme. The difference was that instead of "Mafia" Mary used the term "organized crime."

"Hijacking is a federal crime if it involves interstate commerce, which pretty much covers anything requiring travel on any federal highway anywhere, even for one second. Our businesses lose their investment and income and the governments lose sales taxes. In this case, "governments" includes Thailand. The Thai government is rather pleased to work with us in ridding their nation of foreign gangsters putting locals out of business and then avoiding taxes. Not to mention the possibility that once they are established over here, the Mafia forges ties with other criminal groups, perhaps becoming involved with foreign agents, even if they don't realize it, and it won't be easy to monitor them. We can imagine them providing local gangs services like laundering money or providing weapons. Nothing good can come of their being here, but plenty of bad things can happen."

Glenn took a few bites of his breakfast as Mary explained her mission, and when she was done, he had a question.

"This is all very interesting, but I've heard it before, and I'll say what I said then: this has nothing to do with me, and even if it did, I wouldn't have anything to do with it. I'd love to help Freddie, and I will do what I can now that I know there is a guilty person out there, but that still doesn't mean I can be of help to you. As an FBI agent sworn to tell the truth, I'm certain if Freddie files a habeas corpus petition, you would say in court under oath what you just told me and what will be in my sworn declaration. Are we done?"

"Not yet," Mary said. "You haven't let me finish. Forget about trying to free poor Freddie without me. I'll make sure your sworn declaration never makes it to court and neither do you or your unfortunate former client. Now let's get real, Glenn. We must by necessity work with some Thai law enforcement, even if we have strong suspicions many of its members have been compromised by criminals or by foreign powers. There is one police officer we are certain is honorable and loyal to his country and would be the perfect partner for us. The problem is that this person has a deep and abiding distrust of foreigners, except for one foreigner, who happens to be you. I'm talking about the man you call the Lieutenant."

She's done her homework, Glenn thought. *Like I did when I was a criminal lawyer.* "I see you checked me out," Glenn said. "I'd expect nothing less than this from the FBI."

The most basic investigation would include making a visit to where I live. They'd learn that I am good friends with Lek, the condo concierge, and that his cousin, who my friends and I call the Lieutenant, has worked with me and the General. It's not in Lek's nature to talk about tenants to strangers, especially farang women, so she must have followed Lek, found out about his cousin, and spied on him. I never liked the FBI. I definitely don't like Ms. O'Halloran.

"All you would have to do is hang around me when I'm working with the Lieutenant," Mary explained. "You won't have to say or do a thing. There's not going to be any danger involved, at least not for you."

"You government people bring danger with you wherever you go," Glenn said.

"One tried to kill me, another killed a suspect instead of bringing him back to the U.S. for trial. Now you're gunning for the Mafia. Make sure to include me out."

Mary O'Halloran smiled. She daintily sipped more coffee before responding.

"I'm sorry you had those experiences, but they were with the CIA, and if you didn't learn this as a criminal defense lawyer, I'll tell you now: there's no love lost between the Bureau and the CIA. We consider ourselves law enforcement. We arrest people who do the things they do."

Glenn thought for a second and then nodded in agreement.

"I've cross examined enough of you to fill up a large hall," he said. "You guys are wily, sneaky, smart, and tough on the stand, but for the most part, you're straight shooters who follow the rules and testify truthfully. I respect what you do but just don't want to be part of it." *And I'm not sure you are a straight shooter who follows the rules and tells the truth.*

"But you would like the new evidence on Freddie Trammel brought to the governor's attention forthwith, so he's out and declared innocent. A pardon beats everything, as you know. Am I right about that, Glenn?"

Glenn pictured Freddie Trammel sitting in a cell in Soledad Prison. Freddie would be older now by almost twenty years, and the soft facial features of a twenty-two year old were surely growing into middle age too soon under the harsh regimen of a California prison. *The prison system has never reformed anyone, never deterred anyone, and destroys an innocent person thrown into that hellhole.*

"Let's meet with the Lieutenant," Glenn said. "If he goes along with it, I'm on board. As soon as he agrees, Freddie gets out. But let's make one thing clear: I'm not carrying a gun. I had to use one once and that is it for me." *It's still sometimes hard to sleep even several years later. I'm never touching another gun.*

Mary O'Halloran smiled.

"Don't worry, Glenn. The last thing the Bureau wants is an

amateur like you running around armed. If there's any shooting required, and I really doubt there will be, it'll be the Lieutenant and me pulling the triggers. Don't expect to see any."

Didn't I say they were wily and sneaky? Maybe I should ask the General to loan me one of his bullet proof vests.

EIGHT

A WEEK BEFORE SLEEPY JOE MET THE THREE THUGS, TWO WEEKS BEFORE GLENN MET MARY

The cabbie let Paulie out on the corner of Sukhumvit Road and soi 4, known colloquially as "Soi Nana." Paulie told him he wanted to go to where the go-go bars were, and the driver smiled and drove him to the busiest red light district in the city.

Paulie made his way through crowds so thick he could not see more than a few feet ahead or move more than a few inches at a time. It seemed to him there were only two types of people on Soi Nana: white men, older and most overweight, and young Thai women, most relatively thin and adorned with at least one tattoo. The crowds spilled off the sidewalks and into the street, where vehicular traffic moved far slower than humans on feet. Paulie understood why the cab driver left him off at the corner.

Over the next hour, Paulie sampled a half dozen establishments, most of them go-go bars with dark interiors, capacity crowds, stools and chairs facing a stage where women writhed seductively on poles with discotheque-style music blaring. Paulie hadn't heard such music since old-style discos stopped being popular in Brooklyn. In each bar, he found a seat and waited until a scantily clad server took his order for a beer, always careful to ask them what they wanted to drink. Someone back in the States told him the girls made money for each drink they sold, including ones bought for them. Paulie was comfortable making small talk with each, and when it was clear they would not be the one to tell him what he wanted to know, he left a generous tip and went on to the next place. He assured himself he'd know right away when he found someone who was enough of a hustler to help him. *Hookers are the same all over,* he thought.

On his sixth bar, when he was starting to feel the effects of five previous beers on his mind and his bladder, he visited the restroom, and when he returned saw that the seat he vacated was gone and there were no others available. He was about to leave when he felt a tug on his arm. He turned to face a Thai woman who stood almost as tall as his five foot seven, and while having a difficult time guessing ages of the women, could see this one was a few years older than the ladies hanging from the poles. She asked Paulie if he was looking for a seat. He said yes, and she took him by the hand, led him around the horseshoe-shaped stage where the dancers twisted and wriggled to music that was too loud, and brought him to a vacant stool in the first row of seats not more than two feet from the stage.

"It helps when you have a friend to save your seat," she said with a smile.

Paulie would have felt more comfortable with a friend, but Johnny would never set foot in a place like this and bringing a hothead like Tommy always ran the risk he'd start trouble, and trouble was not what Paulie the Arranger needed when he was trying to make a connection. He'd bring Tommy in after a deal for muscle to supervise was sealed.

The Thai woman told Paulie her name was Nice, and he said his name was Rick. She had been working at this bar for three years, and in the business for nine. *Probably means twelve or more years,* Paulie thought. After the second round of drinks, he paid Nice's bar fine to the *mamasan* and Nice brought him to a cheap by-the-hour hotel. In the brighter light of the hotel lobby, Paulie could see that Nice was definitely older than most of the other girls. He could clearly make out the beginnings of lines at the edges of her eyes and the very beginning of wrinkles along her neck.

He didn't have to pay for more than one hour. Paulie had tried sex with African American and Latino prostitutes in Brooklyn and discovered that the race or color made no difference. He found the same to be true with his first experience with an Asian woman, though it wasn't as exciting to him as making a connection for local tough guys. The truth was that Paulie never really understood other men's obsession with sex, and when he found himself having any, as soon as it began he looked forward to it being over. This time was no different, but he knew he had to paint a different picture if he wanted Nice to help him. *If she's been doing this for nine years like she says, she must know every operator on this street, and this is the kind of street where operators can be found.* He gave her an extra thousand baht over the two thousand he agreed to pay.

"I had a great time," he told Nice as they left the room. "I hope I can see you again tomorrow." Nice smiled and told him to be at the bar at nine p.m. the next night.

No better or worse than any of the others, Paulie thought. *Personally, I think the whole sex thing is overrated.*

The second night Paulie wasted no time in the bar. He paid the bar fine to the mamasan within minutes of arrival and left with Nice. They returned to the same hotel they'd visited the night before. When they were in the room, Nice started to undress before taking the obligatory shower required of every hooker and customer in Thailand. Paulie held up his hand and she stopped.

"I'm not in the mood tonight," he explained. "Nothing wrong with you, it's just one of those days. But you're still getting paid, probably more than you expected." He explained to her that he was in Bangkok to sell security systems, and that required going into some rough neighborhoods. He needed three men who could protect him and his goods. They had to understand English.

"All those years working this street, you must know someone who can find me such men," he said.

Nice nodded.

"I know such a man. He's an American, like you. I can set up a meeting. How much you pay me?"

Paulie handed her five one thousand baht notes.

"There's five more when I meet him," he said.

"Meet me at bar tomorrow night at nine, " Nice said. "We will go see the person."

After Paulie met Nice at the bar and paid the bar fine, she hailed a cab. The driver took them to a dark and winding side soi a quarter mile off Sukhumvit Road. The cab stopped in front of a building with a store of some type - the Thai script meant Paulie couldn't read it - that was closed and had a metal gate protecting its doorway. Paulie thought there might be apartments above the store, but in the dark it was not possible to tell for certain. Nice told Paulie how much to pay the driver, and they left the cab.

Nice walked to the gated door and rattled it loudly several times.

"Wouldn't a doorbell be better?" Paulie asked her.

"He don't have no bell," she replied.

After she rattled the gate the second time, Paulie heard locks being undone and a small Thai man emerged from the building into the small vestibule between the gate and the door. The man unlocked the gate. He spoke to Nice in Thai.

"He's telling us to go upstairs," she explained to Paulie.

They followed the man up a narrow flight of stairs. At the top, the man rapped three times on a metal door. The door opened and another Thai man, this one larger and more muscular than the first, greeted them in English.

"Follow me," was all he said. They followed him through the empty room and faced a third door, which the tough-looking Thai opened. Paulie scanned the room they had just entered. A black man with a shaved head sat behind a desk that didn't have a thing upon it except a whiskey decanter and a small tray of shot glasses. The man rose to greet his visitors.

"You must be Rick," the black man said as he walked around the desk to shake hands with Paulie. He was over six feet tall and was built like the young toughs the Boss hired when he needed extra muscle. "Call me Baxter," he continued. "We're not big on last names around here, so it will be Rick and Baxter. Okay?"

"Fine with me," Paulie replied, wondering if Baxter was the man's first name as he shook his hand. He was surprised to see that Nice's connection was black. He was expecting a Thai. *I've dealt with them back home,* he assured himself. *Times have changed. My father would have never dealt with one.*

"Good firm handshake," Baxter said. "I like that in a man. Better than a credit check or background investigation. You can fool a lot of people about a lot of things, but you can't fool me about a handshake."

Sounds like something the Boss would say, Paulie thought.

Baxter looked at the big Thai who had led Paulie and Nice up the stairs.

"Chong, why don't you take Miss Nice downstairs to the entertainment room and let her watch one of her soap operas while Rick and I discuss business? See if she wants anything to eat or drink." Chong spoke to Nice in Thai, and the two left the room.

"Great lady," Baxter said when he and Paulie were alone. "Was a great lay back in the days, but now I hardly ever make it to any bars. I take it you would agree with me on her skills in bed, but I also bet it's her connection to me that you find most attractive about Nice."

"You're very perceptive," Paulie replied.

"Let me pour us some whiskey and we'll sit down and talk about your needs and how I can help," Baxter said. Without waiting for Paulie to reply, he filled two shot glasses with whiskey from the decanter, sat down behind his desk, and motioned for Paulie to take one of the seats facing him, which Paulie did. He accepted the shot glass Baxter handed him, nodding in thanks. Baxter held out his shot glass and Paulie did the same, meeting Baxter's just when his arm could reach no further.

"*Chok dii khrup,*" Baxter said as the glasses clinked. Paulie had heard that phrase in the bar and figured out it was a Thai toast. He poured half the shot glass down his throat. The whiskey was smooth, with a pleasant aftertaste. *This guy likes the good stuff,* he thought. *Just like the Boss.*

Baxter downed his shot in one movement. He put the empty glass on his desk and looked at Paulie. Paulie saw the man was completely calm and completely in control and surmised it was always this way for Baxter.

"What is it I can do for you, Rick, and whether that's your real name or not doesn't matter to me, as long as your cash is real."

"My cash is good," Paulie answered, equally calm and in control of himself. Bangkok or Brooklyn, Paulie was born to arrange things.

"I have some liquor I'd like to sell to places here in Bangkok," Paulie explained. "It's top shelf stuff, some of it as good as what you just served. We can offer it at very good prices and the customers don't pay us until the booze is delivered to them. We give them thirty days. But I don't know this town the way you do, and I don't want to be known as a guy with lots of good booze and no protection. I'm sure you can understand," Paulie said, then thinking, *since he seems to have more protection than the Boss.*

A wide smile crossed Baxter's face. Paulie notices that except for the lines formed at the corners of his smiling lips, there wasn't a wrinkle to be seen on Baxter's face.

"I like your directness. I also like the way you figured out if you need to speak to a guy like me and you don't know anyone, so you start in the bars, find a streetwise hooker, and sooner or later you'll find who you're looking for. We rarely ever see anyone that smart around here. A smart guy with balls can go really far around here. How do you think I got to be who I am?"

"By being a good judge of character," Paulie said. "Since we've pegged each other for who we are, let's do some business. I need three good men, and I need them right away. They have to be tough enough to scare the shit out of anyone who's thinking about saying no, but they gotta have enough self-control to not cause unnecessary problems. And I have to be able to communicate with them in English."

Baxter poured himself a second shot and filled Paulie's half empty glass. They clinked and toasted again.

"I have just the trio in mind for you," Baxter said after polishing off his second shot in one slug while Paulie sipped his slowly, savoring the mild aftertaste.

"They'll cost you fifteen thousand baht a day, no matter how many hours you have them out pushing your booze. If you want to commit to a week, I can give them to you for ninety thousand baht. You can have them for a whole month for only three hundred thousand."

Paulie's brain quick calculated the conversion to dollars. At the current exchange rate, it would cost a little over four hundred dollars day, around three grand for a week, and under nine thousand bucks for a month. It was cheaper to rent this much muscle for a month in Bangkok than it cost for a week in Brooklyn.

"Sounds like we have a deal in the works," Paulie said. "When do I get to meet them?"

"When I see the money," Baxter said.

Paulie reached into a pants pocket and retrieved a roll of bills, all thousand baht notes. He counted out thirty and placed them on the desk.

"This is for the first two days," he said, "If they're okay, I'll give you another two seventy for the rest of the month."

Baxter held out his hand again.

"We do have a deal," he said. "I'll introduce you to them right now."

"That won't be necessary," Paulie said, with the assurance of a man who had just paid thirty thousand baht.

"They won't be reporting to me. It'll be my business associate who deals with them"

Baxter laughed softly.

"Business associate, you say? I didn't know I was dealing with a corporation. Nice didn't mention anyone else."

"You're not dealing with a corporation," Paulie said. "But we are a business. And I didn't mention my associate to Nice. She only had to know enough to get me to you."

Baxter laughed softly again.

"You've told me enough, Mr. Rick. I think I know the kind of business you're in. No problem on this end."

"On this one either," Paulie replied.

Baxter insisted on one more shot of his fine whiskey. When his shot glass was dry, Paulie told Baxter he had to leave, and asked when his associate could meet the three men he had just hired.

"You bring your friend over to Nice's bar tomorrow at nine and introduce them. Then you leave. Nice will let me know he's there and one of my men will show up outside in a cab. If you want to keep them after the two day trial, show up at Nice's bar the third night with the balance and she'll let me know. We can enjoy more fine scotch."

"It was a pleasure meeting you and doing business," Paulie said as he headed towards the door.

"Any time you need help, you just have Nice get in touch with me," Baxter said. "There's a cab waiting for you downstairs."

Paulie closed the door behind him and nodded to the Thai men he passed on his way out.

When he reached the street, he saw the cab. He told the driver to take him to the Holiday Inn on the corner of Sukhumvit Road and soi 18, from where he would walk to his actual hotel several blocks away. *No reason Baxter has to know where I'm staying,* he thought.

Tommy had no qualms about meeting Baxter and the three hired hands. Johnny was clear: if Paulie the Arranger felt good about Baxter, they would go with his instincts.

"This Baxter guy has no reason to double cross us in any way," Paulie told the other two. "He strikes me one hundred percent as the kind of guy who rents out muscle among his other business interests. He's being well-paid to provide us with some. I don't see how he benefits by screwing us over, or worse."

That evening, Paulie brought Tommy to the go-go bar and introduced Tommy and Nice. Paulie bought the first round of drinks and left when they were done. When he was back on the street, he realized he didn't say goodbye to Nice.

Tommy called Johnny as soon as he was back in his hotel room.

"Everything went as planned," he said. "I got to meet Baxter over at his place. You didn't mention he's black, but that's okay, it's not like I never work with any of them back home.

The three men we're hiring were there too. They seem like they'll do the job. They are all big and they've done this stuff before. Their leader is Russian, speaks real good English, and they got a Thai guy in case someone don't understand English. They're scary looking enough so I don't think they'll ever need to get to the rough stuff."

"Good," Johnny said. "Last thing we need is rough stuff."

NINE

Tommy the Turtle did not like Thai food and saw no reason why he should.

He and Johnny were up at the crack of noon, seated at a table in the dining room of the hotel where the three Brooklynites had taken rooms. Breakfast was over by the time they arrived, but coffee was all they wanted. It was Sunday afternoon, and they drank their coffees while deciding where to go and what to do that evening. Since Paulie the Arranger found the three locals to follow up recalcitrant potential buyers of booze, the three mobsters had more than enough leisure time on their hands. Paulie was off to the local gold dealer, where he would sell more of the Canadian Maple Leaf coins the Boss had given them in addition to the cash to cover expenses.

"No need to declare anything on the way in or out," the Boss explained. "None of you are taking more than ten grand total. And this way there's no record of any transactions, cause it's all in cash, every penny." Every one of those bullion coins would bring in over sixty thousand baht, and each man arrived with five, one around their neck and one on their belt buckles, along with five thousand dollars cash. They weren't running out of money any time soon and in fact were expecting to soon bring in more than the gold.

None of this caused Tommy to change his mind about eating Thai food.

"There's plenty of Italian restaurants in this town," Tommy told Johnny for the tenth time when Johnny suggested trying some of the local cuisine for dinner. "You can eat that shit if you like, but I'm sticking with what I know."

"Suit yourself," Johnny replied. "We've been here over three weeks already and it's about time you accepted it and try enjoying it."

Tommy the Turtle was having none of it.

"Soon as we have the customers lined up and delivery and payment systems working, we're going back to Brooklyn." Paulie would have to figure out some way to get the money changed into dollars and sent to America without being noticed. *Perhaps send the dough back on the ships, if we can trust those people.*

"Don't rush things too quickly," Johnny said. "I'm starting to like it here."

Tommy frowned.

"Johnny, you know the Boss needs you. They don't call you The Brain for nothing."

"I'm in no hurry," Johnny said. "What's there not to like here? They got great food, beautiful women, nightclubs, massages, beautiful beaches a short plane ride away. I could get used to it all."

Tommy got up from his chair and walked behind Johnny. He placed his hands on Johnny's shoulders, gently massaging them.

"Hey pal, I know you been working hard, and let me say, anyone can see brainwork is as tough as the heavy stuff the rest of us do for the Boss. But you're not so tired you forgot we're Brooklyn all the way; Brooklyn and nothing but Brooklyn. I can see why you like it here, but it just ain't for us. Home is Brooklyn and that's where we go, soon as the Boss says the booze business don't need us here. We know that's happening, cause like I said, the Boss needs you."

"Don't I know that," Johnny said. "I also know he's going to have me back and that's for sure. But hey, meanwhile, I'm not the first white guy to dream of a beautiful life in Asia, so let me enjoy it while I'm here."

Tommy placed an unlit Marlboro between his lips, a sign he was getting ready to leave. He spoke through clenched lips.

"This being Sunday, me and Paulie are gonna take some money and head out to the track. Paulie found out they got one here and even though betting on horses is illegal, you can do it at this track. We're gonna grab some lunch at this Italian place before we grab a taxi and play the horses. Interested?"

Johnny shook his head.

"Nah, Tommy, you know I don't bet. And I can eat all the Italian food I want back home. If you gave the Thai food a chance, you might find you like it."

Tommy got up from his chair and faced Johnny.

"The food here sucks," he said. "The only stuff that don't make me barf are the noodles, and they stole that from us Italians." He turned and walked to the apartment door.

"Actually, Tommy, we stole it from the Chinese. Marco Polo. Look it up." Tommy was out the door before Johnny finished.

How did I wind up with such people? he asked himself.

After Tommy and Paulie left, Johnny returned to his room and grabbed several thousand baht notes from the bedside table drawer in his room. He stuffed them into his pants pocket.

Everyone's a millionaire around here, he thought. *Walking around with thousands, even tens of thousands, like it was nothing. It really isn't a whole lot. A thousand baht is not even thirty bucks. If I stayed here, I could never work another day in my life, never have worry, and the only thing making me sweat would be the sun.*

Johnny had to leave the hotel at least once a day as he went about his business, mostly checking in with Paulie to see what new contacts and tidbits he picked up. When they held such discussions, Johnny insisted they be in a large park not far from their hotel. Johnny was not paranoid, but he knew of too many men who didn't think anyone was bugging them until the day were arrested. Johnny was so careful he hadn't even contacted the Boss, and there was no need to unless there was a problem. He knew he wouldn't be in Bangkok unless the Boss had one hundred percent confidence in him. He had some burner cell phones if he really needed to call Brooklyn. He didn't keep notes either; his phenomenal memory was another reason the Boss valued him so much. No one would ever be indicted because of something Johnny Brancini wrote down.

Johnny didn't mind his daily meeting with Paulie, who was smarter and exponentially less violent than Tommy the Turtle. Paulie almost sounded like a cop as he described his daily work, which consisted mainly of trying to get the lay of the land, at least from a gangster's perspective.

"You have lunch and a few drinks at that Foreign Correspondents Club, and I taught myself how to get there on that Skytrain they have here. You ought to try it, Johnny. Makes anything we got back home look like a damn joke. Anyway, those reporters love to talk about themselves, and you'd be surprised what you can pick up. Especially if you tell them you're a writer. Hey, Johnny, I write love notes to my *gumar* when I'm back home. Hang around beer bars shooting pool and drinking with expats who pass along anything they hear, or find a smart, older bar girl with good English and see what you can learn from her. Pay extra and you'll be surprised what they suddenly remember hearing. You'd be surprised how many big mouth guys tell these broads things they never shoulda said."

When they were done talking, Paulie would head back to the hotel or to the nearest massage parlor. Johnny would walk around with no particular plan in mind. Johnny enjoyed walking the streets of Bangkok. It was a world he never knew existed, filled with people he had never imagined existed on this earth. *Maybe Mom was right and I should have gone to college, where I would have known all of this*, he thought the first time he ventured out of the hotel on his own. *Could have, should have, might have been, none of that matters now.*

Johnny began by walking up on side of Sukhumvit Road, crossing at one of the Sky Train overpasses, and then walking back in the other direction. For a week he did this every morning and every evening until he felt comfortable among people who looked, spoke, and acted differently than anyone he'd ever known in Brooklyn. The second week, he ventured onto some of the numbered cross streets, occasionally even meandering down the small side sois off them.

On the third week, he dared to try a piece of grilled chicken on a stick, which he bought from a smiling middle-aged woman who gave him a *wai,* the traditional Thai way of bowing to show respect, when he handed a fifty baht note for a twenty baht piece and indicated putting up a hand that she could keep the change. After that, he made it a point to stop at a different food stand every day and leave a similar gratuity. He came to appreciate not only grilled chicken, but pomegranate juice, watermelon slices where the seeds had been carefully removed, even a packet of sticky rice, which he learned by pantomime from the pretty young women who sold it, was to be eaten while held in the bare hand. By the end of the third week, he had stopped eating lunch or dinner in the hotel and tested several local restaurants. One became his favorite and he had eaten dinner there every day of his fourth week in Bangkok.

Johnny never asked Tommy how his local crew persuaded potential customers. Several agreed to accept shipments and a handful actually made deposits on the liquor. He didn't want to know the details beyond this. The rule in the mob was you only need to know what you need to know, and that axiom prevented generations of busted wise guys from squealing on their bosses.

Johnny knew the idea that mob guys, even made men, don't rat out their crews is a myth, and the law of silence, or omertà, is observed as much in the breach as in the obedience. The rat has been part of the world of criminals as long as there have been people needing to bargain their way out of decades in prison. The main reason there was less of it in the Mafia was because most of the lower level men just didn't know enough to offer the law. That was fine with Johnny, in a relatively exalted position in mob hierarchy, as the Boss's right hand man and very possibly his someday successor. When Johnny was a few years younger, that thought motivated him; but for the past few years, he silently prayed that day never arrived.

The man is twenty years older and at least a hundred pounds more than me. He smokes a half dozen cigars a day, polishes off at least half a bottle of scotch and bottle of red wine along with them. He never exercised a day in his life. On top of that, the law would love to put him away and other wise guys might want to bump him. Any of that happens, I'm the new Boss, looking at the same worries. Years ago, the idea titillated him, but not anymore.

Johnny knew that survival required keeping an eye on all fronts, all possible weak places that could bring a man down. Sometimes taking a light stretch in the joint is better than the mob thinking you were a snitch. The law is much more forgiving and compromising than the mob.

As long as I don't know something, I can't be seen as the rat, Johnny often reminded himself when he thought he might become privy to something there was no reason for him to know. He knew the Boss trusted him implicitly, but he never asked the Boss to tell him anything he didn't need to know to do his work.

One reason I'm still alive and liked.

There was no daylight between him and Tommy on this issue of avoiding any possibility of being turned into a snitch.

"The fewer who know, the less the chance of a rat. Or even someone getting drunk and saying something they shouldn't. I'm really big on keeping the lid on things," Tommy told Johnny when the Brain explained to the Turtle why neither of them needed to know the details about most of Paulie's arrangements other than they were done.

Johnny walked to the little Thai restaurant, a six block stroll from the condo, the one that had become his favorite. It was air-conditioned, and one of the waitresses spoke nearly perfect English. Johnny always made sure to have her take his orders. The last few times he'd eaten there, they exchanged some small talk. She was a young woman with a round face, hair tied in a bun reaching just above the nape of her neck and skin that reminded Johnny of latte. She stood about five foot two, a good half foot shorter than he, and if she weighed over a hundred pounds, he'd be surprised.

As soon as Johnny walked into the restaurant, that very waitress greeted him and led him to a small table. She handed him an English language menu.

"What's good today," he asked.

She smiled at him. She looked young to Johnny, but the other day, when he had lunch at the same restaurant, he struck up a conversation with an Englishman who lived in Bangkok. The friendly Brit informed Johnny that it was rather difficult to pinpoint the age of a Thai woman, and a foreigner could easily be off by as much as ten years, even more. The waitress appeared to be somewhere in her twenties, but he had stored the Brit's advice and withheld judgment.

"You already tried pad thai, larb, som thai, now it's time for you to try something even more spicy for farangs than the som thai. I'll tell them the kitchen to make it less spicy. We call it pad prik king. It is a dry red curry made with red hot chiles and green beans. It's a beautiful dark red. If you want something even spicier, with choice of beef, pork, chicken, or fish, I recommend what we just call pad prik. Of course, it's also time for you to try our most famous soup, tom yum kung, also very spicy. It has lemongrass and ginger as well. This dish is a gorgeous red orange."

Johnny ordered the pad prik with chicken and the soup. He watched the waitress bring his order to the kitchen.

They're never so nice and sweet back in Brooklyn.

Johnny actually enjoyed his meal. He took the waitress's advice and ate slowly, small spoonfuls with rice and water to tamp down any fires in his mouth. The heat was bearable, and he appreciated the subtle taste combinations it brought out. He knew it would take time to become fully acclimated to Thai spice levels, but he deemed it achievable, given sufficient time.

When he was done, the waitress brought the check and asked how he enjoyed his meal. He told her he enjoyed it very much. Then he realized he didn't know her name, so he asked.

"Fah," she replied.

"That's a very nice name," Johnny said. "Does it have any special meaning?"

Fah widened her smile.

"It depends," she said. "It could mean the sky, or it could mean the color of the sky, or it could even be an angel."

This time Johnny smiled.

"Which one are you?" he asked.

Fah blushed.

"Maybe I'm a blue angel," she said.

"You know about the Blue Angels in the U.S. Air Force?" Johnny asked, his surprise obvious in his voice.

"Oh no," Fah replied. "It's the name of a vodka."

Johnny placed one of his thousand baht notes on the little silver tray that held the check. Fah took it to the cashier for change. When she returned, Johnny plucked the five hundred baht note, leaving the two hundred for Fah. She smiled at Johnny as she pocketed the generous gratuity.

"I hope you are enjoying your time in Bangkok, for whatever reason brings you here," she said.

"I'm just here relaxing, taking a break from my busy life back home," he replied.

"Have you seen the sights?" she asked. "The Grand Palace, Wat Arun, Chinatown, the Chao Phraya River?"

"I'm afraid I haven't," Johnny said. "To be honest, I never even heard of any of those places until a few days ago when some guy in my hotel mentioned seeing some of them."

Fah looked at Johnny for a few seconds as a serious look came across her face.

"You really should make sure to see these places before you go home. All my farang customers like them very much."

Johnny looked down in embarrassment.

How could I be so stupid? Passing myself off as a middle-aged

American man enjoying his first long vacation ever, and I don't do a single tourist thing? Not good. Sooner or later I'd trip up.

"I'm not much of a traveler," he explained. "I wouldn't know how to go about getting to any of these places."

Fah laughed.

"Bangkok is easy to get around. Look at all the tourists on the streets, on the Skytrain, the subway, in taxis. There must be a travel agent desk in your hotel. They can set you up with a tour."

Johnny nodded. It was a smart idea that would solve a possible problem. It might even be fun. He thanked Fah. She gave him a slight wai. Tommy walked towards the door, then he stopped, turned around, and walked back to Fah.

"I've got a better idea," he said. "Why don't you be my guide? Then I know I'll enjoy it all."

Fah shook her head and her smile evaporated.

"Sorry, but the boss doesn't like it if the staff dates customers. Creates too many problems he says."

Johnny blushed. He wasn't accustomed to people telling him that he couldn't do what he wanted. He caught himself and forced a weak smile.

"Oh, I fully understand, and we have the same rules back home. But I'm not asking you out on a date. I'm asking you to be my tour guide, and I'd gladly pay for your services."

This time it was Fah who blushed and forced a smile. She nodded slightly.

"That is different," she said. "I will be happy to show you my city, but I won't accept money to do it. Thais want our visitors to enjoy themselves and you seem like a smart man who would enjoy learning our history and culture."

"I'm sure I will," he said. "I couldn't ask for a better guide. You speak English so perfectly, better than a lot of my friends. And I bet you know everything there is to know about the places I'm going to see."

Fah's face matched the serious tone of her voice.

"I should hope I speak English well," she said. "It was my major at university. I was hoping to come to America and study American literature. Then Covid came along."

College girl. I bet she does know all about those things she mentioned.

"So how did your path lead from being a brain to working as a waitress?" he asked. He instantly felt a pang of regret and hoped he hadn't sounded insulting.

"Being an English major at university does not allow one to accumulate a great deal of savings," she said. "I heard about this job where the foreigners tip well and don't bother the women. When I save up some money I can try school again or maybe better paying jobs will come along."

They agreed to meet in the morning at a coffee shop on the corner of Sukhumvit Road and Phra Khanong two days later, when Fah was not working.

While walking back to his hotel room, Johnny realized that this was the first time in his life he was going to have any social interaction with a woman who wasn't mobbed up. Johnny was always considered handsome, and at fifty-two he still had an outside chance at making it in Hollywood on the basis of his looks. His temples and sideburns were graying, he was slightly bulkier than as a youth, but his stood ramrod straight and worked out regularly, even using the crummy little gym at the hotel. He didn't ever think he would have problems finding women, but the life he chose meant they all came from a certain circle, and that circle was called the Mob. He started with the Boss's crew right after college was ruled out, it became a nonstarter, and the Boss made it clear from day one that no one in his crew was to have anything to do with anyone not connected or approved by the Boss. The Giannellis were a rare exception to the rule that to be close to the Boss, you had to be in the Mob. One night stands and hookers were one thing, but a serious girlfriend or a wife necessitated a Mob woman. Even a "gumar," the corruption of the Italian word for mistresses, needed approval.

Johnny didn't like the women the Mob attracted. He had no desire to waste his money on a gumar who didn't love him and wanted only money and good times. He had even less inclination to spend his money and time on prostitutes. Since he didn't drink, he was in bars only for business meetings, and he didn't find barflies particularly desirable. He grew into middle age as a man with limited experience with women, especially when compared to Tommy, and even Paulie. In his entire life, he'd had but one serious relationship; any time his mind tunneled into the deep recesses where those memories were stored, he pulled himself back to the surface.

TEN

As Johnny was walking the even-numbered street side on Sukhumvit Road, Glenn Murray Cohen was walking along in the opposite direction across the boulevard on the odd-numbered streets.

There was something about the FBI agent that wouldn't allow Glenn to stop thinking about her. He wasn't sure what it was - and that bothered him.

It's that criminal lawyer's sixth sense that something was wrong, something hidden below the surface, and if it weren't understood fully it meant trouble. It wasn't simply because once again Glenn was coerced into doing something for his own government that he preferred to completely avoid. *I'm getting used to that happening.*

Was it because this total stranger knew so much about him, yet he only knew what she wanted him to know about herself?

Can't be that, Glenn reasoned. *The feds can find out just about anything they want about anyone on this planet, and I've always known that. They found Osama bin Laden, so how hard could it be to find Glenn Murray Cohen, who isn't really hiding from anyone?*

Glenn considered the possibility that his feelings were triggered by the memory of Freddie, an innocent man who had spent the last two decades in the hellhole of the California Department of Corrections. *No,* he decided. *Every decent criminal lawyer carries inside them the memories of all that went wrong when an innocent person is convicted. Even when a guilty person is convicted but it's done unfairly. I live with this all the time, even if I don't always realize it. Maybe that's part of why I left that life.*

Then Glenn saw the short blonde hair and the blue eyes. The scent of the perfume lingered with him right until he reached the lobby of his condo.

Two days after meeting Mary O'Halloran, as soon as Glenn walked into his building, he was greeted by Lek, the condominium's concierge, and his good friend. Lek had been at this job since before Glenn purchased his apartment, but while Glenn had gained a few pounds, more than a few gray hairs and one or two noticeable wrinkles, Lek had not changed at all.

"My cousin wants to see you later today," Lek informed Glenn. "He said to call him when you come back." Over the past fifteen years, Lek's English had improved to where he spoke with ease. Glenn still knew twenty Thai words at most.

The Lieutenant doesn't waste any time, Glenn thought.

"You are very popular today," Lek added. "A farang lady was also here to see you earlier. I told her you were at the NJA Club because I know you told me when you left."

"Why did you tell her?" Glenn asked, more puzzled than angry. "Ever since some bad guys came looking for me, the deal was no one except Oliver, Sleepy Joe and the General get told where I am."

Lek widened his smile.

"I did it because my cousin told me to. He said a very pretty farang would be asking for you and it was okay to tell her where to find you. Sorry, Glenn, but this is Thailand. When a police lieutenant tells you to do something, you do it. Especially my cousin, who is a good man who likes you, so no problem."

Glenn nodded. Whatever surprise or inconvenience was attached to the news, having Lek as a friend, and also having his police lieutenant cousin on his side, was well worth it. He thanked Lek and took the elevator to his apartment. As soon as he was in the door, he commenced his regular routine of turning on the lights, the air-conditioning, the stereo, or television, and in a very high percentage of instances, smoking a joint.

Maybe not such a good idea with a Thai police lieutenant and an FBI agent dropping by, he thought. Then he remembered weed was in a gray area where it was sold openly as if it were legal, and no one seemed to know for sure if it was.

It didn't require much analysis to conclude the FBI woman would be there with the Lieutenant, as that was the whole purpose of the Thai police officer wanting Glenn present when he was with the agent, or at least that's what that lady agent said. Glenn brewed himself a single cup of coffee and watched the news on CNN while waiting for his international law enforcement delegation.

Glenn didn't care about the stock market experiencing some rough days; relatively little of his money was tied up in equities. Politics was not the red-hot issue it was when Glenn eagerly followed the defeat of Trump and his involuntary exit from the office he never deserved to hold. The midterm elections in the US were more than six months away, and he'd been away from America for so long that many of the contested issues didn't resonate with him as they would were he back in the States. He hoped women kept their right to choose and gay folks didn't lose what rights they finally had recognized in the law. After January 20, 2021, when the world saw Donald Trump's backside (actually they didn't see it, because the ungracious sore loser broke tradition by running out of town when President Biden was inaugurated) the intensity of Glenn's political fires had diminished, awaiting the next titanic confrontation.

"That's only because you're not back in America dealing with sky-high inflation," Oliver, an Australian Conservative Party member, responded when Glenn told him this several months after the disgraced and defeated former President was booted out of office, but continued issuing mouth-foaming rants from Mar-a-Lago, growing more delusional as his disgrace increased and criminal investigations piled up.

"Don't be so hard on our dear friend, Glenn," the General had interjected. "His man Biden had a son who served in the army. Went to Iraq and saw combat. None of your man Trump's boys served a day in uniform." Glenn smiled at this. He knew that the General couldn't care less about American politics, but respected soldiers and loathed those who refused to serve, and he despised leaders who would send another family's son to war but not their own.

He might feel different if he knew Joe Biden himself never served because of allergies, Glenn thought but did not say. *Then again, Trump's old man bought him a deferment for a fake case of bone spurs.*

Sleepy Joe has listened intently and weighed in when the General was finished.

"I don't give a rat's ass about American politics, Australian politics, or Thai politics," he said. "Especially the politicians. They're all a bunch of crooks and liars stealing from hard-working people. But like the General, I like soldiers and their fathers, and I like Glenn, so put me down as a Biden man."

"At least we sensible Aussies know all American politicians are crooks and liars," Oliver said. "Except of course, Ronald Reagan. He would have made a great Australian." Everyone laughed, and the conversation turned to more mundane subjects already forgotten.

The recollections of that day disappeared when the news shifted to Tom Brady retracting his retirement. A warming joy came over Glenn. He wasn't even a Tampa Bay Buccaneers fan, still loyal to the New York Jets he grew up loving, but as a middle-aged man, seeing Tom Brady back on the field meant he himself couldn't be that old. *Even if he is ten years younger than me.*

The jangling of the intercom phone ended Glenn's ruminations. Lek informed him the Lieutenant and the farang lady were in the lobby,

"Send them up," Glenn said.

A few minutes later he ushered them into his apartment. They settled into the living room, with the Lieutenant grabbing the big overstuffed reclining seat. Agent O'Halloran sat on the couch and

Glenn joined her. He noticed that she was wearing a short skirt and a tight blouse cut far lower than Glenn expected from an agent of the Federal Bureau of Investigation. She set her handbag in front of her on Glenn's coffee table. He noticed it was Gucci.

"Didn't realize the FBI paid so well," he said, pointing to the bag. "Unless of course it's a counterfeit bought on Sukhumvit Road."

"Or maybe I have a rich husband," she said. She still had traces of the sunburn he'd seen when he met her, so he couldn't tell if she was angry, embarrassed, or both.

"I don't see a ring," Glenn replied. "Man buys his wife a Gucci bag, he expects her to wear a ring."

Mary stared at Glenn, her eyes locked on his, but her face bearing no trace of emotion.

"Mr. Cohen, I know all there is to know about you, and I knew it before I ever got on the plane. As an experienced criminal defense lawyer, you must know this is how we operate. From what I gather, you are not the person to explain the intricacies of marriage."

Glenn blushed, embarrassed not because he cared about his long-ago marriage and divorce, but because someone had been prowling around in the back alleys of his life.

"But don't take it the wrong way," she said, patting his hand as she spoke. "I'm not that person either, and rest assured, my divorce would be worse than yours." Glenn felt the warmth of her hand on the top of his after she withdrew it. *Does that mean she is married?*

"Can we please get down to business?" the Lieutenant asked. "You two can exchange histories later on." The Lieutenant spoke excellent English, a fact he kept from Glenn for the first half-dozen years they knew each other. *Not a man who tips his hand unless necessary.*

"Since you're the one wanting me involved in whatever it is you're doing with Agent O'Halloran, perhaps you should start," Glenn told the Lieutenant.

"I told you to call me Mary," the FBI agent said. Glenn nodded but said nothing. The Lieutenant began speaking, in a slow, rolling cadence with almost no discernible Thai accent. It sounded more like a British accent. Glenn deduced whoever taught the Lieutenant his English hailed from that Island.

The Lieutenant related what the General had told Glenn, Joe, and Oliver, but added more detail. Based on information shared by the FBI, the Thai police, at least the ones trusted by the Americans, he learned that the mobsters who came to Bangkok originated out of Brooklyn, New York, and they had some means of bringing to Bangkok high quality liquor they hijacked back home.

Agent O'Halloran explained what the FBI believed they themselves had established.

"We've been told by local law enforcement in Brooklyn that there was a liquor truck hijacked a little over a month ago. Two of the liquor wholesalers employees are missing, along with several known organized crime figures believed to have been associated with the crimes. One of our informants on the waterfront told us there was a man asking around about sneaking some booze on board. This informant has always been reliable."

"Isn't that enough to lead back to whoever is behind the whole scheme?" Glenn asked. "I mean from the hijacking to the shipment to the strong-arming going on here."

Mary responded. "The missing mobsters came from a different family and different crews than the ones who masterminded the hijacking. Think of them as contractors hired for a specific job. We think that was done on purpose, to throw us off any trail leading to the ones who are behind it all."

"What about looking to see if any suspicious men entered Thailand recently?" Glenn asked.

"We haven't been able to identify the mobsters who came over," the Lieutenant explained. "Highly unlikely they entered with passports in their own names. Almost certainly genuine U.S. passports but not issued through proper channels."

"It's not all that difficult for a skilled forger to change a passport photo," Mary O'Halloran interjected. "They've got all kinds of ways, some more sophisticated than the CIA. Glenn, I know you don't care for our national intelligence agency, and they're not my favorites either, but when it comes to forging documents, they are the best."

The Lieutenant continued. "We've tried facial recognition, and if there's a match, it will also show they entered on a forged passport, giving us an automatic reason to arrest and interrogate them."

Mary interjected again.

"If their guys came in with passports under different names but using a current photo of themselves, facial recognition won't necessarily give us a reliable hit if all we were given by our own American law enforcement are very old mug shots or poor quality surveillance photos," she said. "We'd have to get an artist to draw what they think the person looks like today."

"Do you think the Mafia is going to send someone who has recently been arrested?" Glenn asked. "No one with recent arrests would be sent over here. I don't care what name or photo they use, a smart mob boss will not allow someone with a case hanging over their heads to get in a situation where they might be detained and questioned abroad without any of the legal protections they'd have back home. That's looking to create a snitch."

"I'd agree with you there, Glenn," Mary O'Halloran said, once again patting Glenn's hand, and once again he felt the heat seeping from his fingertips. "But if they're mobbed up, we've surely got something on them in our databases. It may take time to find the lead we need, but we will. Once we locate even one of them, we'll start learning all we have to know."

The Lieutenant held up a hand, palm facing the Americans. They stopped their conversation and directed their attention to the Lieutenant's smooth, expressionless game.

The Lieutenant explained that whoever the Mafia men may be, they were not directly interacting with the intended victims. A handful of the targets notified the police, and while the thugs went to great lengths to encounter their targets away from surveillance cameras, they slipped up once and the police know what they look like. He told them one was Thai, one was from one of the South Pacific nations, and the third was a farang, conclusively determined to be a Russian.

"I'm just curious," Glenn said. "How is it you're so certain it's a Russian? Couldn't he be any of a number of foreign nationalities? Maybe an American since this is the Brooklyn Mafia at work."

The Lieutenant relaxed his expressionless demeanor enough for a small smile.

"My experience is that with Americans, their decency, intelligence, or fear would make it most unlikely they work as thugs in Bangkok. Russians, on the other hand, lack all three traits, and it's the lack of fear that makes them dangerous. That was caught by the camera."

"Are these conclusions based on your policeman's hunch, or on actual experience?" Glenn asked.

Mary threw Glenn a stern look.

"You shouldn't question a cop's 'hunch,' as you called it," she said.

"He's right," the Lieutenant interjected. "I'm not an expert on ethnicity, but when you have seen the bodies, it's easy to know one when you see one."

The Lieutenant next revealed that several days ago a cleaning lady in an office building heard a loud scuffle coming from a rear alley several stories below. It was still daylight, very early evening, and she told the police what she saw.

"She saw a big white man who spoke English with a Russian accent. She also saw a big Thai man and a third big man who looked Asian but she couldn't say from where. Those were the same three men on that surveillance tape." A wave of silence passed over the two Americans as they absorbed the news. Glenn felt muscles tightening in his chest and wrists as he clenched his fists and leaned towards the Lieutenant.

"You said there was a scuffle reported," Glenn said.

"Yes," the Lieutenant continued. "The cleaning lady saw a fourth man fighting with the others after a brief exchange of words. It all happened very fast, but when it was over, the fourth man was the only one standing. She could not provide any description of that man, other than to say he looked smaller than the others. That's almost every man in Thailand."

"So now we're dealing with more than just some second-string Mafiosos pushing stolen booze," Glenn said while his face flushed. "Now we're talking about murder."

"It was not suicide or accident," the Lieutenant calmly stated. "And it does not sound like self-defense. Nor is it likely the three deceased were the aggressors. Who could kill three people if they were in the process of killing him? No, the killer must have taken them by surprise before they had time to react. Homicide is the only explanation."

"Could it be a gang war?" Mary asked. "Locals sending a message to intruders thinking of cutting into their turf?"

The Lieutenant nodded.

"That's our thinking as of now. We just don't know who. Could be any of a number of sources. Maybe the people already distributing liquor, or maybe some of the intended victims got together and hired a local killer. Sad to say that's not very difficult."

"So, you think it was a professional hit?" the FBI agent asked. Glenn watched the two law enforcement professionals try to paint a fuller picture, much as he did when he was a lawyer defending the kind of people Mary and the Lieutenant wanted to arrest.

"Our initial assessment is that the three deceased were somehow lured or chased into a dead end where there would be little traffic or pedestrians. One was killed with a knife, one had his brains bashed out against a wall and the third died of a broken neck. That sounds like a professional who didn't want the noise of a gun or the possibility of forensics tracing it. Leaving the bodies lying there tells us whoever did it was not afraid and wanted the Mafia to see what happens when they go where they should not."

"What happened after the cleaning lady called your department?" Mary asked the Lieutenant.

"That is the strangest part," he said. "We dispatched a patrol car and two detectives and called for ambulances. When they showed up, there were no bodies. The cleaning lady had moved away from the window after seeing the fight and had no idea what happened after she walked away."

"Any chance the lady was hallucinating?" Glenn asked

"None," the Lieutenant said. "In addition to her descriptions matching the tapes, we found blood and pieces of skull at the site, all fresh. We think this was a professional job and whoever did it had their associates come for the bodies."

I'm getting out of this right now, Glenn thought.

"I was asked to sit through this because the Lieutenant felt comfortable with me there with Agent O'Halloran. It looks to me like you two work well together, and there is no further need for me, so I'll take my leave. Lek can lock up when you two are done." Glenn rose from the couch. Then he felt Mary's hand press down on the top of his thighs, pushing him back to a seated potion.

"Sit down, Glenn, and remember to call me Mary. This isn't just about what makes the Lieutenant comfortable. I also feel better having you here, another American, one who knows this place and knows about mobsters. Your questions are all good."

"I've been gone for over fifteen years," Glenn replied. "A lot has changed since then."

"Not with Brooklyn mobsters," Mary said. "Let's not forget you learned a lot about how organized crime gangs operate, and whether they are Black, Latino, Aryan Brotherhood or Mafia, the structures and rules are surprisingly similar. You can help us figure out better how these gangsters operate,"

Glenn took a deep breath and realized he had little choice. If he wanted to free Freddie, help protect people like Wang and places like the NJA Club, he had to cooperate. He told the two law enforcement officers all he knew about organized criminals, from his days as a criminal lawyer in New York through his last days in San Francisco. After three hours, the Lieutenant and Mary left, telling Glenn they'd be back soon.

"Feel free to cancel," he said as he closed the door behind them.

ELEVEN

THE MORNING AFTER GLENN'S VISIT FROM THE LIEUTENANT AND MARY

Tommy the Turtle was in a foul mood, obvious to Johnny and Paulie by the way he stubbed out his cigarettes as if he were plunging a dagger into a traitor's heart. This was the fourth he'd smoked in the past fifteen minutes. He spoke to Paulie through clenched teeth as they sat around the coffee table in Johnny's hotel room.

"Paulie, you told me these three guys were reliable. I don't think never getting back to me for the past five days is reliable." Paulie signed them up, but after that they reported to Tommy. If there were ever any trouble that required fists or guns, Tommy was the best equipped of the three for such trouble.

Paulie leaned back and exhaled a deep breath through his mouth.

"I tell you two, these men were sent to me by someone whose word I would never have reason to doubt. Hell, Tommy, you met Baxter yourself. Don't worry, there are so many layers between them and us here, no one will ever put it together. I'm going to talk to Baxter, and we'll figure something out. We still have the booze coming, let's not forget that part."

Johnny directed a question to both of his colleagues.

"Is there anything we can think of for what they wouldn't want to report back to Tommy? They get paid whether or not they bring in a lot of business. We can't keep changing our muscles every week, and they should know it. It's easy money for them, a lot safer than going up against other armed wise guys, or whatever they call them here."

"What are you getting at, Johnny?" Tommy asked. *Whatever you think, at least you have a thought. You always do. That's why the Boss loves you and that's why he trusted you to call the shots here. So, what's your take?"*

Johnny the Brain stood up and stretched before answering.

"There are only two possibilities," he began. "One, some outsider, like an angry competitor, the targeted businesses, or a lock gang. Two, Baxter got a better offer for these men and he decided to screw us."

"Which one would you put your money on, Brains?" Tommy asked.

"I'm not a betting man, as you know, Tommy," Johnny replied. "Right now the smart bet is to let the Boss know there's a problem before he finds out some other way."

"He's gonna be pissed," Paulie said.

"He'll be more pissed if we hide the ball from him," Johnny said. "Tommy, why don't you take a break, take a walk, stop at a 7-11 and pick up some beer and booze. You guys look like you need some." *While they're drinking themselves into a stupor, I can call the Boss and maybe make some headway here. I don't see these two being much help right now. Tommy's angry and Paulie is worried. No room for either in my work.*

"Sounds like a plan," Tommy said. "I'll go now. Then me and Paulie can get drunk together. Come to think of it, why don't you take a walk with me, Paulie? I think the brains of this operation needs some time alone."

He's not always as dumb as he looks, Johnny thought.

When Tommy and Paulie were out of the room, Johnny opened up the attaché case he brought with him and retrieved one of the cheap burner phones the Boss had given him. Taped to the phone was the number of a burner phone the Boss held for the sole purpose of receiving calls from Johnny. There would be no voicemail if the Boss wasn't hearing the ring, but no doubt he'd dial Johnny's burner as soon as he saw the missed call. The instructions were clear: report after a month and other than that, call only when necessary. Use each phone only once, and afterward, remove the sim card and slice it into pieces, then smash the phone and dispose of the pieces in different garbage cans. Providing phones turned out to be a wise move, because in Thailand, a foreigner would have to present their passport to buy a sim card.

Johnny dialed and prayed the Boss would answer.

～

At the very moment Johnny Brancini was calling the Boss, Glenn Murray Cohen was smoking a joint.

Bangkok was awash in weed, or *ganja* as the locals called it. Due to the intentional difficulty of interpreting Thai laws, the legal status of the plant was unclear, and it was sold and smoked openly with exponentially increasing frequency. None of this mattered to Glenn, who still received his monthly packet from Sleepy Joe. The Aussie hippie-warrior abandoned dealing when he didn't need the money, but still procured large amounts for his own personal use.

No doubt Mary O'Halloran knows about my weed smoking, he thought. *She knows everything else about me. Maybe I ought to offer her a toke next time I see her. Let her know just whose turf we're playing on and who needs who.*

Let's see how far she gets with the Lieutenant if I'm not around

For reasons Glenn could not fathom, the Lieutenant insisted he be present whenever he met with Mary. If this bothered Mary, she didn't let Glenn see it, but he sensed it rankled her.

What FBI agent wants to be told by a fellow cop they won't be taken seriously unless they have a former criminal defense lawyer riding shotgun? She could get anything I know about the mob from people who have better and more current knowledge. It hurts her that the Lieutenant so openly distrusts her. Glenn never saw a reason for his presence. *It really isn't necessary, but he thinks it is.*

While Mary and the Lieutenant occupied the space in his head, pangs of hunger invaded his stomach. He hadn't eaten breakfast and it was already half past noon. Since he never kept any solid food in his home, he left his apartment and thought of where to eat lunch as the elevator descended to the lobby.

As soon as Glenn walked out of the elevator, Lek called to him from his podium style desk and seat.

"My cousin will come here tonight at eight o clock, with the lady farang. I will order dinner for all of you." Glenn had accounts with several fine eateries. After fifteen years of free-spending culinary hedonism, his credit was platinum with all of them. Getting food wasn't the problem.

"Lek, I don't know your cousin very well, but you do." Glenn knew Lek and the Lieutenant grew up together, sharing hardscrabble young lives in the Northeastern region of Isan, one of the poorest in Thailand. Their bond remained fully intact as they made their way upward in a Bangkok controlled by elites who looked down on the salt-of-the-earth people of the Northeast. Lek wore a custom tailored suit, one of several purchased for him by Glenn in appreciation for years of loyalty above and beyond the job description. His cousin always wore the uniform of a Lieutenant in the Royal Thai Police, or *tamruat haenf chat*.

"My cousin likes you, and he also respects you and trusts you. He does not trust the FBI lady. He tells me all FBI lie all the time."

"That was my position when I was defending people arrested by the FBI," Glenn said, and he and Lek laughed very briefly before Glenn's mood turned serious.

"I don't know if she lies to other cops," Glenn said. "None of this is really my business, Lek, I mean, I'm not a cop and I couldn't help with their problems even if I wanted to, which I do not. But it is your cousin, the Lieutenant, and he has helped me and my friends many times, so it's now time for me to return the favor."

Lek studied his friend for a few seconds.

"That's why he respects you, Kuhn Glenn."

Twenty meters past his door, Glenn settled on Robin Hood, a well-known British restaurant he didn't frequent very often, but was high on his list when he craved genuine and quality Western food in the Green Belt. He liked being surrounded by the kind of farangs he could relate to, businesspeople, well dressed, not likely to float in with a semi-naked hooker on their arm. Glenn had acquired a mild taste for classic British dishes like fish and chips and shepherd's pie, but this place made the best hamburger he'd ever seen anywhere, even in America.

As Glenn walked along Sukhumvit Road, he was not fixed on the sights of the busy Bangkok streets as usual. Even after a decade and a half, Glenn was continually amazed at what he saw each day. Watching street-side cobblers repair the footwear of motorcycle taxi drivers as well as affluent but thrifty farangs, breathing in the smell of fresh barbecued chicken, checking out the watch stand set up where the man on a corner replaced batteries and worn bands, while a mere few feet away on the boulevard, buses wheezed, motorcycles weaved, farangs and Thais alike tried to cross the street without being run over.

The Boss picked up on the third ring.

"What's the good news, pal?" he asked. "Make it quick. I got some people waiting."

Johnny took a deep breath. The Boss didn't like hearing bad news.

"No good news today," he said. "The three guys who were supposed to do the job have gone missing. No one's heard from them in days."

There was a ten second stretch of silence. *He's thinking*, Johnny recognized.

"What the hell went wrong?" the Boss asked, his voice calmer than Johnny expected.

"I don't know for sure," Johnny said. "Way I see it, could only be they or their bosses double-crossed us for some reason I can't figure out, or someone else doesn't want us around."

Another brief silence, broken by the Boss.

"Well, in any event, it ain't the end of the world. It does tell me it was a mistake to try and pull this off, and I should have listened to you. Here's the plan. The stuff should arrive in Bangkok any day, and when it does, you tell the Arranger to sell it as fast as he can, don't get too worried about price, and then you guys get the hell out of there and come back where you belong. I really need you here, Johnny."

The hitch in the Boss's voice told Johnny something was wrong.

"Now that we've wrapped up my end, what's eating you on yours?" he asked the Boss.

"Can't fool you, which is why I need you. I got a real headache on my hands, more like heartache too." The Boss asked Johnny if he knew Bobby Giannelli. Johnny directed his mind to the file cabinet where it kept such generally useless information, but information that might someday be useful.

"Isn't he the son or grandson of some family friend of yours?" he asked the Boss when the file was retrieved.

"Great memory, Brain, He's both. My grandfather and his came over together from the old country. Our families have been real close ever since. I happen to be his godfather."

"So, what's the problem, Godfather?"

"Big one, Brain. Bobby's gone missing, disappeared, not a trace, and I can't get a word out of anybody anywhere, which makes me think no one knows where he went or why. His wife, mother and grandmother are over my house every day, begging my wife to make me find him. What do they think, I know everything?"

No, Johnny thought, *but they know enough to understand if an Italian goes missing in our neighborhood, you know about that.* He said something different.

"You must know something by now. You have eyes and ears everywhere a guy like that might have been. Did he have a girlfriend on the side? Was he into drugs? Was he stealing from his boss?"

"I know he worked as a driver for the booze distributor whose truck Tommy hijacked for you guys to sell in Thailand. Working that evening, though it was supposed to be a day off. Nothing ever happens to the drivers, you know that. Half the time they're in on it, the other half are so happy to get out alive they never remember a thing. That's good for us. Hijacking booze is one thing, killing working stiffs is something else, and the heat would really be on."

"Okay, he works hard," Johnny said. "But was he in on it?"

The Boss snorted a laugh.

"You may have met Bobby, but you don't know him, or you wouldn't ask. Was an altar boy. Goes to Mass every Sunday, I mean really goes, not make-believe. He's the guy that shovels the snow for the ones who can't. If you dropped a hundred dollar bill, he'd pick it up and give it back to you. No way he was in. He's a kid from the neighborhood who would have known what was going on, a smart guy too scared to remember anything."

"How can I help?" Johnny asked.

"I want you to ask the Turtle what he knows. He ran the job, but you guys flew out before I could talk to him."

"That doesn't mean he was there," Johnny said. "He hires a crew."

"But he might have heard something or maybe he will remember what someone said. Anything will help."

"Will do," Johnny said. The Boss told him to call after he spoke with Tommy. They agreed no more than three days.

Johnny knew his two friends would be delighted to hear they were going home, but he himself didn't feel the same. He looked at his watch and saw it was time for lunch. He didn't want to see Fah before she gave him the tour. He had passed a decent looking place the other way, that looked like it served food white people eat. He was certain he could find it if he walked up Sukhumvit Road. He proved this to be correct, and ten minutes later he walked into Robin Hood.

Glenn scanned the first floor of the restaurant and spied a seat at a two person table, facing the street. He preferred the action on Sukhumvit Road to that in the restaurant, so he grabbed the chair. There was a man seated with his back against the window, one table over. Glenn nodded in the way farangs show politeness to each other in Thailand and sat down. At that moment, a waitress appeared from nowhere and handed menus to both men. Glenn handed it back and told her he'd have a hamburger, medium-well done and a diet soft drink. The other man said he needed a few minutes. When the waitress was out of sight, he spoke to Glenn.

"From the way you ordered right away, you must be a regular here. It's my first time. Any recommendations?"

Glenn decided from the man's accent he was a native New Yorker like him, except it hadn't been softened by decades away from the Big Apple.

"Everything here is good," Glenn said, "including the Thai food, but it's three times the normal price. Most of us expats come here for a taste of American or British food. But I bet you have just come from the land of the hamburger, so I'd recommend some of the British food. Shepherd's pie or fish and chips."

"What's a shepherd's pie?" Johnny Brancini asked Glenn.

"Basically a pie made of chopped up meat with mashed potatoes on top," Glenn explained.

Johnny made face as if he had just tasted something unpleasant.

"I'll try the fish and chips," he said. Glenn spotted the waitress waiting behind a pillar and signaled to her. Johnny gave his order with the same soft drink Glenn ordered.

"Would I be correct in assuming this is your first visit to Bangkok?" Glenn asked Johnny.

"Am I that obvious," the Brooklyn mobster said. "What tipped you off?"

"A couple of things," Glenn said. "I can see that look of a man who is trying to understand, a look you see on first timers. It was clear you didn't know this place, which almost every English-speaking resident or long stay gets to know. Then the way you asked me, a fellow American, for suggestions instead of the waitress, as an expat or seasoned visitor does."

Smart guy, Johnny thought. *Not like the two yo-yos I'm stuck with. Outside of being gangsters, they're useless.*

"You've got a hell of a handle on sizing people up fast," Johnny said. "May I ask what line of work you're in?"

Glenn smiled.

"None right now, I'm pleased to say. I'm a retired criminal defense lawyer, with an emphasis on 'retired.'"

Won't take him long to make me, Johnny realized.

"I guess you found this to be a great place to retire," Johnny said.

Glenn nodded twice.

"It's all very subjective," he said. "And there's a lot of reasons that appeal to different people. It's really inexpensive and the dollar goes far. Once you know your way around, you can do just about anything you could do back home. This is a cosmopolitan, international city. The food's good, there's lots of fine music, easy access to beaches, and number one, the Thai people are the best." *Not the time to mention strong and cheap weed.*

"A lawyer's answer," Johnny said. "You didn't mention that the women are drop dead beautiful."

He hasn't said a word about why he's here, Glenn thought.

Glenn leaned a few inches toward Johnny and smiled.

"It's so obvious, it didn't need to be said. Charming as well."

"Good to know," Johnny said. "To be honest with you, I've given some thought to moving here myself. Listening to you makes it more likely."

Glenn knew it was the time to ask the man about himself.

"As long as we're getting so serious about things, we ought to have some names. I'm Glenn Murray Cohen, and I've lived here for several years. I was born in Brooklyn, raised in Queens, went back to Brooklyn for law school, but spent most of my career in San Francisco. Now it's your turn."

Johnny studied Glenn's face, his shirt, his haircut. From the way he spoke and the way he easily entered into a conversation with a total stranger, even one he probably sensed was mobbed up, signaled that he must have been a fine lawyer, and that if he gave Glenn an opening, he'd drive a Mack Truck through a bullshit story.

He gave Glenn his real name. *He could check every criminal data base in the world and he won't see that name. That juvie car bust was erased a long time ago and I've checked my records with New York and the FBI. Clean as can be, at least on paper, a rare guy in the mob. I'm lucky the boss understands his best number one man or consigliere will always be someone no one really knows about unless they have to know. If anyone gave up my name to the law, the day we find out would be their last day on earth. No one is ever seeing my name in the papers, and I'm never anywhere near a place where I might get pinched. Better for Glenn to have my real name instead of the name I came in on or some fake name I forget and slip up down the road. Besides, this guy is a criminal lawyer, right here in Bangkok, and if I do have a problem, he should be the first guy I call.*

"I'm a Brooklyn boy just like you, but I never left. I manage the family properties, mostly apartments my grandfather bought cheaply a long time ago, and you must know about Brooklyn rents these days. I'm over here on vacation, just trying something new after all these years."

"And what do you think so far?" Glenn asked.

"I like it," Johnny said. "In fact, like I said, the thought of staying here has crossed my mind the past few days. Become like you, I guess."

Glenn chuckled.

"Oh, I don't know if I should be your role model," he said. "When it comes to these beautiful ladies you mentioned, I have a fairly poor history. I'm still looking for the right one to come along."

"You and me both, Glenn," Johnny said. "I'm fifty-two and never been married. How many Brooklyn Italians can say that? But I don't understand how a good looking guy like you, smart, probably in good shape money-wise, has a hard time with women."

This guy is good looking and has money. He'd better be careful, Glenn thought.

"It's complicated," Glenn then explained. "I don't want anything to do with the ones who only want money, and the ones who want love don't want me."

Glenn saw the serious look on Johnny's face.

"That's impossible Glenn, not if you've been here a bunch of years. Not a guy like you. Even a loser like me already met somebody who might fit the bill we're looking for."

Now it became Glenn's face with the serious look.

"Hope it works out for you," he said. "I could spend days telling you stories about guys like us who were fooled, starting with me."

"I'd love to hear them sometime," Johnny said, "but here comes our food. Let's pick this up after we eat." For the next ten minutes, they engaged in the smallest of small talk, mostly about the food and the place.

When they were finished and the plates off the table, they resumed their real conversation.

"Before I tell you any stories, tell me about this very lucky lady." *Here's hoping he didn't first see her hanging off a pole at a go-go bar.*

"She's the waitress in the little restaurant I've been going to," Johnny said, feeling uplifted as he thought of Fah and pictured her face.

When Glenn heard the word 'waitress,' he felt anything but uplifted. He saw Kit's face.

"I'm glad to hear you're not like so many of these blindsided fools who think they found the one honorable hooker in Thailand, or even crazier, think they can turn one into something they can never be," he said. "Confirms my initial impression that you are a smart fellow. Aren't all we Brooklyn-born guys?"

"Hey, Glenn, no worries there. I never used hookers back home, why would I start here?"

Maybe because they're cheaper, more available, no trouble with the law, prettier, and they act like they really like you. No need to go there with Johnny. We think the same.

"You and me both," Glenn said, then he remembered his very brief dalliance with a former bargirl-turned-drink server. That was over seven years ago, and he had mosquito bites that lasted longer than that relationship.

Johnny told Glenn what attracted him to Fah.

"First, she's really smart. College grad. Me, I got a high school diploma and never took advantage of all the free colleges in New York City. She speaks English better than most of the Americans I know. She's really sweet. When she saw I was having a hard time figuring out this place, she said she would show me around. We're going to see this Grand Palace and some other places."

"Sounds like you're at the start of something good," Glenn said. "Better start than all these bozos who come here and after a week of trolling the bars they think they found the hooker with the heart of gold."

The waitress brought their checks.

"Let me pick this up," Johnny said. "It's been a pleasure to talk to another guy from Brooklyn, one who knows this place."

Glenn nodded in acceptance. Johnny dropped a five hundred and a one hundred baht note on the little bill tray. Glenn, who knew the prices on the menu, calculated Johnny was leaving over a hundred twenty baht tip.

"This will be one happy waitress," he told Johnny.

"Well, seems like I've got this thing for waitresses," he said as they stood and headed out the door. When they were standing on the corner of Sukhumvit Road and Soi 33/1, Glenn asked Johnny what he was doing that evening. The mobster said he had nothing planned.

"Why don't you join me and my friends at our favorite haunt," he said. " Seven p.m. is when a bunch of us are having dinner. It's a nice little restaurant not all that far from here. The food is pretty good, especially the steak, and the Thai food is also fine. It's got a great bar but looks like you and me aren't making the bars rich." He gave Johnny the name and address of the NJA Club.

"Any cab driver will find it," he explained.

"I might just walk," Johnny said. "I don't know why, but I never get bored walking around this place. See you at seven, Glenn." He and Glenn walked in opposite directions along Sukhumvit Road.

Maybe he will stick around, Glenn thought. *Seems like we could be friends.*

TWELVE

As soon as Johnny was back in his hotel room, he called Tommy and Paulie on the phones Paulie had purchased from a bouncer at one of the go-go bars on Soi Nana. The phones the Boss gave Johnny were only to call him. The bouncer threw in several sim cards so the phone numbers could be changed frequently. For Paulie, it was never difficult to find someone with the right sideline. *Bouncers are the same everywhere,* Paulie understood. They're usually protecting the interests of some big guys making a lot of money, seeing how they live, and it was only natural they would like to make as much as they could for themselves. So long as it didn't cause problems, the big guys don't mind; it means they can pay the muscle men less and let them prosper through their sidelines. It looked to Paulie they only thing they couldn't sell was drugs and that showed how smart the big guys in Bangkok were. He recalled what the Boss told him years ago when explaining why his crew had to stay away from narcotics.

"No one goes away for life or close to it for bookmaking, loansharking, dealing in stolen goods. So long as no one gets killed, the worst anyone is looking at is a few years." The Boss was at first averse to Tommy's plans to focus on hijacking trucks filled with easily sold goods, but the promise of no one being hurt persuaded him to allow it.

"I'll let you do it, and you can use our guys, or any guys you trust, provided you don't involve me, and when it's done and you give me my share. I can arrange for buyers. The first time someone gets hurt, it's all over. I seen guys get ten, twenty years for a simple hijack. We got better lawyers than them, but it's still a possibility. I don't wanna be supporting any guy's family for ten to twenty years, *capice?*"

Paulie spoke to Stanley Scharfman, the best criminal lawyer in Brooklyn, and the grandson and son of the two great Scharfman lawyers before him. The mob wasn't the only organization that believed in family. Stanley confirmed what the Boss claimed.

"Technically, armed hijacking could get you life, but unless someone's killed or hurt really badly, probably ten years tops around here."

When Tommy and Paulie were seated around the coffee table in Johnny's room, he told them of the Boss's order to sell the booze as quickly as possible and get out of Bangkok. Then he added the Boss's personal concern.

"He asked me to find out if Tommy has any idea what might have happened to the Giannelli kid," Johnny said. The late Bobby Giannelli was destined to be remembered as a 'kid,' even though he died at age forty-two.

"We know you keep away from the scene to make sure there's no trail back to the Boss, but maybe you heard something," Johnny added.

"Not a thing," Tommy said. "I was busy getting ready to come here. The crew I put together could do it in their sleep and they leave no trails."

"Exactly," Johnny said. "That's why the Boss wants to talk to them. If you weren't there, this crew are the only ones who can tell us anything that might help the Boss figure this out. Maybe the Giannelli kid or the guy we had inside the company who was also there said something. Maybe the kid pissed off one of the guys in the crew. Maybe the Giannelli kid was in on it and took off with his money, maybe he got tired of the wife and kids and took the chance to blow them off."

Tommy shook his head vigorously.

"These guys I used are with the Santucci Family. You know how old man Santucci is about people working for anyone else. He's totally paranoid and he don't want his people talking to anybody outside the Santuccis. It'd be their death sentence if he finds out they was doing some side stuff for us."

Johnny felt anger growing inside him, like a kindled flame that keeps growing, reaching for bigger pieces of wood. He learned long ago that anger was a distraction. He took a deep breath, let his mind clear for a few seconds, then read Tommy the law.

"You work for the Boss. The only words that matter are his, and the only rules we follow are the ones he gives us. The first rule goes like this: the Boss tells us what he thinks we need to know, but we tell him everything we know. Any problem with this?"

Tommy thought for a moment before answering.

"Of course, I understand, but you and the Boss got to understand also. I got these peoples' lives in my hands. They trusted me to keep the lid on. Tell the Boss I said when I'm back and can protect these guys, I'll tell him anything he wants to know."

Paulie shook his head.

"Johnny can tell him that, but he ain't gonna be happy."

Just be glad you're not the one who's got to tell the Boss, Johnny thought.

Paulie was right. The Boss was not happy at all.

"What do you mean?" he shouted into his burner phone, yelling so loud Johnny had to move his phone a foot from his ear. "Since when does Tommy the Turtle decide when he's gonna listen to me? What kind of bullshit is he trying to pull?"

"He's hiding something," Johnny said calmly, hoping the tone of assurance would bring the Boss down a few degrees. "I don't buy this story about hiring some mugs trying to do an end-run around the Santucci Family being the reason he's clammed up. Whatever Tommy might pay them, it can't be worth their lives, and we both know if Tony Santucci found out they went behind his back against his orders, they'd be dead men. More likely Old Man Santucci was fine with them doing a job for Tommy in the Boss's territory, so long as the Santucci family got a cut. If his men disappeared and he got nothing, that's a different story. We can't yet be sure Tommy did hire any of Santucci's men and if he did, was it really done behind the old man's back?"

The Boss was silent for a good twenty seconds. Tommy heard the sound of lighter being flicked and the sound of an exhale. He pictured the Boss lighting one of his big Churchills and blowing smoke rings as he struggled to calm himself.

"Bobby wasn't even supposed to be working that day. It was a day off for him, and he got called and offered time and a half to fill in for the regular driver, who got in a car accident the night before. A little something extra for his wife and kids. No way Bobby was in on anything. No way he knew there was gonna be a hijacking, no way he had any plans to do anything except go home to his wife and kids with extra dough in his pocket, dough he made driving the truck, not working for Tommy's crew."

"So what do you want me to do?" Johnny asked. He heard another exhale and pictured the Boss sitting behind his big desk, cigar between the thumb and first two fingers, tip glowing bright red, and the Boss's angry face a matching color.

"You get Tommy back here as soon as possible. With those three locals gone missing on you, Tommy's got no crew to run. Soon as Paulie's unloaded the booze, book him a flight back here. Let me know the flight details and I'll have someone meet him at JFK. We're gonna get to the bottom of this one way or the other."

More time to enjoy myself around here. I already have a date and a new friend. Tommy is nothing but trouble and I'm sick of trouble. I'm in no hurry to leave. But the Boss can't know any of this.

"Have you thought about calling Tony Santucci and seeing what he knows? If he's got people dealing behind his back, you'd be doing him a favor by letting him know."

This actually got a laugh out of the Boss.

"Johnny, the last thing I want the Santuccis to know is that I've got someone as close to me as Tommy who I can't trust, someone messing around in his yard. If Tommy hired Santucci's men, he probably was told and he would know Bobby is missing. If it was his guys that whacked Bobby, Santucci's gonna stick by his men. If he didn't know, I'd be telling him and he'd still stick with them. Either way, Santucci will just look for more weak spots. The man is a snake. You know we can't take on the Santuccis."

Johnny did know this. The Santuccis were the biggest crime family in Brooklyn, probably in the whole U.S. Tony Santucci did not share the Boss's aversion to narcotics, which made his family bigger, richer, and more brutal. Whereas the Boss preferred to stay in businesses like loansharking and dealing stolen goods and what little bookmaking was left after legal betting offices and online gambling; the Santuccis were perfectly at ease in shooting wars with rival drug gangs. Most of those rivals were Latino or black gangs, and it was a constant contest between Santucci and them for who could be more violent. The Boss didn't lose many men to violence and Johnny could not recall him ordering a hit, but in the Santucci world, they needed their own funeral home.

Johnny told the Boss he would deliver the order forthwith. The Boss thanked him, told him how much he missed him, and told Johnny to call him when Tommy was on the plane.

"If it turns out he had anything at all to do with Bobby Giannelli disappearing, it's gonna be me calling Santucci for some of his men."

So that's why I never heard of him ordering a hit. Live and learn, Johnny thought.

Glenn was telling his friends at the NJA club how he met a fellow American, a Brooklynite in fact, and invited him to join them for dinner. Real estate management, he explained.

"He's here on vacation." Glenn added. "I doubt he's looking for condos."

Glenn, the General, Oliver and Sleepy Joe dined together at the Club every Wednesday when all were in Bangkok, and this Wednesday Oliver was up from his island retreat on Koh Phanang, and Sleepy Joe was not off on some mysterious assignment for the General. Glenn loved these gatherings with the people who were the closest he had to family. The only damper was Edward joining them without an invitation. Since he and the others knew the General had on certain occasions needed Edward's skills as a money launderer, his presence had to be tolerated. Glenn did not like Edward, because he didn't trust him, and it seriously rankled him that there was always an unfounded suspicion by others that his dislike had to do with Edward being gay.

I need a gay friend to assure the world that's not the case.

At one minute before seven, Johnny walked through the front door of the NJA Club. He spotted Glenn, who saw him and waved, and Johnny walked towards the table. Glenn noticed the expensive brand polo shirt, which he suspected was real and not a street knockoff, and the Italian loafers on Johnny's feet. Glenn owned a pair himself and knew they set Johnny back over three hundred dollars.

Property management is lucrative in Brooklyn, he thought.

After the introductions were made all round, the General asked Johnny what he was drinking, and Johnny told him a diet coke with a lemon.

"No wonder Glenn likes you," the General said. "He's not much of a drinker either, but he'll usually agree to one martini just to please an old man."

"If there's anything I can do for you besides drinking, it will be my pleasure," Johnny replied. "I promised my late mother I would not drink. My old man was a longshoreman, and he drank himself to death when the business on the docks dried up and he lost his job. My mother's been gone some ten years now, but as long as I keep that promise she is still alive inside me." *That's the first true thing I've said about myself since I landed here.*

The table was silent for a moment.

"That's quite admirable," Edward said. "I'm sure your mother is looking down from heaven with pride."

Johnny's face turned red. *She died crying her heart out because of what I became.*

"Thank you, Edward," Johnny said. "I believe it's true."

Ahn was on waitress duty and took their orders. Glenn recommended Johnny try the sirloin steak.

"Wang, the cook and owner, serves the equal of Peter Luger," Glenn said, referring to the venerable Brooklyn steakhouse where he had dined only once, the day of his law school graduation. When he saw the puzzled looks on his friends' faces, he explained that Peter Luger was long held to be the best restaurant in Brooklyn, and Brooklynites deemed it the best steak house in the world.

"Johnny and I are Brooklyn born, and unlike me, Johnny never left. That's a real Brooklynite," Glenn said.

"An Italian boy from Brooklyn?" Oliver called out in a playful voice. "Sure you're not bringing the Mafia into the NJA Club?"

The General shot Oliver a stern look that said not to even joke about that problem.

A series of chimes rang in Glenn's mind. At first they were little more than a tinkle, then rose to the sound level of a jazz xylophone.

Comes from Brooklyn. Really nice haircut. No details on his work, just a vague mention of property management. Italian from Red Hook. Eats at Peter Luger. Shows up just when we are on an alert for the Mafia. Impossible. If he were with that mob gang, he'd never set foot in the NJA Club, not after Wang warned the thugs about the General and then they disappeared. Then again, would he know everyone who those three local goons contacted?

Glenn gave Johnny a quick glance.

But he doesn't drink or smoke, avoids hookers, fell for a smart Thai waitress who's taking him to the Grand Palace. I was a criminal lawyer for a long time and never met a mobster like him. My mind is playing tricks on me. Since the General and that O' Halloran woman dragged me into this, nothing's felt quite right.

Glenn's thoughts were interrupted by the arrival of Edward and a young farang man. Glenn had known Edward long enough to understand the look on his face was a mixture of love and lust. He addressed the table, "Gentlemen, I'd like you to meet Rinaldo. He's from Argentina, but for the time being, he's with me."

"Poor guy," Oliver said. "The good news for Rinaldo is that this won't last long. No one can bear Edward for more than a week."

"We'll see about that," Edward replied. Then he looked at Johnny, who he hadn't even noticed in his zeal in introducing his latest companion.

"Well, who is this fellow?" Edward asked. "Lucky for Rinaldo I met him before I saw this face."

Johnny's face turned beet red. He rose from his seat to his full height.

"What did you say, faggot?" he bellowed at Edward, who froze in place,

The General held up a hand and looked directly at Johnny.

"We'll have none of that here," he said. "You are always welcome at this club, but we are all tolerant people if nothing else. Edward is used to speaking like that around us, and we have learned to ignore him, which is the wisest course of action for all, especially for a newcomer."

"As for you and Rinaldo," the General said staring at Edward. "I'd appreciate your finding another table as far from me as possible." Edward took Rinaldo's arm and steered him to the other side of the NJA Club.

Johnny sat down again, and the redness left his face. When the General spoke, Johnny knew who he was seeing. His decades in the mob taught him to recognize a powerful man, a leader, someone to be obeyed when they gave a command.

"I apologize if I broke your rules," Johnny said. "It's just that where I come from, what he said to me is a tremendous insult and if we were back in Brooklyn, I might have punched him out."

"I know the feeling," Sleepy Joe interjected. "Edward once pissed me off so much I dangled him over a balcony. By his feet."

"It's true," Glenn said. "I was there."

Who the hell am I dealing with? Johnny asked himself. This curiosity caused him to ask Sleepy Joe what Edward might have done to cause such a response. Sleepy Joe didn't look to Johnny like he could dangle a bag of potato chips over a balcony, let alone the pudgy Welshman.

Sleepy Joe smiled in a way that showed his yellowing teeth.

"The little weasel tried to hide the fact that he told some bad guys about Glenn. Glenn could have gotten hurt. Anyone who tries to mess with my mate Glenn has to get through me."

Oliver caught the look of disbelief on Johnny's face.

"Trust me, Johnny, Glenn is safer than the President of the United States with Sleepy Joe watching his back. Joe may look like a refugee from the Sixties, but my fellow Aussie served many years in our Special Forces and if he gets into a fight, it's a debate whether to call an ambulance or a hearse for the other side."

An old hippie who dangles rats off balconies and will kill for his friend Glenn. What the hell have I stumbled into? Another thought crossed his mind and he smiled. *The Boss would love this guy.* Then a thought broke through the mental meandering of times past in Brooklyn.

I wonder what kind of bad guys were asking about Glenn. And why.

After dinner was served, eaten, and its remnants removed from the table, the General called Ahn, and told her to bring his companions the drinks of their choice. A few minutes later, the General hoisted his martini, and Oliver and Sleepy Joe their beers. Glenn and Johnny toasted with their diet soft drinks.

"Here's to Johnny and a bright future, wherever it takes him," the General said over the clinking of the glasses. "He's always welcome in the NJA Club."

A few minutes later Johnny looked at his watch. Glenn saw it was a gold Rolex.

"As they say, time flies when you're having a good time, and that's the case for me tonight," he said. "But it's getting late and I have to meet someone in the morning, so I'll head back to my hotel. Thanks for the good time I had tonight." He stood up and shook hands all around the table.

As Johnny walked towards the door, he passed Edward and

Rinaldo, who sat directly in his line of sight. He avoided eye contact and turned his head to the side so he wouldn't have to see them.

"Don't let the door hit your ass on the way out," Edward called out to Johnny. The gangster stopped in his tracks and turned to face Edward and Rinaldo.

"What did you say?" he asked, his voice encased in iron-strong anger.

"It doesn't matter what I said a second ago," Edward calmly replied. "It's what I'm saying now that matters. Rinaldo came here to study Muay thai and he's been at it for a year. You are damn lucky he didn't break half the bones in your body." Rinaldo grinned at Johnny while holding up his middle finger.

As angry as he was over Edward's comment, Johnny couldn't help but smile at the thought of the slight Rinaldo implying even the most-farfetched threat. Johnny had eight or nine inches in height over him, not to mention forty pounds, much of it muscle from hours at the gym, and several inches in reach.

"I'm going to give you a pass," he said to Edward and Rinaldo. "Everyone else here seems really nice and I don't want to create a disturbance in someone else's house when they invited me and treated me so well. Consider yourself lucky."

"No problem, you two are free to work it out in the back alley," a voice called from behind Johnny, speaking English with a heavy accent. Johnny turned around to face Wang, the cook and owner of the NJA Club. Wang's face showed no trace of whatever emotion was hidden behind his blank stare.

Wang's appearance and suggestion caught Johnny off guard, but he quickly recovered.

Johnny scowled at the cook.

"Why, so the two of you can jump me and call in more of your midget army?" he asked.

A faint smile crossed Wang's face.

"That would not be necessary from either of us," he replied. "Consider yourself lucky you will fight Rinaldo and not me."

"I'll keep that in mind," Johnny said. "Let's go." *These guys can't be serious,* he told himself. *Looks like I could pick any one of them up and dangle them off a balcony just like that hippie did to the big-mouthed queer.*

Johnny and Rinaldo walked to the back door of the club, with Edward and Wang behind them. Glenn started to rise.

"I've got to stop this," he said. He looked to the General. "You can end this now."

"Sit down, Glenn," the General said in an unusually stern voice. "This is not your fight."

"I brought Johnny here," Glenn pleaded. "And I probably turned him against Edward with the way I spoke about him."

Sleepy Joe stood up and moved behind Glenn. He placed his hands on his friend's shoulders to keep him in place.

"I didn't hear you bring up Edward's sexual identity," Joe said. "If your new friend plans to live in Bangkok, he's got to learn to get along with everyone. At least accept everyone. Better to learn on the front end, wouldn't you agree?" Joe released his hands from Glenn's shoulders and went back to his chair. Glenn caught a glimpse of Wang and Edward as they passed through the door to the back alley. He and Joe remained inside the NJA Club.

When the other four men were in the back alley, Rinaldo stood in front of Johnny and stared into his eyes. He had to crane his neck upwards, Wang stepped between them and told Johnny he was going to pat him down.

"This will be a fair fight," he told the gangster.

"He won't lay a hand on me," Johnny said. He sounded like a man trying to come off as menacing but not really confident.

Wang placed a hand under Johnny's neck and held him in place while he patted him down with the other hand. He released Johnny when he was done. It took a matter of seconds. The moment Wang grabbed him, Johnny understood he was not dealing with an old man or a typical cook. Three decades in the Mafia taught him to instinctively know when he met a man who could kill without a second thought.

Glad to be fighting the little faggot and not this guy, he thought.

Wang steeped away, leaving Rinaldo staring again at his opponent. The slightly built Argentinian raised both hands over his head.

"Giving you a chance," he said.

Johnny worked out but had never taken any sort of fighting lessons. He didn't think he would have a need any to handle a clown like Rinaldo.

"You might want to protect your face," he said to Rinaldo. "Your girlfriend might not like it all smashed up."

"Don't worry about my romantic life," Rinaldo said and laughed. The laugh angered Johnny. How many times had the Boss told him that no one should ever laugh at a made man and get away with it.

Johnny placed a foot forward and thew a punch a Rinaldo. He didn't like throwing punches at a shrimp of a man who had both hands above his head, but a lesson needed to be taught.

Johnny's fist passed through air. Rinaldo had moved a few inches to the side. When the Argentinian was back in his line of sight, Johnny lunged at him, planning to grab him by the neck as Wang had done to him. He'd throttle Rinaldo until he was limp like a rag doll and then drop him to let him catch his breath again. He'd seen Tommy do that several times. He never got the chance.

Johnny didn't see it, but he felt Rinaldo's foot as it flew into his crotch. Johnny howled, fell the ground, and writhed in pain he didn't previously imagine was possible.

"Give it ten minutes and you'll be able to walk home," Rinaldo said. "But I wouldn't plan on using your pecker for a full day."

"That's a shame," Edward said as he gazed down on the prone Brooklynite. "Sort of cute, in a thuggish way."

"Not your type, Edward," Wang said. "You like small guys."

Wang walked back into the club and Edward and Rinaldo followed. Johnny took a deep breath and struggled to raise himself from the ground.

"Your friend is not welcome here until he apologizes for insulting my customers," Wang told Glenn. He had pulled up a chair between Glenn and the General. "He is lucky Rinaldo didn't do more than kick him in the balls." Wang chuckled when he saw Glenn grimace.

"Don't worry, ten minutes from now his ego will hurt more than his balls."

"I had no idea he was like that, or I would never have invited him to join us," Glenn said sheepishly. "I'm going to apologize to Edward and Rinaldo, and to you for causing this problem."

Wang flashed a thin smile.

"No apology necessary," Wang replied. "I think you spent too much time with such men in your other life, so they seem normal to you."

Glenn sat up ramrod straight.

"Are you saying Johnny is like one of the crooks I represented when I was a criminal lawyer?"

Wang smiled briefly once again.

"I do not know if they had the Mafia where you worked, but I think all criminals are basically the same inside. Stupid and not as tough as they think they are."

Oliver sipped his beer during this exchange. When Wang was done, he shared his thoughts with his friends.

"The man is in real estate management, you say? Shouldn't be too hard for me to see if that's the case." Glenn and the General nodded, both knowing well that their big Australian friend was the number one purveyor of information in the Kingdom.

"Why are we wasting our time on this?" Sleepy Joe asked.

Oliver stared at his fellow Australian.

"Mate, didn't you tell us just a short while ago how you dangled Edward off a balcony because some bad men came around asking about Glenn and he told them what they wanted to know? What's the harm in knowing who we're dealing with?"

An uneasy feeling came over Glenn, causing his stomach to tighten as did the muscles in his hands and wrists as he gripped the edge of the table.

"Why do we have to get involved in investigating a tourist who stops here for dinner?" he asked. "Isn't it enough that we've been dragged into real Mafia business?"

"Oliver is suggesting that there may be a link between the Mafia who came to town and your new friend," the General said. "The men who tried to strong-arm Wang were not Americans, so we can assume someone hired them, and according to what we learned, mostly from your FBI, they were hired by Mafia from Brooklyn, New York."

Sleepy Joe listened to the discussion and offered his opinion.

"Glenn, you've got to admit it may be more than coincidence that this Johnny fellow is an Italian boy from Brooklyn, with some very vague plans and a rather sketchy explanation for how he makes his money. Can you see that, mate?"

"Perhaps we should ask the lady FBI agent to do this for us," the General said. "She won't charge me like Oliver will." He smiled at the big Aussie, and Oliver understood the General was letting him know he was not serious about the money part.

"That may be best," Wang said. "I'm going back to my kitchen. I'm a cook, not a policeman." He walked away.

Something stirred inside Glenn. For a moment he struggled to grasp this feeling, and he then recalled the words of his criminal procedure professor all those years ago in Brooklyn Law School.

There's a reason why grand jury proceedings are secret. All kinds of hearsay and innuendo wind up being put before the jurors, and it's quite common for innocent people to be the subject of an investigation. Reputations can be ruined and lives destroyed by leaks that are utterly false. If there's no indictment, there's no reason for a single word to be revealed.

"Ms. O'Halloran should be informed only if Oliver comes up with solid evidence that Johnny is mixed up in our problem," he said. "My experience has been that once someone is investigated by the FBI, they suffer because of that fact alone, even if they are as clean as a plate out of Wang's kitchen."

"Glenn's the lawyer, so we'll listen to him on this," the General instructed. "If I recall from my days in America, grand jury leaks can be nastier than Thai gossip."

Oliver glanced at his gold Rolex watch.

"I'll get started tonight," he said. "By the time I get home it will be morning in your country and my connections will be wide awake." He bid his friends good night and left the club.

Minutes after Oliver departed, Edward took his seat. He and

Rinaldo took a table as far from the others as the room allowed. Glenn spoke directly to Edward.

"If you're looking for an apology from me, Edward, you just got it. Had I known this fellow was anything like he turned out to be, I would never have asked him here. I am humiliated that I brought the person who insulted you and Rinaldo the way he did."

Edward smiled and showed his yellowing teeth. Glenn noticed for the first time that several were crooked.

"Don't be so hard on yourself," he told Glenn. "People of better breeding have said worse things. Your Johnny talked like a gangster but went down like a little child. A good kick in the balls can do that, you know."

Glenn smiled back at Edward. *Strange he too should think gangster in connection with Johnny.*

"I'm glad you feel that way, Edward, and I'm proud of Rinaldo for showing Johnny what happens when you open your big mouth to the wrong people. But I do have a question if you don't mind."

"Ask me," Edward said.

"I studied Muay thai for a few years," Glenn said. "We were taught certain rules and one of them was never kick a guy in the nuts. Okay to kick him in the head, the belly, limbs, and shoulders, but stay away from the sensitive parts. So why didn't Rinaldo follow that rule?"

"Strange you should ask, as I posed Rinaldo the same question. And he explained to me that there are different rules when someone calls you a faggot."

"As there well should be," Sleepy Joe interjected.

Edward stared at the man who once dangled him over a balcony railing and who had been a member of the Australian Special Forces, not known as a hotbed of LBGTQ rights advocates, at least in Edward's mind.

"Since when did you become such a champion of our rights? Never would have suspected it."

Sleepy Joe grinned at Edward, showing teeth as yellow and crooked as the Welshman's.

"You spend enough time around a liberal Democrat from San Francisco like my mate Glenn, and some of it rubs off on you."

"Fair enough," Edward said. "But I'm still a Tory. In my country, conservatives don't hate gay people."

"Wish I could say the same," Glenn said. "If Johnny ever shows his face around here again, I'll be the first to tell him to leave."

"Oh, no need for that," Edward said. "If he comes back it means he's learned a lesson and we must give him another chance."

"You're rather forgiving," a surprised Glenn replied

"We don't all carry grudges, Glenn," Edward countered. He went back to Rinaldo

The General said he had an appointment to meet his latest mia noi at the condo he was renting for her. Glenn didn't know her name, couldn't recall if he'd been told, and didn't care. *Even if I did, they're never around long enough to justify the effort.* Glenn found it strange that the Thai term was generally translated not as "mistress," but as "minor wife," as the relationships were not necessarily minor and the woman was definitely not a wife.

When the General was gone, Sleepy Joe turned to Glenn.

"Over to your place for a few joints and a movie?" Sleepy Joe asked.

"Absolutely," Glenn said. "My fingers are itching to do some rolling."

THIRTEEN

P aulie paid Nice two thousand baht to let Baxter know they had to meet as quickly as possible. She made the call, and when she was done, led Paulie along Soi Nana to where it intersected with Sukhumvit Road and hailed a cab, giving the driver specific directions in Thai. He drove Paulie to Baxter's headquarters. Paulie made the trek through the same doors and stairs as before.

"I've got bad news," he told Baxter as soon as they were seated and the whiskeys poured. "The three guys we got from you have gone missing. No one's seen or heard from them in days. We never even got their last report of which places they visited. I was hoping you could help us out."

Baxter's smooth face remained as impassive as usual. *This guy is either the coolest guy I've run across or he's too stupid to know a problem."* Paulie thought. *"I'm going with the first.*

"I'm truly sorry it didn't work out for you," Baxter said. "I realize those three are a little wild, but they've always done well for me. I can find replacements, and of course, you won't have to pay the balance due, but I can't refund what you already paid for the first week."

"I wasn't expecting that," Paulie said. "And it's too late for replacements. We've had a change of plans. What I'd like is for you to help me unload the booze when it arrives, meaning instead of sending men around to every bar or restaurant in town, we sell as much as we can to some big purchasers and get it all done quickly."

Baxter smiled as he poured more drinks.

"That can be arranged," he said. "Of course, if they're buying in bulk, they get a better deal."

"Understood," Paulie replied as he drank his second shot of whiskey. *Good thing I can hold it,* he thought. *This guy's got a wooden leg.*

Baxter explained that he could provide a medium sized truck to ferry the booze to the places he had in mind after they picked it up at the dock.

"You'll have to trust me," he explained to Paulie. "You'll be there when we take the shipment at the docks, but my men and I make the deliveries ourselves. When it's all done, we'll pay you what we owe."

Paulie reflected for a good half minute. If he wanted to comply with the Boss's order to unload the booze and come home, there weren't any other options.

"Okay, but when I make the pickup of the money, I'm bringing Tommy, the guy who was running those three mugs until they disappeared. I don't like going around by myself with all that dough."

Baxter nodded.

"Wouldn't expect you to, and I've already met your friend Tommy, so I'm cool with him watching your back."

The cab was waiting for Paulie when he hit the street, and he again had the driver bring him to the Holiday Inn. He waited inside for five minutes, left by a different exit, and walked to his hotel.

FOURTEEN

Rinaldo was right; the pain in Johnny's testicles subsided to the point where he could walk ten minutes after being kicked, and when he woke up the next morning, the pain was gone. Johnny knew the shame would stay with him longer. Even more disconcerting was the way that big Australian with the shaved head joked about him being in the Mafia.

It's better I never go back there, he thought.

Johnny had not lied when he told Glenn and his friends he had an appointment in the morning. He was about to have breakfast with Tommy and Paulie, to remind them the boat with the booze was docking the next day, and that the liquor needed to be disposed of as quickly as possible. After that, Tommy could leave and he and Paulie would handle the matter of getting the cash to Brooklyn before they could return home. The events of the night before caused Johnny to accept that his thoughts of staying in Bangkok were nothing but flights of fancy. He couldn't remain in a place where people joke about him being in the mob and little gay men kick him in the balls.

Then he remembered he was to meet Fah at noon for his tour of the Grand Palace. He thought for a moment about just not showing up and avoiding her restaurant for the rest of his stay but rejected the thought. *Just because I got embarrassed doesn't mean I can embarrass her.*

Tommy and Paulie insisted on meeting in the nearest McDonald's. While it would not have been their choice back home, in the absence of a genuine Brooklyn diner, the familiar fast food was their fallback. Paulie and Johnny sat at a table while Tommy stood in line to order their breakfast sandwiches and coffees. Johnny used Tommy's absence to question Paulie. The first was whether there was any information about the three missing salesmen, if they could be called such.

"I met this guy in one of the bars, he set me up with a British guy married to a local and her brother was an officer with the cops. Still has connections. He found out a cleaning lady on a high floor of an office building reported watching three big men fight a fourth and smaller man. It lasted only a few seconds, leaving the first three dead. Too dark for any details, but she heard them speaking in English, which she doesn't understand. The lady called it in, but when the cops finally showed up, there were no bodies."

"Sounds like the cleaning lady has a fertile imagination," Johnny said.

"You think Tommy's got something to do with this Bobby Giannelli disappearing?" Paulie asked.

"I don't know what to think," Johnny said. "He won't tell me who he hired for the hijacking, and I don't buy his reasons. Santucci's men would pay the old man his cut and not have to worry about getting whacked for disloyalty. There's some other reason Tommy doesn't want the boss to talk to these guys. He'll have to tell the Boss when asked, although the Boss made it clear over here I'm acting in his place, and he's not being fully on the up-and-up with me. Besides, Paulie, you're the Arranger, and if Tommy wanted to cut some deal with another family, you're the man for that job. Tommy didn't tell me, and it's clear he never discussed it with you or the Boss first. Maybe there's a reason for all this secrecy, but I don't see one unless Tommy's hiding something from us."

Paulie formed his lips into an O, softly expelling air in the universal sign to be quiet. Tommy was no more than twenty feet away.

"Hey, I like the McDonalds over here," he said. "They bring the food right to our table. Almost like a restaurant."

"While we're waiting, let's talk a little about the booze that's arriving tomorrow," Johnny said. "I want you two down at the dock to meet our man on board the ship. Don't worry, he knows what you two look like and he'll find you. Have you arranged for a truck to be waiting with you?"

"Of course," Paulie replied. "After all, I'm the Arranger. Our friend Baxter will again provide men to help us. Anyone tries to track down these guys he sends, good luck.

I can always rely on Paulie, Johnny thought.

"Tommy just has to stand there looking tough when we're dropping off the booze and when I get the money, which comes naturally to him. If anyone is stupid enough to try ripping us off, Tommy uses his discretion."

Tommy nodded, then asked Johnny a question.

"I'm supposed to do all this unarmed? I'm just supposed to scare them?"

"If there's armed men who want the booze or the money, let them have it," Johnny said, explaining what Paulie had told him earlier that day. "A shootout on the docks or the streets won't make it easier in any way, and the law out here will be looking for us if we go that far. Besides, one gun wouldn't do any good against a gang, and that's what it would take to pull off a heist like you're worried about. Don't worry. You looking tough will scare away the small time thieves. Besides, Baxter's men will surely be armed and they'll be with you two until you're safely away from the dock and the booze is being sold."

A pretty young waitress brought the food, carefully placing a Breakfast Mac and cup of scalding hot black coffee before each man. Johnny handed her a fifty baht note, which she accepted with a wide smile and a wai. The moment she was gone, Johnny continued.

"And once we have it in the truck, we need buyers. What's the story there, Paulie"

"Baxter's got a half dozen bars in and around Soi Nana that will take it all, and that's gonna make it go quickly" Paulie said. "The truck will make the drop offs with Tommy and me along for the ride. Baxter's men will unload and collect the money from the bars. No one will see us behind the tinted windows of the truck. I'm keeping a case or two for us to party with, sorry, not you Johnny, and one for the driver and helper, but the rest will be gone. Why shouldn't they be? I'm practically giving it away. It's worth it to be done and gone real soon."

Johnny cleared his throat. Paulie and Tommy knew this meant he was about to deliver an order from the boss.

"The Boss wants Tommy home as soon as possible. Once the money is collected, Tommy goes home right away. While you're unloading the booze, I'll be getting his ticket issued." They had purchased open-ended return flights. "Paulie and I will take care of getting the money to the Boss and making sure we don't leave any traces of our presence here behind us when we leave."

I don't like this, and I bet the Boss doesn't like me right now. Much as I miss home, this does not feel right, Tommy thought. But what he said was, "Of course, Johnny, whatever the Boss wants."

That having been said, the three Brooklyn mobsters quietly ate their Breakfast Macs and drank their coffee. When they were done, Johnny explained that he had an appointment and left. Tommy and Paulie knew better than to ask the Boss's representative with whom he was meeting.

Paulie had to bring Baxter money to rent the trucks, which would be done by Thai men using fake ID cards. He asked Tommy if he had any plans.

"Maybe get another one of them massages," he said with a leer. "Maybe take one of those pool-playing babes from the beer bars back to my room. I ain't gonna see prices like this much longer. Have fun here before I have to go back to Brooklyn and deal with that mess."

He had no intention of doing either.

FIFTEEN

At five minutes to eight, Lek called Glenn to let him know he'd be coming up with dinner for Glenn and his guests. Mary and the Lieutenant would be arriving at eight, and Glenn knew from experience that Lek and his cousin were perpetually on time and assumed an FBI agent would be as well.

"I ordered plain pad thai, not spicy, for the farang lady," Lek explained as he set three places at the table. He knew where to find Glenn's cutlery, as well as their long periods of not escaping the drawer, so he washed each utensil before placing them on the table. He did the same with the plates and glasses.

"There's normal Thai food for you and my cousin," Lek said. "I made sure to get you steamed fish in lemon sauce," he added.

"Thank you. Maybe one day I'll learn to say the name of my favorite Thai dish in Thai.

"*Pla Kra Pong Neung Ma Nau,*" Lek said. "No way you learn to say that. You live here how many years, but you don't know more than twenty words in our language?"

"That's why I keep you around," Glenn said with a smile. "And thanks for taking care of dinner. What do I owe you?"

"Nothing," Lek said. "My cousin gave me money for this last time he was here."

"I bet he paid for it out of his own pocket, because he doesn't trust too many people in his own department," Glenn said. "He wouldn't want to explain his meetings."

"I think you are correct, Khun Glenn. If you're thinking about repaying him, forget it. He's such an honest cop that he won't even let someone pay for dinner - especially not a farang."

Lek then realized he may have insulted Glenn. He apologized and gave Glenn a deep wai.

"Nothing to be sorry about, Lek," Glenn assured his friend. "That's why we respect him."

There was a knock on the door.

"I'll let them in and go back to my desk. My assistant was under instructions to let them in. She knows the Lieutenant."

The female pronoun caught Glenn's attention.

Since when is your assistant a she?" he asked Lek. "I thought it was the nice young man who's been here for a good year."

"Yes, he was a nice young man, but he took another job."

"And what was that new job if I may inquire?" Glenn asked.

"He went to work for the police department," Lek said. "My cousin recruited him."

The doorbell rang, Lek looked through the peephole and then let the Lieutenant and Mary O'Halloran into the apartment. Lek closed the door behind him when he left. The two law enforcement officers joined Glenn at the table.

"You're about to enjoy a good meal," the Lieutenant said to Mary as they seated themselves. "My cousin Lek is on excellent terms with every good Thai restaurant within five kilometers. They pay special attention to his orders."

"I have a bottle of wine, if anyone is interested," Glenn said. While he wasn't interested, he thought his guests might be.

"FBI agents never drink while working," Mary said.

"Most Thai police do, but not this one," the Lieutenant said.

They agreed on water.

. . .

When the meal was over, Glenn suggested they move to the living room. He sat on his beloved armchair, and the other two sat facing him on the couch. They declined Glenn's offer to make coffee.

"We called this meeting because we think you know more about this Mafia business than you're letting on," Mary said. "There's no way the General hasn't heard from the intended victims, and if he did, there's no way he wouldn't seek your counsel."

Glenn stared at the Lieutenant. The Thai policeman showed no signs that he even noticed.

There's no way she knows that except by him telling her.

"My understanding has been that the Lieutenant wants me here because he feels more comfortable with a friendly face in the presence of an FBI agent," Glenn responded. "That lecture on organized crime was a one-off. I'm just here to listen."

"Maybe that's what we thought at first," Mary replied. "We're investigators, and if we think we have a lead, we follow it up."

Glenn's eyes held daggers as they glared at the Lieutenant.

"If our friend the Lieutenant wishes to learn of any conversations between the General and I, he is free to ask the General. That's my only comment."

"I'm sure he can," Mary said coolly. "But I'm doing my own investigation as an FBI agent, and I need to speak to anyone who has relevant information. I can't assume that everything the General said to the Lieutenant is the same as what he told you."

"Nice try," Glenn said. "Let's say my conversations with the General were within the attorney-client privilege."

"As long as we're talking about clients, have we forgotten poor Freddie Trammel?" Mary asked. Glenn sensed the hostility she was suppressing without much success.

"Not at all," Glenn said. "I'm going to hire a lawyer back in California to represent him. I'll put in my declaration as to what you told me, and I'm sure the lawyer will get any information or evidence in the actual or constructive possession of the FBI, not to mention the media." *I sound like a lawyer myself again.*

The Lieutenant intervened.

"I think we've gone as far as we can on this issue of Glenn

revealing what he feels are privileged conversations. Let's ask him if he has gained any insights into some other occurrences we've discovered."

"Fair enough," Mary said. She opened a notebook and reviewed her notes.

"The local police received a call from a cleaning woman who witnessed a fight between four men in an alley. She saw three of the men down and presumed they were dead or dying. She was certain one of them was Russian and one was Thai. Couldn't figure out what the third dead man might be. The fourth man walked away and she never got a very good look at him. When the squad car and ambulance arrived, there were no bodies anywhere in sight, but there was blood and tissue later determined to be human."

"What does this have to do with me?" Glenn asked Mary.

"We don't know that it has anything to do with you," she explained. "We are hoping you heard something about this. Your friends, the General and Oliver, are well informed on anything out of the ordinary taking place in Bangkok."

Glenn smiled.

"Based on some of the things I've experienced the past few years, I'm not sure three men being killed in an alley and disappearing constitutes something out of the ordinary in Bangkok."

The Lieutenant addressed Glenn's point.

"It does when we know that three known hoods-for-hire have also disappeared. I have a few honest men in an organized crime unit and they tell me that's what they are hearing out on the street. And one of the missing men is a Russian, the other a Thai. The third is of unknown origin."

Mary took over from the Lieutenant.

"The Lieutenant's men have canvassed every bar and restaurant with a liquor license," Mary said. "The hoods trying to sell the hijacked booze were careful to avoid security cameras in any establishment and confronted their targets on the streets where they believed there were no cameras. They screwed up once, when they stopped one owner on a street where we have good surveillance cameras. From what we have determined from the footage, the three hoods were a Russian, a Thai and a third guy that looked like he was from somewhere in the South Pacific." She pulled some photos from the notebook and showed them to Glenn. They were grainy and somewhat out of focus, but he could clearly see that one man was a Thai and the other certainly looked like he could be a Russian, and if the Lieutenant's people thought he was, that was good enough for Glenn.

"Never saw any of them," Glenn said.

"Maybe not," Mary said. "But we think you have seen someone else, an American, an Italian man from Brooklyn who some of your friends thought might be in the Mafia. We know you brought him to your favorite haunt, the NJA Club."

She must have spoken to Edward, Glenn thought. He said nothing.

"Will you confirm or deny this?" she asked Glenn. He remained silent.

"It appears you've been monitoring my every movement," Glenn said. He felt anger and heat rising inside him. "I don't appreciate it, especially since you have little to no legal authority in this country. I, as a lawful foreign resident, do have some legal privacy rights, and if these illegal violations continue, I'm going to have to ask the Lieutenant to protect my rights against you." Glenn was not smiling when he said this. The Lieutenant, however, did allow his lips to upturn slightly in their corners.

"Here's what I'm going to do immediately," Glenn said. "I'm no longer going to meet with you or any other representative of American law enforcement. I will, of course, continue to help the Lieutenant in any way he requests, provided I have his assurance he'll share none of what I tell him with you or any other US officials. Maybe then you'll get the idea of just how unimportant you are in this country." He looked at the Lieutenant.

"Are you okay with this?" Glenn asked the Thai police officer, who nodded in the affirmative before addressing Mary.

"My job is to protect the people of Thailand," he explained. "I thought at first it would be beneficial to work with someone from the FBI. I also thought I needed Glenn with me to make certain I was getting the whole truth and some real assistance. I'm not persuaded I'm getting either from you, Agent O'Halloran. You didn't tell me you were spying on Glenn. Not exactly how we get cooperation around here. I have worked with Glenn in the past, and I'm certain I'll work better with him on this case without your help."

Mary stared at the Lieutenant, her mouth wide open as if she were about to either scream or deliver a rebuke. The Lieutenant spoke before she could do either.

"You're dismissed," the Lieutenant told Mary. "Lek will get you a cab."

Mary rose and left the apartment without saying a word. As Glenn watched her walk away, he observed what a shapely behind the FBI agent possessed.

"I guess you were right about not trusting an FBI agent," Glenn said to the Lieutenant when they were alone.

"I was correct to want you here to make certain she didn't lie to me," the Lieutenant replied. "I had no idea she was investigating you or the General."

Glenn remained silent for a moment, then spoke again.

"She's actually right about that guy from Brooklyn I brought to the NJA Club. There were some joking remarks about him being in the Mafia. Who really knows how much of a joke it really is?"

The Lieutenant answered Glenn's question.

"If you don't mind, Glenn, I'd like to look into this, with your help. When you know as little as we do right now, every possible lead must be checked out."

"I'd be happy to help you in any way I can," Glenn said. "The problem is, I don't know how to reach this fellow. All I know is that he's staying somewhere in the Green Belt and found a favorite restaurant where he seems to have fallen for a waitress. He says his name is Johnny Brancini. He is about my age, maybe a few years younger, in good shape. He doesn't drink or smoke. Says he's in property management, but no one believed him."

"I'll have one of our sketch artists pay a visit to the NJA Club and work off of the descriptions we get from the witnesses who met him, starting with you. We'll distribute his likeness through the Green Belt. If we're lucky, some taxi driver or restaurant worker will recall seeing someone who looks like him. That's the best we can do right now."

With that, the Lieutenant bid Glenn a good night and left the apartment.

~

Oliver was still in town, and when Glenn called and asked him to come to his place, the big Aussie said he'd be there in ten minutes. He arrived bearing a gift for Glenn.

"There are stores selling weed all over Bangkok," Oliver said as he handed Glenn a small packet of marijuana buds. "You really don't need Sleepy Joe anymore."

"I'll always need Sleepy Joe," Glenn replied. He put the gifted weed in his pocket. He then told Oliver everything that had transpired between him and his earlier visitors.

"The good news is the Lieutenant will report everything to the General, and your loyalty to him will be duly noted," Oliver said. "The bad news is we now have one of your FBI hounds sniffing around the NJA Club, and you and the General in particular."

"What's your recommendation?" Glenn asked.

Oliver walked over to Glenn's liquor cabinet, filled with bottles of quality spirits. Glenn himself almost never poured a drink, but he kept them for his friends, most of whom enjoyed booze as much as he loved smoking weed. Oliver poured himself a shot glass of Tito's vodka, the only liquor Glenn himself actually liked, because after six distillations, it had virtually no taste. He quaffed it in one big slug.

"Ah, that went down well," Oliver said. "You don't drink much, but as in all else, you have impeccable taste in vodka."

"I'm lighting a joint," Glenn replied, and pulled one from a small box on the coffee table He lit it with the nearby lighter. Oliver waited until Glenn had exhaled the first puff before commenting on Glenn's visit from the two law enforcement officials.

"They told you what we already knew about the fight, the call to the cops, and the absence of the bodies when the cops arrived. We'd love to know who took the bodies, and why, not to mention what they did with them."

"Any thoughts on the 'who' part?" Glenn asked.

"Let's think this through," Oliver replied. "It looks to this analyst that someone was following the three missing hoods, and the man who encountered them must have been a skilled fighter to kill three men without using a gun. Since there was a pool of blood observed, and no gun shots heard and no casings or other signs of a gun were found, it was most likely a knife that killed one of them."

"Which tells you what?" Glenn asked.

"It tells me that whoever that cleaning lady saw kill three big men was, it's most likely, trained to do that sort of thing. It's not a skill one just happens to have, and whoever sent him out there surely used him for those very skills."

"Why do you think someone hired him?" Glenn asked.

"Unlikely the man just happened to encounter them in an alleyway and decided to kill them for no reason," Oliver said. "The bodies were gone before the cops arrived, strongly suggesting the killer's accomplices removed them. Since the cleaning lady left the window after she saw the murders, we have no evidence on who took the bodies away."

Glenn took two deep drags off his joint and reflected on Oliver's words.

"The cleaning lady did say the fourth man, the sole survivor, was noticeably smaller than the other three," he said.

"That fits almost every man in Bangkok, except maybe me," Oliver said.

"How many smaller men do we know who are capable of killing three men while he's unarmed?" Glenn asked.

"I only know of one," Oliver said. He smiled and then softly said the words "Sleepy Joe."

Glenn needed another long drag on his joint before he could pose more questions

"Why would Sleepy Joe want to kill three hoods in a back alley, whether or not they were the ones trying to strong-arm locals into using their hijacked booze?" he asked,

Oliver shook his head in disbelief.

"Have you forgotten how the General explained to us the whole scheme? Remember he said they had even approached Wang and were not dissuaded when the unflappable Wang mentioned the NJA Club was the General's favorite place? And finally, do you remember he told us that they were taken care of? Must I draw you a road map?"

The joint was at Glenn's fingertips thanks to the huge drags he'd taken. He put it in an ashtray.

"Do you think the General sent Sleepy Joe on assignment to get these guys off the backs of the local businessmen, and he sent Joe because he knew he could handle them if they got rough?"

"Something like that," Oliver replied. "I doubt the orders were to kill, but something happened that led to these untimely deaths." Oliver walked to the liquor cabinet and poured himself another shot of vodka, which he downed while sanding, and then returned to his seat.

Glenn shook his head before speaking, just as Oliver had.

"When I was a practicing criminal lawyer, I often didn't ask my clients about what actually happened, because I didn't want to be burdened with the consequences of knowing, and they didn't voluntarily tell me those things. This is such an occasion. Though it makes no sense that the General would not want us to know. It's not like we are unaware of the kind of situations they deal with. The General has a security business and many important clients who face dangerous enemies."

"Agreed," Oliver said. "Let's you and I not work off the assumption that Sleepy Joe killed these men while on assignment for the General because it doesn't make any difference right now. Forget it, put it off to the side somewhere. But we do try to find this Johnny Brancini character. We all thought he was hiding something, and without tooting our own horns too loudly, if you and I plus the General and Sleepy Joe all felt that way, it means he's hiding something."

"The Lieutenant is going to have a sketch artist meet with me and maybe the rest of you, and then the picture will be distributed around the Green Belt," Glenn explained.

"I'll put it out to any source I have that might be able to help. Guys who bum around the Green Belt, some crime reporters in New York, If the likeness is any good and we show it to enough people, we're going to get leads and one of them may turn out to be the one we want."

Oliver told Glenn he had to leave as he had a busy day ahead of him.

"Nothing to do with this mess," he said. "I've been hired by an Australian bank to find a former teller who embezzled several million Aussie dollars from his branch and is somewhere in the Kingdom. I think I've got a lead. Found a credit card transaction in his wife's name in Phuket last week. They're smart to be hiding out amongst other farangs. Too many of these fugitives think it's smarter to head for the hinterlands, where of course, a farang, especially one with money, sticks out like a sore thumb."

Oliver bid Glenn good night and told him they'd meet the following afternoon at the NJA Club, where they would bring the General up to speed on their plan to find Johnny Brancini and use him to make certain the Mafia never again came near the NJA Club.

SIXTEEN

J ohnny had gone to a tailor the week before and had some custom-fitted clothing made. Back in Brooklyn, he always took care to be well-dressed, not gaudy or attention-seeking like the tough guys, but well-dressed in an understated manner. His order from the Bangkok tailor stayed true to Johnny's preferences: olive and khaki casual dress pants, short-sleeved shirts in white, blue, and tan. Tommy and Paulie dressed as if they were still in Brooklyn, favoring heavier pants, long sleeved shirts and sport coats or light jackets, even when the temperature approached a hundred degrees. They really weren't out on the streets all that much, and Bangkok air-conditioning approximated Arctic temperatures.

He chose the new pair of khaki trousers and the white shirt for his date with Fah. He slipped his feet into a pair of comfortable loafers with soles designed for walking. He stopped off at the barbershop a few doors down from the hotel, where the English-speaking Thai barber gave him an outstanding trim and shave. The hot lather felt good on his face and the after-shave lotion the barber slashed on Johnny's face produced both a jolt of energy and a pleasant scent.

He showed up at the coffee shop where they were to meet a full half hour ahead of time. He drank coffee and read the newspapers the shop made available for customers. Fah walked through the door at exactly noon, wearing a yellow and white dress with bare sleeves. Her hair, tied in a bun when working, hung down to her shoulders. A leather bag was draped across her shoulder. She smiled when she saw Johnny.

The coffee shop wasn't far from the Siphon Taksin BTS station, which Johnny had taken. Fah suggested that instead of a cab, they take a river taxi which carried passengers along the Chao Phraya River, making numerous stops. The Grand Palace was the ninth stop, the Tha Chang Pier.

"The only benefit of taking a cab is that because you're with a Thai, the driver won't try the old trick of telling you today is a holiday and the Grand Palace is closed. Then they take you to buy some fake gems. But it's a nice day, and you'll enjoy the boat ride."

Fah led Johnny two blocks to the entrance to the pier. They stood in line for tickets and then a different line for boarding. They walked along the rickety plank bridge onto the crowded long boat and found two seats. Fah told Johnny to sit by the side railing The boat had no walls, only a roof held up by poles spaced far apart, so the view was unobstructed.

The boat's engine was noisy, but the breeze was pleasant, and Johnny did enjoy watching all manner of vessels cruise the wide river. They passed the stately old Oriental Hotel on one side and the modern Hilton on the other. *If the boss were more generous with expenses, I'd be in a place like those,* he thought.

When the boat reached the Tha Chang Pier, Fah edged Johnny and they walked over another rickety plank bridge, through a covered market hawking souvenirs to the multitude of tourists. Johnny hadn't seen as many white people in one place since he arrived, not even in the Green Belt. They walked to the Grand Palace's main gate, and after they passed through a second set of separate gates (with separate admission prices) for foreigners and Thais, they met up.

"The first thing I want you to see is the Emerald Buddha," Fah said when they were together again. "Most of the palaces here are closed to the public. The King doesn't live here anymore, and most of it is now used for the Royal offices."

The Wat was a complex of several buildings. Fah directed Johnny towards the largest one.

"The Emerald Buddha is in here," she said. She explained that they would view it from a distance of several meters.

Fah explained that the Wat complex was not actually a temple, because monks did not reside there. "We call it Wat Phra Kaew," she said.

The area surrounding the Emerald Buddha was crowded and they had to wait their turn to maneuver a clear view. She brought Johnny as close to the famed statue as one was allowed, several yards away, and he could see that it was made of what looked to him to be emerald or jade, but he didn't know enough about precious stones to know the difference, only that both were green. The statue was covered in a gold cloth. Johnny recognized the classic seated Buddha but was surprised to see it was barely two feet tall.

"I thought it would be larger," he told Fah.

"This is our most treasured symbol of our Buddhism," she said solemnly. "It has been in Thailand for seven hundred years. Only our King gets to touch it."

"I meant no disrespect," Johnny said. "Good things come in small packages."

"Don't worry," she said playfully. "Wait until you see the Reclining Buddha not too far away."

As they walked away from Wat Phra Kaew, Johnny eyed the statues of warriors standing throughout the complex. They reminded him of scenes from Japanese anime or the villains in a Marvel universe movie. Fah noticed his interest.

"Those are not really Thai," she explained. "They are Chinese warrior statues. If you travel around Thailand and our neighbors, you can always tell what was built by Chinese and what was built by Indians. They both brought Buddhism here. This is pure Chinese, and most likely they paid for a lot of this construction. At least that's what one of my professors taught."

"Looking at the statues and the architecture makes me think I've walked onto the set of *Star Wars*," Johnny said.

Fah explained that it was only a short walk behind the Emerald

Buddha facility to the Wat Pho complex, where the Reclining Buddha was housed. When they were inside the building, Johnny smiled and nodded, as if to signal that this was the size he was hoping to see. The wooden carving stood fifty feet high, and the Buddha reclined for a total of a hundred fifty feet.

When they were outside again, Fah asked Johnny if he wanted to try a real Thai massage.

"On sacred grounds?" he asked.

Fah laughed.

"We don't see it exactly that way. The most famous school of massage in the Kingdom is right here. They train the best masseuses. We can get massages right here from the students. Very inexpensive."

They walked a short distance and stopped in front of an open-air space with a thatched roof and no sides. Scores of people laid on thin pads as student masseuses massaged the white tourists and the Thais, all with their shirts or blouses on. A young woman escorted Johnny and Fah to two pads upon which they lay. Two young students, a man, and a woman, were summoned. The young man knelt next to Johnny and the young woman next to Fah. Fah spoke to the students in Thai and then explained to Johnny that she'd asked his masseuse to give a medium massage as this was his first time. Within five minutes of his massage, Johnny found himself drifting off to dreamland. He experienced a sense of relaxation he hadn't felt since the one time he smoked weed with Tommy the Turtle over twenty years ago. The weed relaxed Johnny so much that he feared he wouldn't be able to function if he kept smoking it, so he never tried it again. Tommy went back to his usual boozing, and marijuana played no future role in their lives.

An hour later, when the massages were over and Johnny and Fah were leaving the complex, she asked him how he liked the massage.

"It's the first one I've had here," he said. "I always thought the massage parlors were just a front for prostitution."

Fah cast him a stern look.

"That's because you spend most of your time in the farang areas," she said. "That's what the farang men want. But the Thai people just want good massages."

"How do I know which ones are legit?" Johnny asked.

"If they're hanging outside the place dressed like hookers, calling out to passing men, if they have names that sound like a brothel, stay away. Don't go for a massage in a place called 'Honeypot' or 'Love Machine.' Stick with ones that say they are traditional."

"I'll remember those names and try to stay away," Johnny said.

They hailed a cab, and the driver took them to the busy Asoke intersection, where Fah could catch the MRT subway to go home. She was scheduled to work the evening shift and had enough time to change and make it there by four p.m. Johnny would walk the half mile to his hotel.

When they were on the sidewalk, Fah placed a hand on Johnny's forearm.

"I hope I helped you understand a little more about Thailand," she said. "Any time you're interested in doing it again, let me know." She handed him a slip of paper with her phone number. He thought how odd it was that she had arranged to meet him, but they hadn't yet exchanged numbers. He gave the number of his hotel and the room number and told Fah to leave messages if he wasn't in. She knew him by his real name, and if she ever learned that the room was in a different name, he'd come up with something to say.

"I'll call you in a day or two," Johnny said. "I've got some business ends to tie up over the next day or so, then after that, I'm free."

"I'll be waiting for your call," Fah said, and then walked away and melted into the crowd on Sukhumvit Road.

I wonder what the hell of woman like that sees in a guy like me, Johnny thought as he watched Fah disappear into the press of people. *I know what I see in her.*

SEVENTEEN

Tommy the Turtle needed a gun.

He wasn't going back to Brooklyn, and for the time being, he'd be in Thailand, where the only people he knew were Johnny and Paulie. They both worked for the Boss, and right now the Boss was looking for any connection between Tommy and the disappearance of Bobby Giannelli, and maybe by now, several Brooklyn hoods who hadn't been seen for a while. Johnny's job was to help the Boss do what the Boss wanted, and Paulie's job was to make this easier for Johnny. If the Boss wanted Tommy dead, those two would help the Boss.

Despite the boss's orders, delivered through Johnny, Tommy had no intention of leaving Thailand right after the money was delivered to Johnny, or any time soon after. Tommy did not want to be alone in this country without the security of a gun. He'd need one soon, because he intended to wave it in Paulie's face before he took off with the money after the booze was sold. Not all the money; he'd leave something for Paulie and Johnny to share. He wouldn't kill Paulie. Maybe his old friend would decide he too was better off remaining in Asia, instead of facing the wrath of the Boss when he explained how Tommy stole almost everything.

Tommy had watched the security guard every afternoon for a week. At three o'clock sharp, the guard left the main floor of the office building and shopping mall he protected, walked down the small side soi next to the building, and ducked into the back alley for a smoke. Sometimes he made a phone call. Fifteen minutes after he left his post, he was back on duty.

Tommy watched the guard walk into the little alley. When he was certain there were no other people on the side soi, Tommy went into the alley, waving an unlit cigarette. The guard was smoking a lit one

In Tommy's other hand he wore the brass knuckles he'd found a week ago on a table next to fake Viagra, counterfeit Rolexes, and pirated DVDs of current movies. Tommy was amazed such items could be sold openly in view of the police. He curled his fingers in such a way that the weapon was not visible.

"Got a light?" he asked the guard. The guard nodded, and Tommy drew closer.

The guard reached into his pocket for his lighter. When he bent his head slightly, Tommy swung the arm whose hand wore the brass knuckles into the side of the guard's head, right above his eye. The man staggered a step and fell face forward to the ground. The guard lay there, not moving or making any sound. Tommy bent over and removed the gun from its holster, along with the extra bullets on the belt. It was a .32 caliber revolver like the New York city cops used before Giuliani got them Glocks. He also removed the man's wallet, watch, and ring and put them all in the pockets of his sport coat and pants with the bullets. *Makes it look like a street robbery.*

He tucked the revolver into his rear waistband.. He felt the man's pulse and listened to him breathe and was satisfied that he would live. He walked to the entry of the alley, and after looking to see the side soi was still empty, walked out and turned in the opposite direction from which he came. He spotted the huge condo that served as his landmark back to his hotel and walked in that direction.

Six blocks from where he knocked out the guard, Tommy dropped the stolen personal items into a garbage can, keeping the few hundred baht cash.

A block before the hotel, he stopped into a little bar and ordered a double shot of scotch, which he downed in two gulps. He felt the guard's firearm inside his rear waistband, covered by his shirt and jacket, confident no one in the bar would discern the shape of a gun. When his glass was empty, he paid the four hundred baht for the double, left a hundred as a tip, and headed to his room.

It took him only a few minutes to throw everything he had into his small suitcase, except the revolver, which he kept in his waistband.

He called Paulie and Johnny on their room phones. When neither answered, he knew the coast was clear, and left with his suitcase. He walked two blocks from the hotel and hailed a cab. He had the driver take him to his new hotel in the On Nut neighborhood a mile or so from his current hotel. When the booze was sold, he'd return, pick up his bag, and using his fake passport to fly to Brazil. How many times had he been told Brazil had no extradition treaty with the US? Now he'd get to test that theory. Even if it weren't true, Tommy knew of a group of old Mafia hands from Brooklyn who had settled there for various reasons, mostly to get away from prying criminal investigations and grand jury subpoenas.

The next day Paulie and he would accompany Baxter's men as they delivered the booze to the bars. When it was over, he and Paulie would leave with the money. Paulie fully expected they would return to their hotel, where in Johnny's room they would count it again. Paulie would bring it to various currency exchange booths to buy dollars with the baht. They'd lose a little on the exchange rate, of course, but considering they paid nothing for the product and were paying no taxes, they'd do okay for an operation that was on the verge of falling apart with no hope of making any money. Tommy, in accordance with orders, would fly home while the money was being handled.

Of course, that may have been what Paulie and Johnny thought, but that wasn't how it was going to happen. Once Tommy and Paulie were alone, Tommy would seize the satchel of money from Paulie, who was to hold it. He'd point the gun but had no intention of shooting his old friend. In fact, he would hand him a fat stack of baht and tell him to split it with Johnny. They'd also have the remaining gold coins. If they wanted to return to Brooklyn and deal with the mess Tommy had created, that was their choice. If they wanted to stay in Thailand or go elsewhere, they would have enough cash to make a start.

After all, what are friends for?

Eighteen

Mary O'Halloran was furious. Her internal temperature rose until she felt she might explode. This was the worst humiliation she had ever experienced as a Special Agent of the Federal Bureau of Investigation. Witnesses had lied to her, so had local police, even fellow agents. She'd missed clues, followed dead end leads, and pinned the wrong person as a suspect. Nothing before came close to the shame of a civilian, and a shady criminal lawyer at that, causing a foreign law enforcement officer to lose confidence in her. The Lieutenant preferred working with Glenn Murray Cohen to working with her, an experienced agent specializing in organized crime. How was that going to look in her next report to the Deputy Director running this overseas operation? Her dream of being the youngest woman to head an FBI office was about to evaporate. After this, she'd be lucky to operate the motor pool in rural Alaska. When an agent screws up this badly, their options are usually to resign or to spend a considerable stretch in FBI purgatory, which could last years, even decades.

Her call to her immediate supervisor back in the States did not go well.

"What do you mean, you were kicked out of the meeting?" her

boss bellowed after she delivered her account. "You're an investigator, so go investigate on your own. Start by talking to this American who's causing all the trouble. Maybe you'll do better without the Thai cop in the room. This guy won't feel so protected."

Why didn't I think of that? Mary asked herself after the call.

Glenn had stopped at one of the now ubiquitous cannabis stores in Bangkok, this one a few blocks from home. He bought a pre-rolled joint of the most expensive strain they had. He was two thirds of the way through it when the house phone rang.

"The lady farang is on the way to your door," Lek informed Glenn. "She wouldn't stop when I asked her," Lek continued. He sounded embarrassed that it had happened on his watch. Glenn told him it was not a problem, though he knew it was a big one. He let the joint go out in its ashtray.

Glenn looked through the peephole in the front door and saw Mary coming down the hall. He unlocked the door and motioned for her to enter.

"No point creating a scene," he said. "If you don't leave when I ask, I can always call the Lieutenant. Or even worse for you, the General. So, speak your peace and leave."

Mary walked to the living room and sat down on the couch. She patted the space next to her and Glenn sat there, keeping as far away as possible from Mary.

"You had no right to act like a petulant child," she said. "You know I'm an FBI agent, specializing in organized crime, and you of all people should know what it means when we investigate. I'm here because of what looks like an international conspiracy to hijack liquor in America, smuggle it into Thailand, and sell it with strong-arm tactics. The whole thing has Mafia written all over it. In the middle of all this, you run into an American, an Italian American at that, who happens to come from Brooklyn and can't convince you he's being straight about who he is or what he does. You're going to be mad at me for following up on a lead like this one?"

Glenn contracted his face as he thought this over, pursing his lips, narrowing his eyes, and furrowing his brow. He knew she was right, and any agent would pursue a lead like that, no matter whose toes they had to step on. Johnny had never sought legal advice from Glenn, so there was no attorney-client confidentiality at issue. He insulted gay people in the NJA Club and got into a brawl in the back alley. Everything about him pointed to him having something to hide, and that something was growing more likely to be mob connections. He might be mixed up with the same people who tried to strong-arm Wang and killed another owner who refused to buy from them.

What exactly am I trying to protect, and why?

"I tell you what," Glenn finally said to Mary. "The Lieutenant and the General have people looking for Johnny Brancini, if that is his real name. I met with a police sketch artist and the drawing has been widely distributed to all law enforcement in Bangkok. The street cops, the Tourist Police, the cops at the harbors and airports, even at the train stations. On top of that, the General has the top operatives from his security company working the streets. He will be found, and when he is, I'll make sure you get to question him. I have two prerequisites: one, you have to follow through on your promise to free Freddie so that I don't have to hire a lawyer, and two, you must promise never to ask Edward another question about me."

"I agree to both," Mary replied. "Freddie will soon be a free man, and as for Edward, don't worry, he already told me everything he knows about you. It filled up a whole notebook."

Glenn hoped he did not show the anger he was feeling towards Edward. He understood the anger was irrelevant and he had struck his deal with the FBI agent.

"I wish I could say it's been a pleasure doing business with you," Glenn said to Mary. "All I'm willing to say is it will be a genuine pleasure when it's all done."

Mary leaned over so that her body was inches from Glenn.

"I'm sorry you feel that way, Glenn. For a city known for its pleasures, I'm not experiencing much."

Glenn focused on Mary's hemline, which rose midway between her knee and her waist. She wore a tight-fitting halter top with a low-cut neckline.

"Do you always dress this way on business?" Glen asked. "Where do you keep your badge and your gun?"

"They're in my purse," she said. "I didn't come here thinking I'd need either."

"I'm not sure if that's a compliment," Glenn replied.

Mary laughed.

"Glenn, I checked you out with agents from the Bureau who knew you from your days as a lawyer in San Francisco. Most of them have since retired, but I was able to speak with some current and former agents who filled me in on you. They all say you were one of the best, and especially noted how smart you are. The general consensus was that you didn't miss a thing, and if there was a hole anywhere in the government case, you'd drive a Mack truck through it."

"Now that I take as a compliment," Glenn said. He really did feel good to know his old adversaries felt that way about him.

"However, I believe they may have overestimated your perceptive abilities," Mary said.

"Why would you feel that way, especially after I've been vetted by your colleagues?" Glenn asked.

"They knew you a long time ago, Glenn. You've been gone more than fifteen years. I'm judging you by what I see right now before my very own eyes," she replied.

What the hell is she talking about? Glenn asked himself. *She's gotten everything she wanted.*

"I'll think about what I might be missing here," Glenn told Mary. "In the meantime, I'll bid you good night and am going to smoke a fat joint and fall asleep. It's legal here, you know."

Mary looked at Glenn as if she had just seen a Neanderthal walking down Sukhumvit Road.

"Of course, I know," she replied. "Or at least it looks legal, with a pot shop on almost every street. If it weren't for the risk of a random drug test on the job, I'd try some myself."

"I can get you herbs that beat any drug test on earth," Glenn said. "My friend Sleepy Joe, who you of course know all about, has been supplying people with it for years. Cops, military, government workers, and corporate people, all smoke and don't want to get caught. Even sold to some people working at our Embassy, so if they passed their tests, you should as well."

"You would really get it for me? "Mary asked as she leaned a half inch closer to Glenn, who felt every centimeter of her movement as if it were a rising degree of his body temperature.

"I'll send a text to Sleepy Joe, and it'll be here tomorrow," Glenn said.

"In that case, light one up," Mary replied.

Glenn withdrew a thickly rolled joint from a small box on the coffee table. He lit it with a lighter from the table, took a deep inhale, and when the tip was glowing red and white smoke flowed from his mouth, he handed the joint to Mary.

"I've been vaccinated and boosted, so you won't get COVID sharing this with me," he said as he passed the joint.

Mary smiled and placed the joint between her lips. She closed her eyes as she inhaled. A second later, she coughed several times and spit small clouds of smoke from her mouth.

"My first time," she said when she recovered her composure. "Since high school, I knew I wanted to be an FBI agent, so I never took a puff."

"Now you can make up for lost time," Glenn said.

Mary's eyes were blazing red. Glenn had been smoking weed for so long his eyes no longer turned crimson to any degree. She laid down on the couch with her knees bent and pointing upward, her skirt hiked three-quarters up her thighs. She was smiling and sleeping.

Glenn was in a quandary. He didn't feel it was right to wake her up and send her on her way in such a condition. On the other hand, he didn't relish the idea of an FBI agent rooting around his apartment while he slept, especially one who had investigated him.

Glenn went into his bedroom closet and found a blanket and a pillow stored in the crowded recesses of a shelf. He returned to the living room, gently placed Mary's legs flat on the couch. He felt a tingling sensation when he touched her thighs in the process. He then placed a pillow under her head, put the blanket on top of her, and went back to his bedroom. He set his iPhone to the music function and selected *Speak No Evil*, the 1965 jazz album featuring the great Wayne Shorter on sax, the incomparable Herbie Hancock on piano, with legendary bassist Ron Carter, Elvin Jones on drums, and Freddie Hubbard on trumpet. He fell asleep twenty minutes later to the sound of "Speak No Evil." the title song which began the second side when people still listened to physical albums.

Glenn dreamed that a woman was in bed with him and had pulled down his underpants, her hand on his penis, trying to stimulate him as he slept. In the dream, he grew harder until his male organ bolted upward like a sleeping sentry rising to salute an officer.

When he felt a long nail scratching against his manhood, he was shocked out of his sleep. It was then he saw he had not been dreaming, and a naked Special Agent Mary O'Halloran lie next to him, naked as the day she was born, and not-so-gently stroking the body part that had caused Glenn Murray Cohen so much anguish because of where it sometimes led him. He looked at her smiling face, her eyes as crimson as when he left her sleeping on his living room couch.

"You are indeed a sound sleeper, Counselor," Mary said when she saw Glenn was conscious. "I was beginning to think my hand would fall off before I grabbed your attention."

"So you started out by grabbing my dick?" Glenn asked. "Is that what they teach in the FBI Academy?"

Mary let go of Glenn, turned to face him, and propped herself up on an arm.

"Everything I learned about sex, I learned in my private life, and may I say, without bragging, I was a great student and learned quite a bit. I'm more than happy to share my knowledge with you."

"Let's start Lesson One," Glenn said as he rolled over to face Mary, embraced her, and started kissing her. She responded in kind, sticking her tongue so far down Glenn's throat he feared he might choke. He ran his hands over her body, feeling her breasts-which were larger than they seemed when she was dressed- and grabbing her buttocks.

After several minutes of foreplay, Mary managed to roll under Glenn and guided his member into her. For the next ten minutes, Glenn's bedroom was filled with the sound of a creaking bed, a moaning Mary, and a Glenn breathing so hard he might have passed for the wolf who could huff and puff and blow a house down.

When Glenn awoke, it took him a minute to wipe the sleep from his body and his eyes. Enough light filtered through the small space between the window curtains and the open bedroom door that he realized Mary was not in his bed. He called her name and received no response. He got out of bed, flipped on the light switch, and walked around the room. He saw no sign Mary was in the apartment. He saw no clothing, handbags, or other sign of a woman in his home. A quick examination of the bathroom, living room and kitchen yielded the same result.

Glenn rubbed the last remnants of sleep from his eyes. It was early morning, the clock showing it was just a few minutes past seven. Glenn instinctively moved to his coffee-making area, his regular habit upon awakening. As he pondered which coffee to brew, he simultaneously pondered what occurred during the night.

Could I have just imagined the entire thing? Is the stuff they sell at the new weed shop laced with something?

He decided on pricey Ethiopian Highland he'd purchased at Food Villa the week before. That store was an expensive favorite of expats who could afford it, and their coffee selection was among the best in Bangkok. Glenn placed a few scoopfuls of beans in his grinder and turned it on. He also turned on his electric water heater, which he had just filled with water. When it was ground, he used a small spoon to scoop the ground beans into a paper filter placed in a plastic one-cup holder, seated upon Glenn's favorite mug. As he had been doing for the past several months, he had arranged the setup the night before, prior to Mary's arrival, if she had in fact been there.

When the water boiled, Glenn poured a small amount over the beans, waited for it to drip through, and then filled the plastic cone and waited for all the water to pass through. It took less than a minute. He grabbed the hot mug and walked to his living room, where he flipped on the television, already set to CNN. Glenn sat in his easy chair and listened to the news.

There were going to be Congressional elections back in America later that year, but Glenn was not following them with anything close to the interest he showed during the past two Presidential elections, where he had been crushed when Trump won and ecstatic when the voters tossed him out of office by a clear and very healthy margin. He just couldn't work up the same partisan or personal emotions this time; perhaps it was because he'd been away from America for so long that he didn't feel or even fully grasp the issues facing voters. He'd get his absentee ballot and vote the straight Democratic ticket, but it would be a mechanical act, not the act of devotion and passion he felt when he twice voted against Donald Trump. Besides, he no longer had to engage in friendly banter with Oliver, an arch-conservative supporter of the Australian Conservative Party. Oliver had been a fan of Trump until January 6, 2021. With Trump out of office and out of his debates with Oliver, Glenn lost interest in U.S. politics. His friends had even stopped referring to him as "the bleeding-heart liberal" or "the San Francisco Democrat." Glenn was always surprised by how much Oliver, the General, and even Sleepy Joe knew about American politics.

I guess since everyone in the world is affected by what America does, the smart people know.

The rest of the news from America was about inflation, especially the rising price of gasoline. The President and his team were assuring the American people they had the matter under control, and inflation was a temporary annoyance that would soon go away. Living on the baht as a rich farang, inflation meant nothing to Glenn personally, but he recalled enough economics from college to understand the inflation would not disappear overnight or anytime soon.

When he was done with his coffee, Glenn turned off the television and took a shower. As the hot water poured over him, he felt the traces of Mary. He couldn't put a finger on exactly what it was: a trace of a scent, a feeling of another person's bodily fluids on him, or the memories of something that really occurred.

I don't think I could imagine the whole thing.

When he was dressed and ready for a second cup, the house phone rang. It was Lek, who had been on the job for well over an hour.

"The lady farang left a letter for you with the night security guard," Lek said. "He gave it to me when I arrived."

Good, Glenn thought. *Maybe the night guy didn't tell him she'd spent the night here if she actually stayed long enough to be described that way.*

"I'll be down in a little while and I'll pick it up," Glenn said. He didn't want Lek to think he was too anxious to see what Mary had to say.

Lek handed Glenn the letter without saying a word. Glenn nodded, folded the envelope, and put it in his pants pocket. He left the condo building and started walking to Benjasiri Park, his favorite outdoor location for thinking.

It was a fifteen-minute walk to the park, and every few blocks Glenn felt for the letter in his pocket, as if the feel of the paper envelope would summon the feel of Mary's body as they wrestled with spirited passion the night before. When he reached his destination, he walked past the huge gold coin that watched over the pleasant green space in the midst of busy Bangkok. Glenn spotted an empty bench under several tall trees, and he parked himself there. He reached for the envelope, which had his name printed in capital block letters. He peeled it open, withdrew the single page, and read what Mary had written in the same capital block letters.

I don't know if it was the weed, or my sexual longings for a man who attracted me the minute I laid eyes upon him. It doesn't matter because it never should have happened. I never told you clearly I was married, but I am, and being unfaithful to my husband is not something of which I am proud. When we meet again, it will be purely professional.

Glenn read the letter twice more, then crumpled it and the

envelope into a small ball rose from the bench and walked to a nearby trash can, into which he dropped the wadded paper.

She wrote in block letters and didn't mention her name or mine because she didn't want anyone to know what she had done and that if anyone thought they had such evidence, no one would be able to recognize her handwriting, Glenn thought as he walked out of the park. *Her secret is safe with me.*

NINETEEN

Johnny Brancini was happy that morning. He was to meet Fah for lunch at a Japanese restaurant she suggested, located on the fourth floor of Terminal Twenty One, the big complex of stores and restaurants right at the Asoke BTS station along Sukhumvit Road. His elation at spending more time with the charming and attractive young Thai woman lifted his spirits even as he knew once the booze was sold, it would be time for Tommy to head back to Brooklyn and face the wrath of the Boss. Johnny knew the Boss smelled a connection between Tommy, the hijacking, and the disappearance of his family friend. Whether Tommy obeyed the order to return, or refused, it was going to be a major headache for Johnny. If the Boss decided he'd had enough of Tommy the Turtle, it would take time and effort to replace him, and if Tommy failed to appear for his meeting with the Boss, he could never rule out the possibility that there was a new and very dangerous enemy on the loose. Tommy knew every move and every haunt of the Boss as well as of Johnny, and this would mean at the very least a lifetime of looking over their shoulders wherever they went.

Even more of a reason to stay here, Johnny thought. *Maybe I'll get somewhere with Fah.* He had yet to touch her, but that didn't dissuade him. He understood he was in Bangkok, not Brooklyn, and Fah was not American, and certainly not like the women with whom Tommy and Paulie had brief encounters.

Johnny was a few steps past the Dunkin' Donut stand outside the Sukhumvit Road street level entrance to Terminal 21 when the uniformed policeman stepped from behind to turn and face him. The officer showed a blank face. His crisply pressed uniform and the insignias on it led Johnny to understand he was staring at a higher officer, not a street cop. Thirty years in the mob created in Johnny a sixth sense about police officers.

"Give a cop your name, and nothing else," the Boss had taught Johnny when he started working for him. "Then ask to call your lawyer." The Boss handed Johnny a Scharfman Law Firm card. "Been using them for almost a hundred years," he explained. "The grandfather represented my grandfather on four different cases. Got him off every time. They know we're good for the money, so you call them, they come."

The Scharfmans were on the other side of the globe. The only lawyer he knew here was that Glenn Cohen fellow, and after what happened after Glenn invited him to his hangout, it was doubtful Glenn would help, even if he could reach him. Glenn was not a Thai lawyer, but he was smart and knew the system, so he'd be able to help. At least, that's what Johnny hoped. Johnny just assumed he was in deep trouble.

"Mr. Johnny Brancini?" the police officer asked. "There's no point in denying it," he added. He had a rolled-up paper in his hand, and when he unrolled it, he showed Johnny the police sketch artist's drawing. Johnny studied it for ten seconds.

"Amazing likeness," he said.

"That's because it's you," the cop replied. "But to be on the safe side, I'm bringing you where there can be a positive identification."

"I want to speak to my lawyer," Johnny replied in the calm voice the Boss had instructed him to use in such a situation. "His name is Glenn Cohen. He lives here. You're a cop, in fact, an officer. You can find him."

A smile crossed the Lieutenant's face.

"Absolutely," the Lieutenant said. "Just come with me and we'll make certain you see Mr. Cohen." At that moment, two more uniformed officers appeared one at each side of Johnny.

"There's no need for handcuffs or my officer to hang on to your arms, is there, Mr. Brancini? Can I rely on you to walk over to that police car at the curb and get into the back seat without any problems?"

"Let's go," Johnny said. *I hope they really bring Cohen to see me.*

At the very moment, Johnny agreed to enter the police car without restraints, Fah was crossing Asoke in the direction of Terminal 21, on the other side from the MTR subway stop she had just left. She could have entered the Terminal 21 complex through a series of tunnels and stairs, but she felt claustrophobic after the subway ride and preferred the open air. Just as she stepped over the curb onto the other side, she saw Johnny walking towards the police car with three uniformed police around him. She hurried her pace and in seconds was a foot from the four men.

"What is going on here?" she asked Johnny in a voice laced with fear. Thais knew encounters with their police were seldom for the betterment of the other party, be they Thai or farang.

"It's okay, Fah," Johnny replied. "It's nothing serious. I'm just helping these officers with some information about something I may have seen. I'm sorry we have to cancel lunch, but I'll call you as soon as I'm done."

Fah turned to the Lieutenant. She knew from his uniform he was an officer and in charge. She'd served enough cops-most of whom refused to pay or leave a tip-to recognize the uniform of an officer.

"Why are you bothering him?" she asked in Thai. "He's done nothing wrong. He was just coming to meet me for lunch. If you don't let him go right now, I'm calling a lawyer. I'd rather see him pay a lawyer than pay you."

"I'm sorry you have such a low opinion of your police," the Lieutenant replied in Thai. "We don't want any of your boyfriend's money. We just need to ask him a few questions, and if he answers truthfully, I see no problem. And by the way, I'm impressed with your English. It's probably better than mine, with even less of an accent."

"It ought to be," Fah said, shooting the Lieutenant an angry look. "I'm a graduate of Thammasat University, with a major in English."

The Lieutenant smiled.

"So am I," he said. "A few years ahead of you, no doubt. Since you're a fellow alumnus, I'm going to be straight with you. We think Johnny Brancini has information that can help us solve some very serious crimes. He has asked for his lawyer to be present, and we of course agreed. We have nothing to hide, and we trust neither does your boyfriend."

"He's not my boyfriend!" Fah exclaimed in a voice loud enough to catch the attention of Johnny and the passersby who stopped to take in the scene. "And you probably think every Thai woman with a farang man is a bargirl."

"I'd be right almost ninety percent of the time," the Lieutenant replied. "It's clear this falls into the other ten percent, which is why I treat you like an equal and the fact that you would know him means he goes up in my eyes."

The Lieutenant asked Fah how she and Johnny met. She gave a brief summary of knowing him as a customer at the restaurant, and how she had shown him the Grand Palace and Wat Pho, and they were planning to see Wat Arun and the floating markets over the next few days.

"I don't suppose you have much information on his employment," the Lieutenant said. Fah replied that so far as she knew, he owned or managed real estate back in America.

"We can't keep standing here," the Lieutenant said. He handed his card to Fah.

"If he isn't out by dinner, call me. He'll call you when he's done." Without another word, the three police and Johnny got into the squad car and it drove off, leaving Fah staring in wonder.

Who am I getting involved with?

Fah was not the only one in Johnny's circle to watch him slide into a squad car, apparently of his own volition, with no handcuffs or cops holding onto him. Tommy the Turtle munched on a donut, thirty feet to the side of the Dunkin' kiosk, not visible to Johnny because of the constant flow of people and the fact that Tommy was wearing mirror sunglasses, a baseball cap, and a t-shirt declaring "Good Boys Go to Heaven, Bad Boys Go to Soi Nana."

Tommy had been worrying about Johnny ever since he hit him with the double-barreled shocks of revealing his growing desire to remain in Thailand, and his laying the groundwork for the Boss's investigation into the disappearance of Bobby Giannelli. If Johnny stayed in Thailand, that would make it difficult for Tommy to do the same. Even if Johnny remained in Bangkok, his loyalty would always be to the Boss and not Tommy the Turtle. Returning home was certain to end with Tommy's corpse taking a trip to Little Sal's. Sooner or later, the Boss would put it all together. All of these reasons combined led to Tommy disguising himself and following Johnny when Mr. Brancini said he was going to take a walk and grab some Thai food.

Now Johnny's getting into a cop car, and who is that lady talking to the cops? What else don't I know about Johnny?

Tommy saw a line of orange-vested motorcycle taxis lined up not more than twenty meters from where the police car was parked. Tommy had never taken one before, and he couldn't recall ever riding on a motorcycle of any size as a passenger or a driver. *There's always a first time,* he told himself,

The driver understood Tommy's English, but when asked to follow a police car, hesitated.

"Don't want problems," he said,

Tommy waved three one thousand baht notes under the driver's nose. Almost eighty dollars at the current exchange rate. The driver grabbed the money and told Tommy to hop on the back. They took off, weaving between the buses, trucks and cars that choked Sukhumvit Road.

Johnny was taken to a small substation on the edge far northern of the city. The sergeant in charge had been promoted with help from the Lieutenant and was an honorable cop who didn't take bribes and didn't abuse citizens or foreigners. When the Lieutenant called and said he'd need his office for a few hours, the sergeant was delighted to assist the man who added thousands of baht a month to his paycheck.

The Lieutenant called Glenn and Mary and dispatched plain clothes officers and cars to pick them up. He and Johnny were barely settled into the small office when the plainclothes officers ushered the two farangs into the office. Johnny smiled when he saw Glenn. He looked Mary over and determined he'd never seen her before.

"I'd like a few moments alone with my client," Glenn said, before he or Mary were seated. The Lieutenant nodded, and he and the FBI agent left the room. Mary hadn't yet looked directly at Glenn, and he was trying his best to act as if she weren't present.

"I've been informed you want me as your lawyer," Glenn said.

"It's not like I know a whole lot of mouthpieces in this town," Johnny said. "You seem like a good guy and a standup guy. You can get past the little scene I created at your hangout. If it means anything, I'm sorry. In fact, I'm ashamed. We're not in Brooklyn, and you and your friends are good people who should be treated respectfully."

"Maybe not Edward," Glenn said and then smiled. "It's okay, Johnny, criminal lawyers don't have to like their clients, they just have to fight for them. In your case, the big issue is not your behavior. It's that there's a bit of a conflict of interest. I have to be up front with you, Johnny. I was initially consulted with, to try and find whoever was behind this booze extortion racket. I was working with the Lieutenant who brought you in, along with that woman you just saw, who happens to be Special Agent Mary O'Halloran of the FBI. In other words, you're trying to hire a lawyer who has been working the other side of the street."

"Can't you just cross over? I don't care how you started out. Obviously you didn't help them very much because I was right under your nose, and you didn't know who I am."

"No, but we had a fairly good idea, and we were working on it. Needless to say, we succeeded because here you are. I'm the one who gave the police the description that wound up catching you. That sketch was distributed to every cop within a hundred kilometers. Some sharp-eyed tourist cop grabbing a donut at Dunkin' spotted you and as luck would have it, the Lieutenant was with some men around the corner on Soi Cowboy, interviewing a witness to a homicide."

"My good luck," Johnny commented.

"It actually was," Glenn said. "If the Lieutenant hadn't been able to make it there quickly, the tourist cop would have turned you over to the nearest street cop, and the two of them would have tried to jack you up for as much as they could get out of you, and then haul you off to jail while the Lieutenant made his way to see you. They wouldn't have arranged for me to be here, and they surely would not have treated your girlfriend so respectfully."

"Let's see how long my luck holds up. Are you my lawyer?"

"If you will sign a written waiver of any conflict of interest, which I just happen to have with me, I will be delighted. We don't yet need a waiver from the government because we're in Thailand and an FBI agent can't agree to waive squat. Only a federal prosecutor can do that, and if any of them ever got hold of this case, I'd be too involved as your lawyer for them to boot me off."

"You're my lawyer, so tell me what I need to know," Johnny said.

"Sit down while I explain the facts of life to you, Johnny," Glenn replied.

Glenn told Johnny that the Lieutenant and the FBI agent knew he was with the Brooklyn Mafia and involved in trying to force local businesses to buy hijacked booze from America. He explained how they had tapes of the three local thugs and knew that the three had apparently been killed and their bodies taken away before the police arrived.

"What do you mean by a session with an FBI agent?" Johnny asked when Glenn said one was being scheduled for as soon as possible.

Glenn explained that he was trying to negotiate a deal whereby Johnny would tell the Lieutenant and Mary everything he knew about both the booze scheme and the Brooklyn Mob-the latter of interest only to Mary-and in exchange, the Thai and American governments would leave him alone forever so long as he committed no new crimes.

"How do I know we can trust them?" Johnny asked.

"It's not really about trusting them," Glenn explained. "It's more about understanding what cards each side is holding. You have all the information they want and need, and there's no other way to get any of it except from you. You can help them shut down this current extortion plot, and make sure no more happens here. That's going to please the Lieutenant and the Thais. Mary is going to be able to use what you tell her in order to get search warrants and to follow your former colleagues and sooner or later catch them in the act if they haven't already been indicted on what you gave up plus what we can expect to be countless other charges to be uncovered. There will be no need for you to testify, assuming the U.S. could make the Thais give you to them."

Glenn thought about the Russian gangster he'd help kidnap when the Thais didn't want to extradite him, but the Thais looked the other way, and Johnny Brancini was nowhere nearly as important a fugitive as that arms dealing murderer.

"Wouldn't the defendants have the right to question me?" Johnny asked.

Glenn explained it was extremely unlikely.

"Only if they can get the Thai government to send you over, which I said isn't going to happen. They have no automatic right to call the informant behind a search warrant, and with the kind of information you give them, they'll be able to put together a case without your testimony. We know the booze was hijacked, we know it's heading here, so all that is needed to nail your old gang is proof that they were involved. That's where you come in. You're going to lead us to your buddies and Agent O'Halloran is going to be a witness to all that gets discovered. Do you get it all?"

Johnny thought it over for a minute while Glenn sat quietly, until Johnny spoke.

"Let me sign that waiver, Glenn."

～

For the next five hours, Johnny told the Lieutenant and Mary everything he knew about the hijacking and the plans to sell the booze in Bangkok. He told them how Paulie hired three local hoods and they had disappeared without a trace, believed to have been murdered. Neither law officer nor Glenn gave a hint they already knew this.

Johnny told them the name of the hotel and provided detailed descriptions of Tommy and Paulie. Mary told him they were probably in the FBI criminal database.

"You're an unusual case, not being listed as a mob member or affiliate. I'm impressed you've never been busted." Even the FBI didn't have access to his sealed juvenile record.

He also told them everything he knew about the Brooklyn Mob. He stopped to compose himself several times when he realized he was probably sending the Boss and most of his closest friends to prison for the rest of their lives. Mary noticed his difficulty, and asked him the problem, which he candidly explained just as she thought.

"They're not your friends," she said. "They're your business associates at best, and they'd sell you out if it were to their benefit, and they'd put a bullet in your head if ordered to do so."

Johnny nodded. He knew she was right, and he knew what he was doing then and there was right.

Most significantly, Johnny told them how Tommy and Paulie were to meet Baxter at the docks, where someone from the ship would recognize them and make sure the hijacked liquor was loaded on the trucks Baxter was providing.

"I know of Baxter," the Lieutenant said. "I'm not surprised these gangsters found their way to him."

Mary interrupted to advise the others that her office had sent her photos of Tommy and Paulie. Johnny immediately identified them.

The Lieutenant explained that he and Mary would be surveilling the gang at the docks and would follow them during their deliveries. At the end of the day, when all the money was collected, the Lieutenant would step in and make an arrest.

Mary would not be armed. Back in America, she was told the Thais were reluctant to grant permission to carry firearms to American law enforcement, who they viewed as too trigger happy. The last thing the Thai government wanted was a Thai citizen killed by foreign law enforcement.

"I'll have several armed officers backing me up, and we're expecting that when faced with overwhelming odds against them, this Turtle and this Arranger will throw up their hands and surrender peacefully."

"What about Baxter's men?" Johnny asked.

"That's good thinking, and it's exactly what I was concerned about," the Lieutenant explained. "That's why we're going to let Baxter's men take his share of the sale proceeds and leave. We'll arrest your friends after they have separated. We'll worry about Baxter some other day."

Mary took copious notes, and the Lieutenant was recording the session and would have it transcribed overnight.

It's hard finding really competent interpreters and transcribers, he thought. *This gangster's girlfriend spoke English beautifully and I picked up right away she's smart. Maybe when this is all worked out, I'll talk to her about coming to work for us. That's one way to keep an eye on Johnny.*

At five thirty, when they'd been going for five and a half hours, the Lieutenant spoke to the other three.

"I assured Ms. Fah that we'd have Johnny back to her for dinner or I'd call her. My suggestion is we have her brought here, have dinner sent in, and she can join us. After dinner, we need a very short period of time with Glenn and Johnny, and then I'm certain we can all be on our separate ways."

Mary shot the Lieutenant a puzzled glance.

"We're just going to let this guy out of our sight and trust him to stick around for follow-through?" she asked.

"Who said anything about letting him out of our sight?" the Lieutenant asked. "I said he could be on his way, that's all."

Fah was not surprised when the policeman called on her cell phone and told her to be outside her apartment building in five minutes, and that she was going to join Johnny and some friends for dinner. *In Thailand, the police can get any information they need. There's no right to privacy here.*

She was driven to the remote substation and taken to the room where Johnny, the Lieutenant, Mary, and Glenn were seated around a small table filled with plates of food. The Lieutenant rose and offered her a chair, which he placed next to Johnny. Fah smiled at the Brooklynite. Introductions were made.

"So, it looks like everything is alright," she said. "Otherwise, the police wouldn't be providing such a fine meal. Unless they're making you pay for it."

"This one is paid for by my department," the Lieutenant said. "It's the least we could do for such a cooperative and helpful farang and his charming companion."

"If the police are paying for it, it's only because they stole the money from some innocent citizen or tourist," Fah retorted.

Glenn paused loading his plate with pad thai and som tom thai.

"If it were any other policeman in Thailand, I'd agree with you," he said to Fah. "But I've known the Lieutenant for some time, and I assure you, he is as honest as anyone could ever be."

Fah addressed the Lieutenant in Thai.

"Then it is my great pleasure to meet the only honest policeman in the Kingdom."

The Lieutenant was eyeing the plate of larb. He turned his gaze to Fah and spoke in their language.

"And I am deeply honored to meet a respectable and honorable Thai woman involved with a farang. You're not the usual type they find. They seem to look for women hanging from poles in bars, who charge them money to make believe they care about them."

"You don't like the sex trade?" Fah asked.

"I think our women could do better than serving the sick fantasies of mentally deranged foreigners," the Lieutenant replied.

Fah let out a short laugh. "You're the police. If you don't like it, close it down."

"I would if I could," the Lieutenant said. "But as I'm sure you know, too many powerful people make a lot of money off the misery of our young women. I'd like to see the day when they have to answer for what they have permitted and even encouraged."

"I doubt either of us live that long," Fah said.

"Excuse me," Mary O'Halloran interjected. "I expected this proceeding to be conducted in English."

"The investigation is over for today, and Mr. Johnny Brancini is free to leave any time he wishes. We Thais are certainly entitled to speak in our own language when it has nothing to do with this case. This is our country, after all."

Mary's face turned red.

"Maybe you can give me a translation," she said.

"Maybe this doesn't concern you, which is why we spoke in our own language," the Lieutenant replied.

He wasn't kidding when he said he wanted me around, Glenn thought. *He really does not like the FBI.*

Mary's face turned even redder.

TWENTY

When Tommy saw the police car stop in front of a small station house, he told the motorcycle taxi driver to stop. Tommy could identify a police station anywhere, especially when there were a half dozen squad cars parked in front. He felt secure, certain that no one was paying attention to a farang getting off a motorcycle a block away. Fortunately for Tommy, there was a small outdoor coffee stand across the street from the station, a cart manned by an old woman who had set a few plastic chairs and small tables around the area. Tommy walked over, ordered a coffee, and sat down, watching the station. He saw Johnny leave the car, and walk into the station on his own, the police walking behind him. Ten minutes later, he watched as another police car let out a blond woman dressed in a business-like skirt and blouse. Five minutes after that, a middle-aged, well-built white man was similarly delivered to the station.

After two hours of sitting at the coffee stand and watching the station while drinking three cups of coffee, Tommy's bladder signaled a readiness to empty itself. He asked the old woman behind the coffee cart where he might find a bathroom. She understood enough English to point to the police station.

"Tell them you my customer. Police all buy my coffee. They let you pee."

Tommy dropped a hundred baht note in the tip jar on the cart, smiled when the old woman gave a wai, and crossed the street.

Just as the old woman said, the officer at the desk pointed to a restroom when Tommy explained he was coming from the coffee cart. The cop behind the front desk didn't speak much English, but when Tommy pointed in the direction of the coffee cart and made a face telling any other man of his bladder urgency, the officer understood. Tommy went to the restroom and relieved himself.

Just as Tommy was walking to the door to leave the restroom, it opened and in walked the American Tommy had seen enter the station earlier. They looked at each other, both surprised to find another white man in the bathroom of an obscure Thai police substation in the outer edge of Bangkok.

"Do you speak English?" Tommy asked.

"I hope so, though my Aussie friends might beg to differ," Glenn said with a smile. He extended his hand and gave his name. Tommy shook it vigorously.

"Pleased to meet you, Glenn. My name is Bobby Giannelli, from Massapequa, on Long Island, New York."

"You don't say," Glenn replied. "I was also born on Long Island, in Brooklyn, graduated Brooklyn Law School. Spent most of my adult life in San Francisco, but I live here now."

"And did you just come in to use the restroom like we customers at the coffee cart across the street?" Tommy asked.

"Not quite," Glenn said. "I've got some business here. I'm a lawyer."

Tommy's face did not show what he was thinking.

If Johnny's got an American lawyer here at the police station, it's got to mean he's ratting us out. I bet that blonde is from the U.S. government. Probably a federal prosecutor.

"It's nice meeting you, Mr. Cohen," Tommy said as he wiped his hands on what passed for a paper towel in Thailand, really just a roll of toilet paper.

"Enjoy your time in Thailand, Bobby," Glenn said as he watched

Tommy walk away.

Glenn went back to the office, where the Lieutenant, Mary, Johnny, and Fah were piling plates with food spread on the little table and desk in the room. Glenn filled his plate with pad thai and the fish with lemon sauce and sat down next to Johnny.

"What a small world it is," he told Johnny. "When I was in the head, I ran into another guy from our neck of the woods. Massapequa, Long Island."

The Lieutenant overheard Glenn.

"Did he say what he was doing here," he asked Glenn. "They don't get a lot of farang tourists around here, and I don't know of any living in this area, though it's possible."

"This guy was no expat," Glenn said. He described the t shirt and the fact that the man wore mirror sunglasses indoors in the bathroom. "All he said was he was drinking coffee across the street and had to pee, and the owner told him it was okay to use the restroom here."

"Actually, it isn't," the Lieutenant explained. "the man at the desk probably figured if a farang came here, it must be important and didn't bother him. Especially after two others came here.

"I find it strange that a farang like that would come all the way out here just to drink coffee. Did he tell you anything else?"

Glenn thought for a moment.

"Only that his name was Bobby Giannelli. I hope I'm pronouncing it right."

Johnny Brancini shot up like a lightning bolt in reverse.

"That's the name he gave? Bobby Giannelli? Are you absolutely certain?" Johnny asked Glenn, and Glenn said he was. Johnny explained that Bobby Giannelli was one of the two employees of the hijacked liquor company, who had disappeared and was never heard from again. He explained that the Boss, the head of his crew, was a personal friend of Bobby's family, and that Tommy the Turtle was suspected of being involved somehow. Glenn said he had told the man his name, that he was a lawyer in the nation on business.

"Probably not the brightest thing to say," Glenn told the others.

Mary showed Glenn the photo of Tommy. He studied it for a half a minute.

"It's hard to tell for certain, with him wearing those sunglasses and a cap. But the nose, the mouth, the shape of the jaw, they are exactly what I saw."

The Lieutenant held up his hand.

"It didn't matter what you said. If this fellow is Tommy the Turtle and he found us here, he knows there's a connection and it can't be good for him. From this moment on, Glenn, I'm placing you under twenty-four hour police protection. I have men I can trust with your life."

"That's most appreciated, Lieutenant, but I'd feel safer if it was Sleepy Joe watching over me."

"Fair enough," the Lieutenant said. "He'd do anything to protect you and it will free up some manpower for me. I'll have my men regularly check your condo and the NJA Club, and if you go to any music or dining establishments, let me know and I'll station someone there. Other than that, you're in the hands of Sleepy Joe."

Who probably killed the three locals Johnny and his men hired.

For the rest of the dinner, the five of them acted as if the encounter with Tommy had not occurred. The Lieutenant was most interested in Fah's education and experience. He was intrigued to learn she had done research for a financial investigative service before COVID cost her the job.

She could be more than an interpreter.

Tommy left the station and walked a block to the left, where he'd seen a small market earlier when the motorcycle taxi slowed down like the police car he was following. He smiled when he saw a stall with a rack of shirts. There were only two that fit him, and one was a pale green, not likely to draw undue attention. He bought it. He peeled off his t-shirt, removed his hat and sunglasses, and dropped them in a trash basket next to the shirts. He put on his new shirt, tucked it into his black trousers, and walked off.

Between the little market and the police substation was a line of motorcycle taxis. Tommy saw the first one carrying a spare helmet on the back seat, something Tommy was certain was the law but was honored more in the breach than in practice. He approached the driver, and between broken English and hand movements, Tommy was able to get across that he wanted the driver to wait until his friend came out of the station and then followed him. Tommy put on the helmet, handed the driver a five hundred baht note, and accepted a wai.

Five minutes later, Tommy watched as Glenn and Mary left the station and walked into a cab that had just pulled up. Tommy told the driver to follow the cab.

Even if one of them notices there's a motorcycle taxi following them, they'll most likely think he's heading in the same direction. No way that lawyer will make the passenger on the bike with a normal shirt and a helmet as the same guy he met in the bathroom dressed like a fool.

The motorcycle taxi driver weaved between large and small vehicles, running a few red lights and stop signs, and screaming at jaywalking Thai pedestrians. Twenty minutes later, the cab stopped in front of the Rembrandt Hotel, far down off Sukhumvit Road on soi 18.

Smart move putting her up here, Tommy thought. *Street not too busy, not too many ways on or off. If she's a federal prosecutor or investigator like I figure, the local cops are probably keeping an eye on the place. By now, thanks to Johnny, they probably have pictures of us, so getting in there to take care of her won't be easy. But it can be done.*

The cab then drove Glenn to his condo, Tommy's motorcycle taxi always keeping it in sight. Tommy made a mental note of the streets he needed to take to find the condo again.

He gave the motorcycle taxi driver an extra five hundred baht note and watched him leave. Tommy's body ached too much after all that time on the back of a 125-cc motorcycle. He needed a massage. He knew he'd find one if he walked along Sukhumvit Road a short bit. He didn't care if the place didn't offer a "happy ending." All Tommy wanted was to get the soreness out of his muscles and tendons.

Tommy found a massage parlor within five minutes. The stocky middle-aged masseuse washed his feet, led him upstairs to a cubicle, and handed him the pajama-type garments used in Thailand. While there was no happy ending, there was a tissue-penetrating massage for which Tommy's body was grateful. When the massage was over and Tommy was drinking a cup of tea downstairs, he decided he had to contact Baxter and let him know of Johnny's betrayal. The only problem was that he didn't have a number for Baxter, just an instruction to be at the dock the following morning.

Tommy knew how to find the bargirl who led Paulie to Baxter could reach him. It was close to eight p.m., and she'd probably be starting her shift. As soon as he finished his tea, he paid for the massage, handed the masseuse a generous tip, and was soon back on Sukhumvit Road, where he hailed a cab which took him to Soi Nana.

Nice recognized Tommy as soon as she saw him walk through the door of the bar, and walked to him.

"Decided to try me?" she asked.

"That's a great idea, and definitely in the plans, but not tonight. I need you for something else."

He explained that he wanted her to contact Baxter and tell him Tommy needed to speak with him right away. He handed her a thousand baht note. Nice's eye's widened as she stared at the note.

"That's a lot of money just to make a call," she said.

"There's not a lot of people I know who can dial up Mr. Baxter and get him on the first try," Tommy said.

Nice shook her head, which Tommy took to mean she didn't understand these crazy farangs, but it was easy money. Tommy listened as Nice spoke in Thai to someone on the other line, hopefully Baxter. *I guess if you live around here, you learn to speak the language,* he thought.

Nice handed Tommy the phone. He put it to his ear.

"What the fuck is up, that you have to track down one of my street eyes to call me the night before our deal goes down?" Tommy recognized Baxter's voice at once.

Tommy explained everything he'd seen that day.

"Johnny's been making noises about staying here cause he likes it so much. Looks like he's got a girlfriend, a Thai lady. Then I see him go off with some police, free as a bird, no cuffs, no nothing, and turns out he's already got himself a lawyer. When you been around as long as me, you know how to put together the pieces of a puzzle. Here we got a guy looking for a way to stay here, maybe with that lady, and he's talking to cops with his lawyer and a lady that has to be a fed of some sort."

"Are you suggesting we end the plan?" Baxter asked.

"No, definitely not," Tommy replied. "We can make some money if we can get around them knowing where to look for us. If you can figure out some way to do it, let's go for it. I need the money. I didn't come here on vacation, you know."

Baxter chuckled softly, so softly Tommy didn't know it was a chuckle and thought Baxter had cleared his throat.

"Don't worry about it, Tommy. You and Paulie just do as I say and everything will be fine. What I want you to do is show up with Paulie as planned. I'm going to have someone there to speak to your contact from the ship, and it will all be handled. I guarantee you that no cop in this country or anywhere will have any reason to bother you in any way. But that won't stop them from trying. I'm sure you can handle dealing with them when they've got nothing on you. Just trust me.

"When it's done, you and Paulie will be taken to a safe street corner, safe because my men are watching it. The driver of the truck with the booze in it, which won't be the same booze you see loaded, will tell you what to do, and you listen to him because he will be the one to bring you the money. We won't be meeting or speaking again. Goodbye, Tommy, and good luck wherever you wind up." The call ended and Tommy handed the phone back to Nice and turned towards the door.

"You sure you don't want me to go with you?" Nice asked, taking Tommy's hand. The mobster smiled at her.

"Sorry, not today. I'll be back in a few days, I promise."

He walked out into the stifling heat and humidity of the Bangkok night.

TWENTY-ONE

Johnny and Fah were alone with the Lieutenant in the office at the substation. The Lieutenant spoke to Fah in Thai, as if Johnny were not there.

"How much do you know about this man?" he asked. "About what he does in America?"

"He told me he was a businessman who managed real estate," she replied. "But from what I understand now, that's not exactly the case."

The Lieutenant smiled.

"He may be able to call himself a businessman, but his product is not real estate. It's human misery. Gambling, loan sharking, hijacking. It's all backed up by corruption and violence."

Fah's face turned several shades lighter.

"Are you telling me Johnny is a gangster, like the kind we have here? The kind you arrest?"

"When we can," the Lieutenant said. "But you have the picture."

Fah paused in thought for twenty seconds and then asked if the Lieutenant knew why Johnny came to Thailand. The Lieutenant explained how Johnny was in charge of an American Mafia scheme to sell stolen liquor to Thai businesses, whether they wanted to buy it or not.

"So far at least one honest businessman has been murdered, and several local gangsters are missing. Just today we got a report of a security officer being knocked out in an alley and his gun taken. My policeman's nose tells me they are all related somehow, even if I can't prove it yet."

The Lieutenant saw how uncomfortable Fah had become. It looked as if she were having a hard time breathing.

"Can I get you anything? the Lieutenant asked. "A glass of water, some tissues?" Fah shook her head no,

"What the hell is going on here?" Johnny asked. "What are you telling Fah about me?"

"Quite perceptive, Johnny," the Lieutenant said, shifting effortlessly to English. "I'm simply telling her the truth about you. Shouldn't a woman know the truth about her man?"

"Maybe she should, but it's up to the man to tell her, not a cop!" Johnny said in a loud voice.

"It is a police officer's job to protect the Thai people against foreigners coming here to do bad things," the Lieutenant replied without a trace of emotion. "I'm sure you were going to tell her everything about your career as the number two man in a criminal gang in America. Not just any gang, the Mafia. Surely you were about to explain all the crimes you've committed and all the lives you've ruined and all the people who are dead because of you." This time there was a trace of anger in the Lieutenant's voice.

Johnny sat without saying a word.

"Were you going to tell me?" Fah shouted.

"Eventually," Johnny said sheepishly. "But it doesn't matter now that you know. It's all true what he said. It's also true that coming here and meeting you changed me. I'm not that person anymore."

"It will take time to prove that conclusively," the Lieutenant interjected. "But you've taken a huge step forward by coming to us and helping us stop these very dangerous men."

Fah's eyes were red though no tears had appeared. She stared hard at Johnny before speaking.

"You don't understand karma, but you will if you start here," she said slowly. "You have gathered a lot of bad karma, but if you have truly become a new and different person, you can start gathering some good karma. It's up to you."

"We can protect you here in Thailand," the Lieutenant said. "There are no guarantees in life, but my suspicion is that no matter what problems you cause the Mafia back in America, they won't be coming here looking for you. These men will cut their losses, as you say back in your country."

"I certainly hope so," Johnny replied.

The Lieutenant arranged for Johnny to have a room for the next week at a small hotel just off Siam Square. In addition to its own fine Israeli-trained hotel security force, there would be police on site, some in plainclothes, and an undercover vehicle parked within thirty meters of the entrance.

The Lieutenant personally drove Johnny and Fah to the hotel to make sure there were no problems. He and Fah walked Johnny to the front desk and the instant the concierge saw the Lieutenant in his uniform, he scurried over to make certain the check-in went smoothly and that the security team assigned to protect Johnny knew he was in the house.

"I'll wait outside in the car while you two figure out the next step," he said with a smile.

A half hour later, when Fah did not emerge through the front doors of the hotel, the Lieutenant told his driver to bring him to his own station house.

Ray the Bartender was about to begin one of his patented stories. The unwritten NJA Club rule, vigorously enforced, required the full attention of all present when the story began. NJA Club regulars knew that if one sat at tables farthest from the bar, and spoke in a whisper, they could get away with a violation, but if Ray caught them, his withering stare was more painful than being denied drinks for the rest of the night.

Glenn sat on a stool at the bar, Sleepy Joe on his left and Edward sitting to his right. The General stood behind Glenn, and at the old officer's insistence, Glenn had a martini in front of him, made with Tito's Vodka, distilled six times in Austin, Texas, and the only liquor Glenn could tolerate, mainly because it had no taste. The General held the same drink in his hand. Sleepy Joe was working on a pint of Fosters, and Edward a single malt scotch. Two dozen other customers hung around the bar, absorbing Ray's fabled skills as a raconteur.

Ray's thick Irish brogue, delivered between a tenor and baritone, filled the bar area. Ray had been the evening bartender at the club ever since Glenn arrived over fifteen years ago, and in all those years, he never told the same story twice, and he never told a story that didn't get a rise out of all who listened. Considering that he told two or three tales every week, Ray had quite a backlog of material.

"Being a bartender is a lot like being a criminal lawyer," Glenn once remarked to Ray after hearing such a tale. "We hear fantastic things from people, and we can't wait to tell others. The difference is that there's no legal confidentiality rule for bartenders."

"And a good thing there isn't," Ray said. "Otherwise, my job would be rather boring. And a good thing there is one for your trade, Glenn, otherwise no client would ever talk to you."

This story was about a man Ray called "a sap," a Canadian living in Pattaya.

"Living in Pattaya?" Edward exclaimed. "Doesn't that tell us all we have to know?"

"Not by a long shot," Ray answered and continued his narrative.

"So, this unlucky bloke loses his heart to a Filipina grifter about a third his age," Ray said, when a Scottish-accented voice called out from the crowd.

"You're telling us a man from Pattaya has to import a prostitute? There aren't enough of them in Pattaya?"

"I never said she was a prostitute," Ray said sternly. "A prostitute is an honorable profession, where she sells sex to a willing buyer, and everyone knows what's going on and there's no misunderstandings, mind you. A grifter on the other hand is a thieving liar who makes you think she cares about you so she can clean out your bank account."

"Let Ray tell the story!" Sleepy Joe yelled.

"Thank you, Joe, and I will," Ray said, and he did.

"The poor fool has to fly to the Philippines because her country won't let her leave. Something to do with showing America they're fighting human trafficking. The poor sap tells her he's taking her to the most expensive resort in the country, but when he gets there and finds out how much it costs, it's got him and the grifter out of there and into some fleabag hotel in Manila."

"Cheap doesn't play well in Southeast Asia," a Frenchman called out. He and his Thai girlfriend had been frequenting the NJA club for the past few weeks.

"Where does it play well?" the General whispered to Glenn.

Ray banged his big fist on the bar to let the crowd know it was time for them to shut up.

"Anyway, when the two of them are in this dumpy hotel, the grifter takes the bloke's shorts, the only pants he brought, and tosses them into the rubbish bin by the elevators while he's showering. When he realizes he's without pants, the grifter tells him they must have fallen into the little trash can in the room and the cleaning lady took it away. Sap believes this without question.

"Don't you worry," she tells him. "Around here people go outside and about in their underwear all the time. Shopping, eating, even work. It's no problem." So, for the next two days, everywhere this sap goes, he's wearing one of his boxer shorts. When he tries to go through airport security to fly home, they make him buy a pair of sweatpants from one of the airport stores."

Glenn raised his hand. Ray smiled and recognized him, telling him he had the floor.

"Why would the grifter do this to her mark?" he asked.

"Hell hath no fury like a woman scorned," Ray said. "I'm sure the grifter bragged to all her friends how she hit on a mark who was going to lead her to the big time, starting with that fancy resort. Maybe hoped she'd meet a young, handsome bloke at this rich person's resort and kiss off the sap. Then he makes her look like a fool. She gets even, knowing this idiot is too dumb to see what's going on. A Cheap Charlie gets no quarter in this part of the world."

"Can I ask one more question?" Glenn said

"Of course, Counselor," Ray replied.

"Did this really happen?" Glenn asked. "Who would ever claim it's okay to walk around town in your underwear, and who on earth would believe it?"

"I am one hundred percent certain it happened. This sap posted the whole thing on the internet, complete with story and pictures," Ray said. "Someone who knows I love to tell a good story shared it with me."

"Who could be such an idiot as this sap?" the Frenchman asked.

"A man who lives in Pattaya and has to go to the Philippines to find a woman to take his money," Ray replied.

Glenn pictured an older, overweight Canadian waltzing around an Asian city in his underwear. He couldn't decide if it was that image or the weed he smoked before coming to the NJA Club that caused him to break out in laughter while the others applauded Ray's storytelling.

TWENTY-TWO

As soon as Johnny and Fah were in the room, he called Paulie on one of the local burner phones Paulie had given him.

"I'm not going to be coming to the hotel for a few hours," he said. "Remember I told you about that young lady I'd been seeing? Well, I'm with her tonight. I'll catch you and Tommy later in the day tomorrow, after you get back with the money. Just be careful."

"Always am," Paulie replied. "When that's done with, we have to figure out how we're going to deal with this problem between Tommy and the Boss. I just don't like the way it's going."

"Me either," Johnny said. "But one day at a time. Once we let the Boss know we have some money and everything is done, he's probably going to cool off a bit."

There was a pause on the line.

"I don't know about that," Johnny," Paulie said. "The Boss is really close with the Giannelli family. This ain't about business, and when something ain't about business, but it's personal, that's when even the coolest wise guy can go off the rails. I wouldn't want to be Tommy, and I'm getting the feeling that right now Tommy would like to be someone else for a while. I'm not getting the feeling that he's a man getting ready to face the Boss back in Brooklyn."

"One day at a time, Paulie," Johnny said. "One day at a time."

They agreed to meet at Johnny's room the following day at five p.m. Johnny would personally count the money. Paulie would immediately bring it to a currency changer in Chinatown referred by Baxter, one who could handle this amount, and after Johnny counted the U.S. currency, he would inform the Boss all was well and done. He would have the travel agent downstairs arrange for them to be on the next flight to New York City. At least that was what Johnny told Paulie.

"I'll try to talk Tommy into leaving first, soon as we have the dough, but if he balks, we'll just have to make sure he comes back with the two of us."

Glad my friend Johnny's finally cutting loose for a change, Paulie thought after the call ended. *This business between Tommy and the Boss has to be rough on him. He's got a stick up his ass half the time, and a little time with a woman might fix that for a while.*

Johnny always awoke at six a.m., and now that his body and brain were adapted to local Bangkok time, he maintained the habit. He saw that Fah was not in bed, and none of her clothing or her handbag were where they'd been when he fell asleep four hours ago. The bathroom light was off, but he called her name anyway. When there was no reply, he checked the bathroom and the closet, and when he was totally convinced she had left in shame and he would never see her again, he spotted the folded paper on the pillow where she had slept. He grabbed it and opened it.

I have to be home before anyone sees me coming in. Call me when you are wide awake. Everything will be good.

Love,
Fah

Johnny stood in the hotel room, smiling, and clutching the letter to his chest. He felt something inside himself he could not identify, other than that it was what his late mother called "a feeling." A woman far above him in every way had just committed her love for him to writing. *When was the last time a woman other than his mother told Johnny Brancini she loved him?* He couldn't remember.

Johnny had been cautious and slow to change throughout his entire life, devoted to his work and to the Boss. The Boss called this "reliability." Tommy referred to it as "no fun." Paulie came the closest to the truth: Johnny was, in his words, "a company man." The company was the Mafia, and he was the Boss's direct report. *Just like I played by the rules of the Mob, I can play by the rules of normal people,* Johnny assured himself.

He knew the die was cast. There was no turning back, no return to the warm embrace of the Boss, no reliance on protection by Tommy or arrangements by Paulie. The feds he feared his whole life now protected him, thanks to that sharp lawyer, Glenn Cohen, and that hard-assed but really smart Thai cop. The Lieutenant was a straight shooter, no doubt in Johnny's mind. He didn't trust the FBI agent, and knew if he ever returned to the States, she'd make his life a living hell, no matter what promises were made today. Johnny was comforted by the thought that he wasn't returning to America any time soon.

Johnny accepted that Tommy deserved whatever happened to him, and while Paulie was a better person, he too should pay for the pain and suffering he had helped cause so many innocent people. The same could be said about Johnny, but as Fah explained, he had time to accumulate "good karma" to offset all the bad variety he'd accumulated. The idea that he had a chance to redeem himself and make up for all the bad he had done, gave him hope that his life in Thailand would be good and he would be with Fah, largely based on his actions. He sensed perhaps there was something to this Buddhist religion.

I've been a Catholic my whole life, along with Tommy, Paulie, and the Boss. Our asses have sat many hours on those hard wooden pews, listening to words we ignore every day of our lives. I never felt good for one minute in a church. But the idea that I can change if I want and don't have to worry about going to Purgatory or Hell is a nice thought. Those priests don't know what they're talking about anyway. How do they know what the hell happens when you die? It's not like anyone came back and told them.

The Lieutenant had been clear that Johnny was not to leave the hotel room until the mobsters were arrested. Fah, Glenn, and the Lieutenant were the only other people allowed into the room. The officer stationed on his hotel floor would make certain any room service really came from the hotel kitchen. Johnny looked over the room service menu, called in his breakfast order, and lay down on the bed to rest until the food arrived.

By evening, it would be over. Tommy and Paulie would be in custody, and the feds back in Brooklyn would move in on the Boss and his family as well as any others they could charge criminally. While this was happening in Brooklyn, Johnny would be settling into a new life in Thailand.

Tommy and Paulie drank coffee in Tommy's room. Paulie explained that Johnny was spending the night with the Thai woman he'd met.

"It doesn't matter if he makes it here or not right now," Paulie said. "His job don't start until late afternoon, when we have all the baht."

Tommy said nothing.

"Once he confirms the total, I'll get it changed into dollars and Johnny and me are gonna have to figure out how to get it to America," Paulie continued. "Johnny and me can each carry up to ten grand with us on the plane. If some nosy customs agent asks what we're doing with so much cash, we've got a whole bunch of stories. We will have a lot more than twenty grand, so I may need Baxter's help on this."

I'll keep the baht for a while, Tommy thought. *As long as I'm here, that's all I need.*

They finished their coffee and left the hotel. They walked several blocks and hailed a cab to the docks out at the port. They followed the instructions Johnny had gotten from the Boss and were able to locate the right ship without any problems. They waited in the relative coolness of the early Bangkok morning, hoping there really was an American contact who would recognize and approach them.

Seating was cramped inside the van, and Glenn's thigh pressed against Mary's. He tried to look at Johnny or the Lieutenant. Johnny was there to make a positive and absolute identification of his two colleagues in crime. There was no reason for Glenn to be there except that Johnny spent his entire adult life in the Mafia and wasn't about to be trapped in a van with all these police officers without his lawyer present. The Lieutenant, of course, also felt more comfortable with at least one farang proven to be honorable.

The van's windows allowed people inside to see out, but not from outside, so people in the dock area would have no idea the van was not really from a noodle company awaiting its shipment but was really a sophisticated surveillance tool available only to the most trusted members of the Royal Thai Police. Of the almost quarter million members of the national force, no more than two dozen would ever be allowed to come near this gift from America's Central Intelligence Agency.

"Zoom in on the two men who just got out of that cab," the Lieutenant said to the plainclothes officer at his side, who was manipulating an iPad. Within seconds, the small screen on the monitor hanging on the side of the van showed two white men.

"That's Tommy Turterello on the right and Paulie Arginotti on the left," Johnny said.

"They look just like in the photos," Glenn added.

"They should," Mary said. "Our own surveillance team in Brooklyn took those shots a few weeks before they came here. Our good luck. We're always monitoring these mobsters, but we hardly ever come up with anything. This time we have."

"Tell the A team to keep their eyes on those two, and their ears on their cell phones to hear me call them to make the arrests," the Lieutenant instructed the plainclothes officer.

"Is there a B team?" Mary asked.

"There is," the Lieutenant said. "You don't want to meet them, because they are only coming in if the A team is about to be wiped out. At some point, Baxter's people may want to check out this noodle company van sitting in the line of sight of them loading up the stolen liquor. If we can't get away, the B Team appears."

"What exactly happens if Baxter's people do come over here?" Glenn asked, the quiver in his voice obvious to the others.

"The driver will try to get away, and his partner in the front seat may decide to start firing out his window if he can. If there's no way out, like if they block the roadway out of here, then we have a shoot-out on our hands. If the B Team gets here quickly, they can put down the attackers, but our first option is to drive away, our second possibility is to start defending ourselves before the B Team starts firing at the bad guys. I'm armed, so are my three officers, and I know Mary has a gun she's not supposed to have, given to her by the same CIA that previously gave us this van, so I cannot complain." He smiled. Mary frowned. "Glenn and Johnny, look under your seats and take out what's down there."

The two did as instructed and each held a helmet with a face-covering visor and a Kevlar vest.

"They are not a hundred percent guaranteed, but they'll stop most bullets fired from a distance beyond five meters. All of us will put these on when I send out the A team to make the arrests. No reason for you two to be in even the slightest danger. You're civilians. If they attack this van or we have to get out to fight them, you two stay inside and run away as soon as you can."

"I'm not running away," Johnny said. "When I ran away from my life in Brooklyn, that was the last time I ran. I'll help in any way I can. I'll tackle a man if need be."

"It's not your fight," the Lieutenant said softly. "You have been most helpful, and I'm hoping you really are a changed man. But this is Thailand, and it's a Thai problem."

"A Thai problem with an FBI agent?" Johnny asked. "How come she can be part if this and I can't?" Johnny asked.

"How dare you compare yourself to me," Mary said, struggling to avoid yelling. "You're a gangster and I'm Special Agent of the FBI.

You're the whole reason we're here in the first place. You and your Mafia gang back in Brooklyn." She glared at Johnny, who looked back at her without showing any emotion.

"You're totally right," he said. "It is my fault this all happened. Without me, the Boss would never have set this whole thing up. That's why I have to help if you are all in danger." *And a good reason why I shouldn't go back to Brooklyn and deal with you.*

"That is very decent of you, Johnny," the Lieutenant said," but it won't be necessary. This is our job and this is what we are trained to do. You and Glenn cannot be expected to stand up against someone like Tommy the Turtle or Baxter's thugs."

"What are you talking about?" Johnny asked. "I was Tommy's superior in the Mob. I tell him what to do."

"Not anymore," the Lieutenant said. "Besides, you are not a natural killer like Tommy the Turtle. You would think for a second before shooting someone you know well. Not Tommy. He'd pull the trigger automatically. Same with his new friends. That's what natural killers do."

"I agree with the Lieutenant," Glenn said. "This is not our fight, Johnny, and we are not trained for it. We pose more of a threat to the safety of these police by being here than if we left now. Which is what I suggest. There's no sign of them noticing this van, let alone thinking Johnny and I are in here. It's not yet completely light outside, and once we're out of this van we can walk on the other side of all those trucks parked along the road facing the dock area. They'll never see us. An unmarked car can pick us up in minutes."

"Nobody is going anywhere right now," the Lieutenant said, looking at the screen. "Looks like Johnny's information still holds true. That appears to be the contact from the ship going towards them."

The others looked at the screen. A big white man in gauzy blue pants and a white t shirt came down the gangplank of the cargo ship and headed straight to where Tommy and Paulie stood, at the side of a large, gleaming blue tractor attached to a very long trailer, the kind that unload several shipments for different clients and delivers them throughout the Bangkok region. *Not that different from how it works back home, at least it did when the docks were big business for the Boss and the other families,* Johnny reminisced. The driver stepped out of the tractor's cabin and spoke with Tommy and Paulie.

Inside the van, the Lieutenant and his crew watched the big white man approach the two Brooklyn mobsters.

"Do you recognize him?" the Lieutenant asked Johnny.

"He looks an awful lot like a guy on the waterfront back home who did a lot of freelance work for us. I knew him as Richie. Mostly this kind of stuff, getting things on and off ships that you don't want Uncle Sam to know about. I didn't know he also went out to sea."

"What would make you certain it's him?" Mary asked.

"The guy I'm thinking of had a tattoo of an anchor on the left side of his neck," Johnny said. The Lieutenant ordered the plainclothes cop to focus on that part of the man's body. Johnny identified the tattoo as soon as it appeared.

"Thank you, Johnny," Mary said. "You've helped a lot with this case. The hoods out there are from Brooklyn, not to mention we have you right here. The booze is sure to be from Brooklyn. Now your friends just happen to show up at the docks to meet the ship that's carrying the booze, and guess who's there to greet them? Good old Richie from the Brooklyn docks. Sounds like we've made our case."

She'd still love to put me away with the rest of them if she could, Johnny thought. *I'll be okay living here, but I know she's never going to stop thinking about the one that got away. I guess I'll always have that worry in the back of my mind.*

Everyone in the van watched Richie speak with Tommy, Paulie, and the driver, and then shake hands with all three before he walked back to the gangplank. They didn't see the folded up note the Thai driver slipped into Rich's hand when they shook.

"What's that note say?" Tommy asked the English-speaking driver.

"I didn't read it," the driver replied. "Baxter told me it explains what has to be done to fool the police. If your friend really did betray us, they are going to be here. They probably are watching us right now. But don't worry. We outnumber and outgun them, and they know this. Besides, it's never getting to that point. Trust Baxter."

Tommy scanned the dock, cluttered with forklifts and small electric trucks. He studied the road running alongside it, filled with trucks and cars on both sides. Scores of people scurried about on the dock area and the service road. The noodle company van did not stand out and he paid it no special attention.

"Could be anywhere out there, watching us every minute," Tommy said.

"Just like home," Paulie said.

Richie unfolded the note as soon as he was inside the ship. When he was done reading it the second time, he tore it into tiny pieces and dropped them into a trash can a few meters away. He smiled as he walked to the entrance to the elevator to the cargo hold.

A half-hour later, Richie returned to the truck, this time riding in the passenger seat of an electric vehicle towing stacks of plain brown boxes taken from the hold of the ship. A half dozen men followed the vehicle on foot, and when it stopped by Baxter's truck, they too stopped and waited for Baxter's driver to open the rear of the trailer. They began transferring boxes from the electric vehicle to the trailer.

The Lieutenant counted three hundred thirty-five cases on the electric vehicle. He did this by adding the number of stacks and the number of boxes in each until all were on Baxter's truck.

"Should have been three hundred fifty," Johnny said. "The guys at the docks took a few for themselves."

The van was silent as the inhabitants' eyes were glued to the screen. As soon as the last box was placed into Baxter's truck, the Lieutenant told the plainclothes officer to send in Team A. The Lieutenant and Mary left the van, followed by the cop in the front passenger seats. The plainclothesman slid the van door closed on his way out. All three drew their weapons. Glenn and Johnny watched the events through the windows and on the screen.

"Freeze!" Mary shouted as she held her Glock with both hands, pointed straight at Tommy. The Lieutenant shouted the same command in Thai, and then in English told the American gangsters not to make a move, that there were snipers covering every one of them. A half-dozen black-clad Thai police with baklavas covering their faces and semiautomatic rifles in their arms ran towards them. *The A Team,* Johnny thought as he watched. The truck driver threw up his arms when the plainclothesman glared at him with his pistol aimed at his head, and the Thai workers who unloaded the boxes followed suit. Paulie stood there calmly, as if he were dealing with a visit from the phone company coming to check a line.

"What seems to be the problem here?" Paulie asked the Lieutenant. *He speaks English and seems to be in charge,* he thought.

The Lieutenant said nothing. Two of the men in black started tearing open the cardboard boxes. When each had ripped open half a dozen, they called out to the Lieutenant, who summoned Mary to join him in inspecting the boxes. The Lieutenant reached in and withdrew a bottle of cold pressed virgin olive oil. They ripped open several other boxes, all filled with bottles of olive oil.

"What's this? he shouted at Paulie, waving his pistol in the gangster's face.

"I dunno what the problem is," Paulie replied. "I'm just here to supervise a shipment. I work for an olive oil distributor in America. In case you don't know, olives don't grow in Thailand, but you need the oil for cooking. Is that now against the law? You guys allow weed but not olive oil? You got something against us Italians?"

Mary bit her lower lip. She knew well that olive oil importation was a classic business cover and money laundering scheme for the Mafia. *I wonder if Johnny set us up. Is he somehow still with the Mafia? I never trusted him because you can't trust an Italian mobster, not ever.*

"You have the paperwork to prove this is yours?" she asked Paulie.

The Brooklyn mobster smiled at the angry FBI agent.

"Lady, we don't need to prove shit to you. Whoever the hell you are, whether you're NYPD or a fed, you ain't got no authority here"

"Well, he does," Mary said, pointing to the Lieutenant.

"I'm not so sure about that," Paulie replied. "We are at the Bangkok Port. I understand them to be a fully independent organization responsible for its own security. Unless this gentleman is authorized by the Port to harass its customers, I'd say he doesn't have much more authority here than you."

"Let's call the Port management," the Lieutenant said, remaining calm. "If there is any need for an official stamp of approval, we'll get it." The plainclothes officer holstered his pistol and made the call. The black clad men kept their rifles aimed at Paulie, Tommy, and the Thais.

Tommy, who hadn't uttered a word, looked at his friend Paulie.

Guy has balls. I'll give him a little extra for his troubles.

Minutes later an officious looking man in a severe dark suit and tie appeared with a Port security guard at his side. The official spoke briefly in Thai with the Lieutenant, and then with Paulie in English. He then sent the Port security guard up the gangplank to find Richie.

Paulie and Tommy smoked cigarettes while waiting for Richie. The Lieutenant conferred with the plainclothesman in Thai. Mary stared at Tommy and Paulie and then flashed her badge.

"FBI," she said. "No matter how this little escapade ends, you two are going to be locked up the second you land in America. We know everything you did." *And hopefully someday your friend Johnny will join you.*

Tommy finally spoke.

"The only thing we're doing when we get home is sue your ass for trying to ruin our business and embarrass us in front of our Thai employees." Paulie nodded in agreement.

The Port security guard returned with Richie in tow. Richie held a sheaf of papers. They showed that the olive oil had been ordered by a Thai distributor and were to be picked up by the company representatives.

"And the paperwork shows the connection between these two goons and some real Thai company?" Mary asked.

The Bangkok Port official's round face flashed a smug smile.

"Madam, if you or anyone else wish to investigate the ownership or employment records of a local company, you are of course free to do so, but not on our docks. We have loading and unloading to perform, which is our job. On behalf of the Bangkok Port, I wish you the best of luck with your investigation, but please permit our customers to use our facilities as they were intended, just as you may use your police headquarters for whatever purposes you deem necessary. Have a very pleasant day, and if you like, I can have cups of coffee brought here so you can enjoy them on your ride out." When no one took him up on the offer, he smiled again and speaking Thai, told the Lieutenant it was time to leave.

"Once again, stupid farangs who think they know everything make a problem for us," the Port official said in Thai to the Lieutenant.

"It remains to be seen who is making a problem for whom," the Lieutenant said. He signaled for the men in black and the people from the van to leave, and they obeyed. The Port official shook his head as he watched the police walk away.

Three hundred meters away from where the Lieutenant suffered his humiliation, Baxter's men loaded the liquor onto another of his trucks, one about the size of a large Fed Ex delivery truck, one unit, nothing close to the size of the trailer truck with the olive oil. They'd brought the liquor down a different gangplank on the other end of the big ship, and no one raised an eyebrow at cargo being unloaded off a cargo ship. When the last of the three hundred fifty boxes was loaded, the driver's assistant locked the rear of the truck hopped back into the passenger seat in the front of the truck, and waved goodbye to the Thai dockworkers as he drove off. Neither the Lieutenant, Mary, nor any of the other law enforcement officers paid any attention to one of many trucks leaving the docks.

Fifteen minutes later, a Mercedes dropped Tommy and Paulie off on a side street near Soi Nana. During the ride, Tommy explained to Paulie why there were olive oil bottles and not liquor in the boxes. His explanation did not include the fact of Johnny's betrayal. Instead, he said that Baxter's policy was always to change things around a bit at the end, to make sure that if anyone had gotten hold of the plans, it would do them no good. That was why they would not go back to the hotel to count the money but would go to a safe place belonging to Baxter.

Is that where Johnny will meet us?" Paulie asked.

"I hope so," Tommy replied with a smile.

They waited on the corner for five minutes and the truck with the liquor pulled up next to them. The driver, a young man with his hair tied in a ponytail and a sneer on his lips, rolled down his window and spoke to them in heavily accented English.

"Go around the corner on Sukhumvit Road. Find someplace to eat and drink. Come back here in one hour and wait for me. I bring you your money." He rolled up the window and drove off.

After they turned the corner onto Sukhumvit Road, they stopped in front of a place advertising itself as a genuine New York City deli. The menu offered Big Apple deli staples like corned beef, pastrami, tongue, and even matzoh ball soup.

"Wanna give it a try?" Tommy asked. "Got to admit the Italian food around here ain't half bad, gotta hand it to these Thais, they know how to cook. Maybe this kosher deli stuff is okay, too." Paulie agreed.

Tommy wolfed down his pastrami on rye, declaring it to be a suitable substitute. Paulie nibbled at his chopped liver on a pumpernickel.

"Doesn't it worry you that we haven't seen or heard from Johnny in almost two days?" he asked. Paulie had absolute faith in Johnny, but it was unlike him to take such a hands-off approach at such a critical point in the operation. *Maybe that's what a woman did to him.*

Tommy put the last bite-sized piece of sandwich on his plate.

"Nah, he's shacking up with some broad he met here. Best thing in the world for him. He'll be back at the hotel later today to count the money and make sure the Boss gets it. That's his job."

Paulie nodded.

"You're right, Tommy," he said. "Johnny is the Boss's number one, his consigliere as well, and for good reason. He's real smart, real loyal, and he always gets the job done."

Maybe not so loyal, Tommy thought. *And Johnny being really smart and always getting the job done had me worried. I knew he would tell the* cops about the meeting on the docks. Baxter fixed that one. I'm sure he told them we're to meet later at the hotel with the money. Neither he nor Paulie know we are not going back to that hotel to meet. Tommy's belongings were in the hotel room he'd secretly taken, his remaining cash and gold in the new room's safe. He did a quick calculation, and they came to almost eight thousand US dollars total. *The cops will get Paulie's stash, that's for sure. I'll give him enough of the booze money to make up for it when I explain it all to him later.*

Paulie shared some additional thoughts.

"Just think about it, this whole mess will be over in a few hours. No more worrying about finding people to buy booze, no more dealing with guys like Baxter, no more not knowing what everyone around us is saying and most of them not understanding us. Brooklyn seems better than ever."

Tommy said nothing.

"You still worried about that Bobby Giannelli thing?" Paulie asked Tommy. "Forget about it. When the Boss gets this money, which he probably thought was down the drain, he's gonna forget all about Bobby Giannelli."

"I'm not so sure," Tommy said. "This is a personal thing, not business."

"Everything is business with guys like the Boss," Paulie said. "Guys like you are good for business. You just proved it."

Paulie don't know about the three dissolved mob guys on top of Bobby and the guy who set up the hijack for us. The Boss hates losing people on the inside, which will be bad, but even worse if he ever found out one of his men killed three of Tony Santucci's main guys . . .

Richie stood on the ship's deck, facing the water. He smoked a fat joint, the last of his stash. He had heard things had loosened up in Thailand, and weed was being sold openly everywhere. Baxter's men would return the big tractor-trailer truck he'd "borrowed" from an unsuspecting trucker still out with last night's hooker. Richie would have the dockworkers transfer the olive oil back to the ship, and the local purchaser would never know their olive oil had been used as a prop.

Richie patted the wad in the upper slashed pocket of is cargo pants. He felt the folded hundred-dollar bills Baxter's driver had slipped him before he left. Thirty of them. He could easily afford whatever prices they charged for weed in Bangkok. Or hookers. Or anything else he craved.

TWENTY-THREE

J ohnny and Glenn were ensconced in the latter's condo apartment. The Lieutenant had personally escorted them to the residence.

"It's the safest place for you right now," the Lieutenant advised. "My cousin Lek won't miss a thing out of the ordinary, and my own station is right nearby. I've got some men who are totally loyal to me on call if needed. One will be somewhere in the building at all times, checking out all the floors, checking in with Lek."

"Plus, I've got Sleepy Joc," Glenn said. Joe was already in the lobby when the Lieutenant personally delivered them to Lek. Joe smiled upon hearing these words.

Before he left, the Lieutenant studied Johnny from top to bottom.

"Mr. Johnny, I do believe you are the rare criminal who can be redeemed."

Johnny blushed.

"That's not what I've expected to hear from a police officer. I wish my mother were alive to hear your words."

The Lieutenant smiled.

"I regret your mother is not here to see a man she would now be proud to have as her son. However, you are fortunate to have another very good woman in your life." Johnny blushed again.

"Another reason for me to stay on the straight and narrow," he said, looking at the Lieutenant. "I wouldn't ever want to break Fah's heart. I could never forgive myself."

"Nor could I ever forgive you," the Lieutenant said. "Remember that I am a Lieutenant in the Royal Thai Police. You don't want me angry at you."

"In this new life, I don't ever plan to do anything that would make a policeman mad at me," Johnny replied.

"Especially if that policeman is angry because you mistreated one of his best employees," The Lieutenant said.

A puzzled look crossed Johnny's face.

"Fah doesn't work for you," Johnny said, uncertainty in his voice. "She's a waitress at the restaurant where I met her."

"Not as of tomorrow morning," the Lieutenant said. "She's starting as a civilian police interpreter and a special assistant to me, also doing research, maybe even some interviews."

"Fah never said anything about working for you," Johnny said.

"That's because she didn't know," the Lieutenant explained. "I'll call her later today."

"How do you know she'll accept?" Johnny asked. "After this, she may not exactly crave the life of a police employee."

"Don't worry, Johnny, she won't be out on the streets risking her life. She is going to be safer than anyone in this country because she will be working with the most honest cops in Asia. And as for acceptance of this offer, let me remind you, Johnny, that in this country, when a policeman asks you to do something, you do it." He smiled at Johnny, and his eyes flashed a brief and flickering twinkle.

Tommy paid for the delicatessen meal and left a sizable tip.

"Come back again!" the smiling waiter shouted as the two gangsters left the restaurant.

They walked back to the corner where they were to meet Baxter's driver. Both smoked cigarettes as they walked.

"The Marlboros here don't taste the same as the ones back home," Tommy complained.

"That's why I started smoking these cheap Thai butts," Paulie said. "If the taste ain't there, no sense paying full freight." He exhaled a big cloud of smoke to emphasize his point.

They stopped a half a block before they turned off Sukhumvit Road, put their cigarette butts on the sidewalk, crushed them with their shoes, then picked them up and dropped them into a nearby garbage can. They had seen two instances where a Thai cop approached tourists who dropped butts on the sidewalk. The offending farangs were offered the choice of picking butts off the next several blocks or paying the cops five hundred baht. Both victims paid, cursed the cops, and went on their way. Tommy and Paulie wanted no more encounters with the police.

They waited at the appointed time and place for no more than five minutes before the delivery truck reappeared. Paulie walked to the driver's side and Baxter's ponytailed associate pressed a button to unlock the door. On the passenger seat lay two small rolling suitcases, the kind with wheels and handles that can be carried on a plane. An envelope was placed on top of one. Ponytail told Paulie to open the passenger door and take them. He explained the money was in the suitcases and the envelope held the address and keys for a condo owned by Baxter, where they would stay until they left for home. When Tommy and Paulie each had a suitcase with the handles pulled up, the driver stretched his arm across the passenger seat and closed the door, rolled up his window and drove off without saying a word.

"Not much longer and we're back in Brooklyn again," Paulie said, almost musical in tone. "I'm never leaving again."

Maybe you're going back to Brooklyn, Tommy thought. *But you go alone.* Tommy couldn't imagine that Johnny was planning to return, at least not now. *That's probably the deal he cut with the feds and the Thais.*

"Aren't we sitting ducks for a rip-off? Paulie asked. "Standing on a side street with suitcases filled with money?"

"Don't worry," Tommy said. "Baxter's got this street covered. We wouldn't be here otherwise."

The microphone hidden on a tree a few feet from where the two Brooklyn men stood transmitted the conversation to Baxter, who lounged comfortably on the couch in a small apartment not more than half a block away. He turned to his aide, a muscular Swede with shoulder-length hair and tattoos running up and down both arms.

"That's what they pay me for," he said with a smile as he patted the canvas bag at his side, full of his share of the booze sale money.

At the corner with Sukhumvit Road, Tommy spotted a cab dropping off a passenger. A middle-aged white couple rushed to the cab. Tommy lurched in front of them.

"We got this one," he said menacingly.

"I'm sorry, but I hailed this cab," the man said in an English accent.

"Well, get another one," Paulie interjected. He handed the man a five hundred baht note.

"For your troubles," he said. "We really need this cab now." He and Tommy got in, squeezing themselves and the suitcases in the back seat. The two English tourists stood at the curb, the man's mouth wide open and a five hundred baht note in his hand.

Baxter's safe house was small but furnished with everything Tommy or Paulie would need for a day or two. It was in a neighborhood heavy with farangs, so they wouldn't stand out. Tommy pulled a Chang beer from the refrigerator and opened it, drinking straight from the bottle. Paulie lit a cigarette and pondered the situation.

"We wait here for Johnny, then he counts the dough and I take it over to Baxter's man in Chinatown to get it changed into dollars," he said. "Johnny's not here to count it and he ain't gotten you your ticket home yet."

"No need to wait for Johnny," Tommy said. "Let's get the money changed now. What difference does it make? After the money is changed into dollars, Johnny will be able to see we sold all the bottles at the prices Baxter promised, minus his take. A well-earned take, I have to say."

Paulie shook his head.

"No, we have to wait for Johnny. Remember, when we're here, it's like he's the Boss, and we'd never change the money without the Boss counting it first. If Johnny okays it, we're off the hook even if there was some problem with the total."

Tommy laughed.

"I bet the first thing the Boss would think if any money were short is we stole it even if that ain't the case."

"Still, we ought to wait for Johnny and do it by the book," Paulie said. "Them's the orders, Tommy."

"I don't agree," Tommy countered. "Who the hell knows when Johnny gets tired of this babe he's with? We could be stuck here for days, and every one of those days gives that mean-looking Thai cop and that hot-looking fed more time to come after us. I say change the money now and then you get the tickets for all three of us if Johnny ain't back. What does it matter who changes the money or buys the tickets? However you look at it, it's you handling the money change. You're Paulie the Arranger. You can handle all of this.

"Let's do it now," Tommy said. "You know how to get to this place in Chinatown?"

"We can't," Paulie said, a trace of anger in his voice. "Don't you think you're in enough trouble with the Boss already? You think it gets better if you don't follow his orders, which were that we do what Johnny says. And Johnny says he counts the money, both before and after it's changed."

Tommy replied with an equal trace of anger in his tone.

"Why? You afraid he doesn't trust us? Or the Boss doesn't?" Paulie said nothing. They both knew the Boss suspected Tommy was involved in the disappearance of Bobby Giannelli and possibly the hoods who did the hijacking, as well as the insider who set it up. That definitely fell into the category of the Boss not trusting Tommy.

"Besides," Paulie said, "I'm the one the Boss will be mad with if I am the one who changed the money before Johnny counted it. Easy for you but not for me."

"As I figured," Tommy snarled. "Tell you what, Paulie. I'll take one bag, go change it, even if I have to go to dozens of small places to get it all done. You can have the other, wait for Johnny and back home, you can tell the Boss how bad I am. He'll be happy to see the money."

"That won't work, Tommy. I can't let you take anything. Just wait for Johnny. He'll be here any minute." Then a thought crossed Paulie's mind.

If Johnny's been sacked up the past day, how did he get word that the plans have changed and he's to meet us here? I've been with Tommy almost every minute the past twenty-four hours and he didn't get any messages or calls from Johnny. Besides, Johnny would call me, not Tommy.

"Johnny's not showing up, is he?" Paulie asked.

Tommy started to say something, then stopped and collected his thoughts. He knew he eventually had to tell the truth about Johnny not showing up but wasn't sure about explaining the reason why. He had known Paulie since they were young twenty-somethings making their way up the mob ladder the way a normal citizen might work their way up in the bank or civil service. Paulie was the Arranger, and like Johnny, his value to the Boss was in his brains, not his muscles. A man did not have to be brave to do what Johnny and Paulie did, Tommy reasoned, but they had to be very smart. The smart ones rarely faced danger, and their courage and loyalty were almost never tested or developed because they were almost never in police custody.

But being quiet wouldn't do the trick in this situation. If Paulie knew Johnny was working with the feds, he would immediately understand why Baxter changed the game plan. Paulie was definitely sharp enough to realize no matter how careful Baxter was, Johnny could tell the feds far more than they would need to find him. It might be one thing if Paulie were grabbed in America; he'd call Scharfman and would probably be home for dinner before the arresting officers finished their paperwork. Not here in Thailand. Tommy wondered how a softer mob guy like Paulie would hold up in a Thai precinct or jail cell.

Not very well. He'd talk. I can come up with something that works for both of us.

Tommy didn't tell Paulie the real reason why Johnny wasn't joining them. He gave no reason.

"Don't worry about Johnny," Tommy said. "He's in charge here, he can contact the Boss any time he wants. He knows we have the money, and he knows we can be trusted. So, let's just act like Johnny was here and was counting everything. How about if you go to Chinatown with one of the suitcases and change it while I wait here? If Johnny shows up, I can show him this money and explain we started changing it because we didn't hear from him. And if anything goes wrong, if you have to separate from this suitcase for any reason, we still have this one here. Like I said, that can be changed by me going to lots of local places later on. Johnny will see we used good judgment."

Paulie considered Tommy's suggestion. *It wasn't too bad for such a lunkhead.*

"I could make two trips to Chinatown," Paulie said, "but then again, it's easier to maneuver with only one of these cases and like you say, we don't know for sure who's out there and why and leaving a case of baht here is sort of insurance. I ain't gonna die for the money in the one I'll be lugging if I have a choice."

"You'll be fine," Tommy said. "Have the guy at the front desk get you a cab. Tell him you want the driver to wait for you in Chinatown and you'll pay well for his time. Johnny don't know the safest way." *Johnny don't know the place so he couldn't tell the cops.*

Paulie decided that since it would look like he was going into an office building, a suitcase case full of money might not jump out at anyone.

"I like it," Paulie said, though he wasn't sure if he really liked it or saw no better option.

Ten minutes after Paulie left the condo, Tommy made sure the gun was still secure in his rear waistband, covered by his polo shirt covering the waist, and a sport jacket on top. He walked down the building's stairs and exited through a side door used by building employees. He wheeled his suitcase of cash beside him as he wandered down Sukhumvit Road, looking for a hotel with a cab line. He carefully maneuvered his suitcase between pedestrians, motorcyclists who jumped the curb to ride along the sidewalk instead of stand-still street traffic, and vendors hawking everything from pirated food to clothing, from counterfeit Rolex watches and Gucci handbags to the ubiquitous pirated DVDs and fake Viagra. After perambulating a few blocks, he found what he was looking for, hopped into the first cab on the line, and gave the name of the hotel in On Nut. He kept the suitcase in the back seat next to him.

I wasn't thinking of splitting the money evenly with Paulie, Tommy thought. *It worked out the easiest. I didn't want to have to kill one of my only friends ever. I hope he winds up okay. It won't be easy for Paulie to explain to the Boss that Johnny is a rat and Tommy killed Bobby Giannelli plus three of Santucci's men and stole half the booze money.*

Tommy knew he couldn't go back home, and he couldn't stay in Bangkok. If he returned anywhere in America, sooner or later the Brooklyn Mob would find him if the cops didn't. They always do. His best move for the time being was to stay in Thailand, away from Bangkok. He had a suitcase full of baht and some hundreds and gold. He could live in Asia a very long time on what he had, maybe the rest of his life.

There were only three people who had the ability and the reasons to interfere with Tommy's plans: the blonde fed who showed up at the docks, who he trailed to the Rembrandt Hotel; Glenn, the arrogant but cheery American lawyer he met in the restroom at the police station; and the Lieutenant who came to the docks and was in charge.

Glenn the lawyer wasn't going to be a problem, Tommy decided. Lawyers really don't have any personal interest in a case aside from getting paid. Besides, lawyers can't talk about what their clients told them. Today he helps a rat, tomorrow he defends a wise guy at trial. Tommy understood lawyers. As in his work, it was never personal, just business. He didn't understand how an American criminal lawyer had a case in Thailand or why he lived here, but all of this pointed to Glenn the lawyer forgetting all about this case the minute it was over. Killing him risked creating problems where there otherwise wouldn't be any.

With Johnny, the damage was already done. By now, he must have revealed to the fed lady and the Thai cop every secret he had about the Boss's family and their operations. He was certain to be given protection, maybe even money, probably hidden where Tommy would never find him, especially not in this country. All Tommy could do was save himself, not seek revenge. especially since the Boss was sure to have Tommy killed if he ever got his hands on him. *If Johnny's squealing puts the Boss away, that's best for me.*

Nothing could be done about the Lieutenant. If a farang killed a Thai cop in the Kingdom, there wouldn't be a noodle stand in the provinces where he wasn't sought. That lieutenant managed to sink the booze sale operation, which was his only concern. The Mafia was for the lady fed to chase down back in her own country. Tommy decided it was over and done with for the Thai lieutenant.

That left the lady fed, the FBI agent. Killing a fed would definitely not be something that goes away, and the death of an FBI agent in Bangkok would be investigated by both nations, even if it led nowhere. The Boss would never approve the hit, but Tommy no longer worked for him. Surely, Tommy would be the prime suspect, indeed the only one, despite the lack of any proof, meaning they couldn't charge him with her murder even if they found him. They could put him away for the hijacking, but only if he were dumb enough to return to the States.

Tommy didn't fancy himself an expert on Thai people but had a solid sense that the death of an American FBI agent might be an embarrassment to the Thais but would arouse little outrage among the police or the public. The Royal Thai Police would say they are looking for the killer even if they were not. If a Brooklyn Mafia killer murdered an American cop in Bangkok, Tommy sensed so long as no Thais were hurt, it was considered an American problem, and the Thais would just as soon be left out of it completely.

He saw how easily Baxter maneuvered in this system, and in their own ways, so did the missing Russian and Samoan. Tommy saw how the police gave the gangsters a wide swathe to operate, so long as they paid them and didn't kill them. Tommy decided the knowledge that FBI agents could not be guaranteed safety in Thailand would mean eventually, the dogs would be called off. Digging deeper wasn't going to give them anything more to work with. Tommy once saw a news feature about the wall of plaques at FBI headquarters honoring FBI agents killed in the line of duty. She'd get a plaque at FBI headquarters and the matter would be forgotten.

Tommy had the front desk of the On Nut hotel call a cab and he told the driver to leave him off by the Phrom Phong BTS station, where by now he knew his way around and could take care of some pressing errands

Tommy ran his errands for almost two hours. His first stop was a barbershop with a red pole in front. He was able to convey that he wanted his head shaved. He left after seeing himself in the mirror and not recognizing himself at first. He tipped the barber well for having accomplished more than Tommy hoped for.

His second stop was a store selling over-the-counter sunglasses and contact lenses that did nothing but change the color of eyes. Johnny wanted his brown eyes to be blue. He walked out carrying a pair of mirror sunglasses and wearing the contacts that turned a black haired, brown eyed man into a shaved head man with blue eyes.

His third stop was a luggage store where he purchased a sleek attaché case and small backpack. He passed several street vendors selling clothing and was able to find two button-up shirts that fit him as well as a pair of knock-off Levi's purportedly in his size. The woman vendor suggested Tommy try it on by ducking behind a curtain adjacent to her stand, but Tommy declined, confident the pants would fit. He picked up socks and underwear at another stand. He stuffed his clothing purchases into his backpack and cabbed back to his hotel room. If his change of appearance registered with the staff at the front desk, it didn't show. One could not use the elevator without a room key in any event, so there was little incentive to scrutinize guests.

In the room, Tommy placed his gun in one of the upper compartments of the attaché case. He put on one of his new shirts and jeans and was soon leaving the room, attaché case in hand. When he returned from his missions, he would leave Bangkok. He hadn't yet decided where, but maybe that was best. No leaks if he himself didn't know.

Tommy arrived at the Rembrandt Hotel wearing his sport coat over one of the button-up shirts he'd bought. As he reached the end of the long curved driveway that fronted the hotel, he took note of the security cameras in front and to the sides of the lobby so he could avoid them. He spotted several in the lobby and sat in a chair away from any allowing a clear view of his face. If anyone noticed, they would have seen a blue-eyed man with a shaved head set his attaché case next to the armchair in the lobby where he parked himself, reading the English language newspaper he'd bought on the street.

Sooner or later, she's got to show up if she's not here already. Sooner or later, she'll have to come to the lobby or leave the hotel. That's my chance. If I have to stay here all night, I will.

He didn't even have to wait an hour. He was finishing the beer he ordered when he saw the blonde woman walk into the lobby flanked on each side by a Thai man in a suit. Tommy knew police guards when he saw them.

I should have thought about the possibility of cops guarding her in the hotel, walking her right to and from her room. Makes things difficult. He knew he couldn't risk shooting a Thai cop or even a civilian. That would not be easily forgotten here, like the shooting of an FBI agent would be.

I'll have to get a good shot when she's outside, he thought. It wouldn't be easy because Tommy wasn't as familiar with revolvers as he was with pistols. Revolvers were clumsier and less accurate, with less range. He'd have to get up close to have enough room to hit her and no one else.

Mary went to the elevators, followed by one of the cops. The other took a chair in the lobby, about twenty meters from Tommy. The cop wasn't looking in Tommy's direction, and the gangster returned to reading the paper.

Twenty minutes later, Mary and the cops returned to the lobby. She had changed from the severe business suit of the docks to a light cotton summer dress that she had clinched around her waist. *Good lookin' babe,* Tommy thought. *Almost a shame, but it's her or me. If she's alive, sooner or later she'll find me. I've seen that type of cop. Dead, the heat's on for a while then all will be clear. Couldn't whack a cop back home, but I ain't home and neither is she.* Tommy quickly made the sign of the cross on his chest, hoping it would help.

Tommy knew this woman would never let go until he was either dead or behind bars. He saw that in the look on her face when she was humiliated back at the docks. Behind the humiliation Tommy sensed revenge. The way she promised to pursue him back home. *Good luck, because I'll be gone, and you'll be dead.*

He again assured himself the Thai cop would forget the whole thing so long as none of his people were hurt. He had learned one thing in the almost two months he'd been in Thailand: if something was embarrassing, the Thais would like to forget about it and sweep it under the rug. As long as no one made a big deal about it, the Thai cops were not likely to do much. After all, there were no forced booze sales, one gangster went over to the feds and the other two were about to disappear, one to Brooklyn, one to who-knows where. If there was a problem, it was the Americans' problem, not the Thais'. That's how the Thais would see it.

Tommy didn't think the Americans were going to put a lot of time and energy looking for him if they had no idea where he was. The hijack victim got their money from insurance and all of the dead except Bobby Giannelli were mobbed up, not upstanding citizens.

At least, that's what Tommy hoped.

If Johnny stayed here, he too was safe. It rankled Tommy, but he knew this was part of the life he lived. Rats do surface regularly. It was Johnny's hypocrisy that upset Tommy the Turtle. *The nerve of the guy. He's telling me I gotta go back home and face the Boss and meanwhile he's the biggest rat of all.*

Mary left the lobby with a cop at each side. Tommy removed his jacket and left it on the chair. He unbuttoned his shirt as he walked towards the lobby doors, and when he was outside on the curbed driveway, removed and balled it up and dropped it into the trash can to the side of the lobby entrance. He made sure not to have his face in the camera sights. He was now wearing a white tank top t-shirt, known back in Brooklyn as a wife-beater. At the curb, he spotted Mary, and the Thai cops a half block away, walking towards Sukhumvit Road. *Probably going to a nearby restaurant.*

Tommy saw the line of motorcycle taxis lined up across the street. The first one in line had a helmet for passengers. Tommy hurried over, put the helmet on his head and pointed to the three people walking on the other side of the street, explaining he wanted to drive by them slowly because they were his friends. The driver knew enough English and pantomime to understand that he was to drive by them slowly. There wasn't much traffic on the street, and visibility was fine. As Tommy mounted the rear of the motorcycle taxi, he opened the attaché case locks. As the driver started to pull out to make the U-turn, Tommy opened the case and felt for the gun, which he withdrew and dropped the empty case on the street just as the motorcycle came within fifteen feet of Mary. The ride was too bumpy for Tommy to aim properly. Tommy yelled at the driver to slow down, and the motorcycle came to a near halt three feet from where Mary walked. Aside from the two cops, there were no people within twenty feet of her.

Good, Tommy thought. *I crossed myself because I don't want to kill any innocent people.*

Tommy steadied his shooting hand in the crook of his other elbow and found Mary's head within the line of the gun's sight. He pulled the trigger and the .32 caliber bullet entered Mary's neck on one side and came out the other, stopped by the wall of a building to Mary's right. Mary clutched her neck as blood flowed out and she pitched forward. The two cops hadn't figured out from where the shot came, and scanned the street in all directions, giving Tommy enough time to fire again, this time hitting Mary in the side of her head. She fell to the sidewalk. The cops were scanning the street, looking at the motorcycles and cars passing by, unable to see much detail in the gathering evening darkness. Tommy could see the pool of blood where Mary's head touched the sidewalk twenty feet away.

"Go!" Tommy screamed at the motorcycle taxi driver, who was not aware Tommy had fired the shots until he saw the gun Tommy was pointing at his face when he turned around to look at the gangster. The driver sped off. Two blocks later, within twenty meters of Sukhumvit Road, Tommy yelled at him to stop. The terrified driver put his hands in prayer position, gave Tommy a wai, and said one word: "Please."

Tommy laughed.

"I ain't gonna hurt you," he said. He reached into his pocket and handed the driver several thousand baht notes. "For the ride and the helmet," he said as he walked away. The driver pocketed the notes and sped away recklessly, thanking fate that there wasn't much traffic. He didn't look back. He was shaking, but he also knew the crazy farang with the gun had handed him for a two block ride more than he could earn in two weeks.

Tommy smiled as he watched the motorcycle driver flee the scene.

Glad it worked out well for him. And he never got any sort of look at me that would help identify the shooter.

They'll never match the bald guy with the nice jacket and shirt and attaché case with the guy on the motorcycle wearing a helmet and a wife beater. That nasty bitch FBI agent won't be making her report back home. They'll figure it was me did the broad, but the feds will never find me in Asia, and if they did, what's the proof? Not the way I'm gonna hide out. I bet Baxter can help me. Get me a passport, maybe some plastic surgery. I can pay him. The locals will forget me soon. I didn't whack any of them. And that guy at the Port already said we weren't doing anything wrong by being there. I'll be fine.

Tommy stuffed the gun back down the rear of his waistband. He removed the helmet as he walked. He passed yet another vendor selling shirts on the street. He bought a dark blue shirt that was just a tiny bit tight on him but covered the gun, even without his sport coat when he stuffed it a little further down. He put the helmet on the sidewalk as he tried on the shirt and left it there as if he had forgotten it. A few blocks away he passed an old man selling hats. He bought a cheap straw fedora. He put it on his shaved head and called out to a passing cab. Ten minutes later he was back in On nut and his secret hotel room.

Tommy was pleased with himself. He sat in his room, drinking a beer from the mini bar. He'd done well, better than Johnny or Paulie could have done.

The Thai cops and any feds would be looking for the Tommy Turterello like in the surveillance photo from Brooklyn, with a full head of wavy black hair and dark eyes. The hotel staff would have noted only a businessman in a nice jacket and shirt, with a shaved head and if anyone noticed, blue eyes, thanks to the contact lenses. The killer on the motorcycle wore a helmet and a wife beater. The guy who returned to the hotel had on a blue shirt and a straw hat.

I've driven them crazy.

There were no guarantees in life, as the Boss liked to remind his men. Tommy understood this but felt the way he handled this current problem was the closest thing to a guarantee he could realistically achieve. The course of Tommy's life was to be determined by two factors: first, how much effort the American government was going to apply in trying to solve the murder of an incompetent agent who should have stayed home in the first place; second, if the Thai officer, who seemed to be a lieutenant or a captain, would even think about this mess once all the foreign players were gone. Tommy's quarter century of working his way up in the mob convinced him neither was likely to happen.

Twenty-Four

"Don't worry, you'll get use to everything over here. Pretty soon it will be home to you," Glenn told Johnny after the Brooklyn native expressed his concerns about spending the rest of his life in a strange new country. Glenn spoke on the phone with the speaker on as he and Sleepy Joe sat around Glenn's dining room table drinking coffee. Johnny was in his hotel room.

"It's not that I don't like it, I do, but down the road, I don't speak the language, I don't look like the people here, I don't have their religion, I don't even know the names of their foods," Johnny said.

"The food part will come and it's the easiest," Sleepy Joe said. "And you don't need the language, look at me and Glenn. As for the religion, these people are cool about that, they don't care what religion someone is and they don't get all bent out of shape if someone is different, like you Catholics do." Johnny ignored the dig. He was learning not to take seriously everything Sleepy Joe said.

"There's another thing I'm afraid of," Johnny said. "I think that FBI lady has it in for me. Even after helping break up the liquor game and giving her everything I know about the Boss, she still looks at me like she'd like to put me away forever."

"I'm sure she does," Glenn said. "Another good reason to stay here in Thailand. Between the Lieutenant and the General, even if the U.S. takes any interest in you, they're getting nowhere."

"Enough of this depressing talk," Joe said loudly. "Let's smoke a joint." He flashed a large, rerolled joint he'd bought at one of the countless weed shops dotting the city.

Joe lit the joint, took two huge drags, and passed it to Glenn.

"Too bad you're not here with us, Johnny," Joe said. "We've got some fine weed."

"Never did smoke pot," he explained.

"You don't drink either, do you?" Glenn asked. Johnny said he never had a drop of alcohol.

"Do you at least use whores?" Joe asked, to which Johnny replied he did not.

"What kind of gangster are you?" Joe asked, and the three of them laughed.

The Lieutenant sped through the city in a squad car, horn sirens blaring and lights flashing as the driver ran through red lights. The minute he received the call, he ran out of his station house screaming for his best driver.

Ten minutes later the Lieutenant stood over Mary's body, covered by a blanket from the Hotel Rembrandt. He was careful not to step in the puddle of blood. Forensics was already on the scene, taking photos and gathering such evidence as they could, which included the bullet in the wall. The coroner at the Police Hospital would remove the one in her head.

The Lieutenant spoke with the officers he assigned to guard Mary. One had immediately started interviewing everyone on the street, and when the forensics team arrived, the other officer went up and down the street with a technician, checking security cameras. The only leads the two cops gathered were two people who heard a shot coming from the area from where they saw a motorcycle taxi speed away. The security cameras did not catch any of this. *The killer was lucky and stopped at the perfect location to avoid the cameras,* the Lieutenant thought. *Or was it more than luck?*

The Lieutenant shook his head. He was sorry about the farang woman's death, but when he thought about it longer, he understood it was her mistake. She threatened and insulted the American gangsters at the docks, just as she had insulted and humiliated Johnny. A good police officer, a smart one, never loses their composure on the job. Anger and threats are for the movies, not for real police work. Same with arrogance and thinking because you are law enforcement, you're better than everyone else. She did not understand that criminals are not normal people, they don't live by the rules of any society but their own, and that in their world, insults and humiliations have to be avenged. This was a life-threatening failure for a police officer, and Special Agent O'Halloran proved that to be true. He was glad to be done with this American problem.

Two somber looking representatives from the American Embassy arrived on the scene. One was a middle-aged woman with a short gray hair, clearly the senior official. She smoked several cigarettes while questioning the two officers assigned to protect Mary. The American woman spoke excellent Thai, which she then used to speak with the Lieutenant.

"I cannot tell you strongly enough just how disappointed my government is that one of our agents was murdered on a public street while supposedly protected by your people. Even more distressing, we were notified first by the hotel, not by the police or a government ministry."

The Lieutenant stood silent for ten seconds, and then smiled at the woman from the Embassy. He addressed her in English. He saw the startled look on her face when she heard his nearly accent-less English.

"Don't feel bad. I wanted to personally verify what happened before reporting anything to our American allies. My government is also disappointed. You allowed your domestic criminals to steal liquor, murder people, and then come here to threaten our businesses and steal our money by not paying taxes. Your FBI sent a fool to investigate, and she got herself killed. That's on your government, not ours. None of my men were harmed. Now please stop interfering in our investigation and go back to whatever it is you're doing when you're not getting in my way. And above all, stop sending us your criminals and your stolen goods. I have enough here, I don't need yours."

The man from the Embassy glared at the Lieutenant. He was Asian but not Thai, much younger than his colleague, short and wiry with close cropped hair, so gaunt he looked like a recent escapee from North Korea.

"You have no right to address an official from the United States Embassy in such a manner," he said. "I'm a liaison with your government, and I insist upon an apology right now." He offered his card to the Lieutenant, who waved him away.

"I'm too busy for you people," he said to the Americans. "You're interfering with a crime scene. Leave or I'll have you arrested."

"We are entitled to diplomatic immunity," the young American man huffed.

"You can bring that up with your lawyer in about a month, if we let you have a lawyer," the Lieutenant said, his smile even wider.

"You'll be hearing from us," the American man shouted as the two chastened Foreign Service Officers scurried away.

The ambulance took Mary's body to the police hospital. The U.S. Embassy would arrange for the remains to be repatriated, and none of this would be Thailand's problem any further.

When the Americans were gone, the Lieutenant asked his two officers why Mary was out on the streets when she knew his people were looking for the American gangsters and Tommy the Turtle was looking for Johnny and quite possibly her. The older of the two, a corporal in his late twenties, reminded the Lieutenant that his orders were to stay at Mary's side wherever she went. Why would that be said if she were to be confined to her room? And could the Thai police restrain an American FBI agent who came into the country with certain limited law enforcement privileges?

I'm keeping my eye on this one, the Lieutenant thought. *A mind like that can't stay on the streets forever. Make sure he takes the next sergeant exam.*

The Lieutenant thanked them for their service, apologized for making them think he doubted their capabilities.

"You're right, I couldn't order her to do anything she didn't want to do so long as she wasn't breaking our laws, in which case she could be detained. She was supposed to be an experienced expert on the Mafia, yet she throws away every precaution at the most dangerous moment."

"She was very arrogant," one of the cops said. "Always telling us how to do our job, how we Thais were a century behind the Americans in policing. Look where that got her."

The Lieutenant shook his head.

"Why can't all Americans be like Glenn?" he silently asked himself.

The General told the Lieutenant not to worry. He took the Lieutenant's call just as he was about to enter the lobby of the building where he was housing his latest mia noi, an up-and-coming actress on a Thai soap opera.

"Remember my dear old friend, Colonel Somchai?" the General asked, phone pressed to his ear as he entered the building. "He was a top intelligence officer for decades, and he still keeps his ties to the Americans he worked with. One of them just so happens to be the current American Ambassador's chief of staff. A well-placed call from Somchai, and those two will be on a plane back to the states within twenty four hours."

"I don't want that to happen," the Lieutenant said. "I'm not interested in punishing them or ruining their careers. I just want them to treat Thais with more respect."

"I've taken note of that," the General replied. "Now I've got to go."

I'm getting too soft, the Lieutenant thought as he put his phone back in his pocket.

Paulie accepted Tommy's idea that the safest course of action was to change one suitcase full of baht into dollars while waiting for Johnny, but he did not fully accept that Tommy would still be there when he returned. *At least I'll have half the money, and if the Boss is already thinking Tommy is a traitor and a problem, he'll be thankful I saved it.* He had no regrets now about having asked Baxter to get him the Glock and a few clips of ammunition. Baxter was at first hesitant, but one of the gold coins and a half dozen hundred dollar bills changed his mind. He felt more secure with it while he dragged a suitcase full of baht, which would soon be a suitcase full of dollars. He needed a cab to take him to Chinatown.

He knew there was a cab line in front of the big, fancy hotel around the corner from his own. His suitcase's wheels glided effortlessly over the granite floors of his hotel lobby, but on the street, the cracked and broken pavement slowed him down. When he reached the curb, he stepped over it, pulled the suitcase filled with baht over as well, and once he was in the street itself, he turned to look left, just as he always did in Brooklyn.

The problem was, he wasn't in Brooklyn, he was in Bangkok Thailand, where they drive on the opposite side of America, so he should have looked to his right. He had been made aware of this difference from the U.S., but a lifetime of living in a right-side world of drivers caused him momentary lapses. In Thailand, such lapses are regularly noted in the English and Thai language newspapers.

This lapse meant Paulie did not see the yellow cab speeding down the numbered soi, uncharacteristically free of clogged traffic. The driver saw Paulie, and honked vigorously, but there wasn't enough space between the front of his cab and Paulie to avoid a collision.

Paulie's last thought before his head struck the pavement thirty feet away and cracked open like a coconut was how Tommy should have been with him to grab the suitcase.

The cab drove off without stopping.

Dang stood two feet behind the farang as they both waited to cross the street. Dang's mind was not on the farang, whom she didn't notice. Dang reflected on the reality that she'd been working as a junior accountant for three years and had not saved even half of what was needed to complete the full transition. Dang was fortunate to work in an office where most people were educated Thais who used the term "transgender" rather than the ultimately disrespectful "*katoy,*" or the equally insulting and degrading "ladyboy." When Dang said she wished to be referred to in the feminine gender, there was no resistance. The problem was trying to save for the procedures and at the same time save for the nice house she promised her parents in Isan.

Dang turned towards the sound of the noise, a very loud thump followed by the scream of a farang man. Dang knew it was a farang man because after several years of working with foreign customers, the lack of real tone and accent was always present in their voices, even when they screamed. Dang watched the man fly through the air and land on his head on the other side of the yellow line in the middle of the street that divided traffic moving in different directions. He landed in such a way that for a moment it looked to Dang as if he were doing a headstand before his head collapsed onto the asphalt, one side of his face pressing against the black surface. His body folded over so that his toes and knees reached the ground. He looked like a truncated and inverted letter V, his head lying at that impossible angle.

There wasn't much traffic, so Dang hurried over to where the body lay. When Dang was within a few feet, she saw the blood pooling under the head had formed a fast-growing puddle. Dang was quite certain the farang man broke his neck upon landing. There was no doubt this white-skinned, black-haired man was a farang. There was also no doubt he was dead.

The suitcase was no more than a foot from Dang's feet, as was the gun lying next to the dead man. Dang knew farangs were not supposed to have guns in the Kingdom, so something was wrong.

Dang eyed the suitcase lying where the cab had struck the farang. There were no people between her and the suitcase, and she didn't see anyone else looking at it.

There are no police officers to turn it over to, Dang reflected. *If there were, they'd probably keep it for themselves anyway. Maybe there's something I can sell. The suitcase looks expensive, probably worth a few thousand baht.*

Dang set the suitcase upright, gripped the handle, and rolled it away.

There weren't many people on the sidewalks and the few that were present were either shocked or disinterested, so taking the suitcase and moving forward was easy. No one said a word and she wasn't aware of anyone watching her. Any interested eyes were on the dead farang in the middle of the street.

After wheeling the suitcase for a block, Dang spotted a motorcycle taxi waiting at the corner. The driver put the suitcase in the space between him and the front of the motorcycle and Dang took the back seat. The driver stopped in front of Dang's building five minutes later, handed her the suitcase, and smiled at the generous tip. A minute later, Dang and the suitcase were in the elevator going up, and two minutes after that, both were safely ensconced in Dang's studio apartment.

The suitcase was zipped but not locked. Dang opened it and fainted upon seeing the piles of thousand baht notes.

TEN MINUTES LATER

"I'm getting tired of looking at dead farangs," the Lieutenant said to his driver-plainclothes officer as they stood over Paulie. "Such a violent people," he said, shaking his head as he stared at the gangster's broken body. The Lieutenant took a picture of the dead man's face, which he of recognized, and sent it to Johnny on the secure phone he left him. He typed a short question under the photo: "No doubt?"

"Excuse me sir, but it does appear both the deceased were the victims of violence, not the perpetrators," the plainclothes officer replied. "This one may be an accident. He was surely struck by a vehicle, which some observers say was a cab, but no one has a plate number or any other description. There weren't many people out on this street at that time and no one was paying attention to this farang. No one even noticed him until he went sailing through the air, and that was after he was struck, so little information on the vehicle. Whoever it was just drove away."

"Well, then it's their karma," the Lieutenant said. "I'd like to know what a victim is doing running around with a loaded Glock. How did he get one?" *He does know Baxter,* the Lieutenant reminded himself.

A member of the forensic team gingerly lifted the gun from the street in gloved hands and deposited it into an evidence bag. A minute later Johnny returned the call and told the Lieutenant it was surely Paulie "The Arranger" Arginotti. The Lieutenant detected sadness in Johnny's voice.

When the body was taken away, the Lieutenant turned to the plainclothesman.

"Paulie is dead, and Johnny is with us. That leaves only Tommy the Turtle."

"Is he now the focus of a manhunt?" the younger policeman asked.

"No," the Lieutenant replied. "Based on my experience, a farang criminal on their own will meet with one of two outcomes. Either he will disappear into our crowded nation and cause no trouble, or he will be killed. Either way, it's not a problem for Thailand."

"It's not a problem to have a criminal running around on the loose?" the plainclothesman asked. "Even if he is not presently a threat, are we to allow a criminal to walk free without a worry in the world?"

"He can join the crowd," the Lieutenant replied.

Tommy the Turtle adjusted the seat belt so that it stretched over his large body. The driver of the SUV pulled away from the curb in front of the hotel in On Nut. Tommy didn't look back. He'd be in Hua Hin in less than three hours.

Tommy was still amazed at how cheap everything was in Thailand. This private car was taking him to the seaside resort in Hua Hin, three hours away, for little more than he would pay for a Saturday night cab ride from Little Italy back to Brooklyn. Baxter assured him he would love the accommodations. Baxter warned Tommy that the beaches in Hua Hin were fine to walk along, but they were rocky and not really the best beaches in Thailand. Tommy didn't care because he was at heart a night person who generally avoided the sun and thus was not a true beach person.

Baxter also arranged for Tommy to visit a plastic surgeon in Hua Hin. The small seaside city was very affluent, and a favorite retreat for wealthier Thais and farangs. In Thailand, as everywhere, medical services were drawn to money like bears to honey, and there was no shortage of top specialists in Hua Hin.

"No one will recognize you after this guy is done," Baxter assured Tommy. The fee would be less than ten thousand dollars, leaving Tommy with more than enough for what he was now referring to as his "transition." Tommy understood that plastic surgery would not alter his fingerprints or his DNA, but if he was not spotted and identified, no one would be checking either. Tommy had no intention of being caught.

Glenn and the General were finishing their dinner at the NJA Club when Edward joined them without asking.

"Any word from your belligerent and homophobic countryman?" Edward asked Glenn. "If you hear from him, let him know we believe in second chances here at the NJA Club."

"Now that's something I can agree with," Glenn said."

"But your agreement does not answer my question," Edward replied.

The General cast his gaze on Edward.

"Glenn has indeed answered the question," the General said. "The absence of a positive response can in this instance mean that Glenn has not heard from Johnny or that Glenn doesn't want you to know anything. You have your answer."

"Which is?" Edward asked.

"None of your business," the General answered.

After the waitress removed the dinner plates, the General bought Edward a drink to show he meant nothing by his banter. Edward ordered the most expensive single malt scotch the bar stocked. Ray the Bartender once told Glenn it was among the best in the world. The General didn't seem to care. He also knew Glenn had reached his limit of one drink a day when they had pre-dinner martinis, so he told the waitress to refill Glenn's glass of sugar-free soda.

"Edward, I know you hear rumors, many of them," the General said. "What I can tell you is that any you may have heard about American Mafia thugs trying to force stolen liquor on Thai buyers are nothing to be concerned about. The matter has been resolved."

"What makes you think I hear rumors?" Edward asked.

"Because I do," the General said.

The drinks arrived and the three men toasted by clinking their glasses. Glenn spoke.

"Edward, let me clarify things. You will eventually see Johnny, most likely right here at the NJA Club. I am convinced he is a changed person, and he would never act the way he did that night. I usually don't buy battlefield conversions, but this one I believe. All I ask is for you and Rinaldo to give him a chance."

"I already told you we're over it. At least I am. Can't say how Rinaldo feels at this moment, since he's back in Argentina."

"I hope it was not due to any problems, either with the Thai government or with you," Glenn said.

Edward sipped his drink before replying. The General and Glenn saw from the look on Edward's face how much the costly single malt scotch pleased him.

I couldn't tell the difference between the good stuff and the cheapest crap, Glenn thought. *They all taste like paint thinner to me.*

"Ricardo's dream is to own a chain of martial arts studios in his country," Edward said. "I like it here in Thailand."

Glenn and the General nodded. They knew of many foreigners who lived in Thailand only a short time before returning to their homelands. Edward and Glenn were among those in for the long haul.

"Seems like we've worked out everything," the General said. "Edward has no problem with Johnny coming here, and from now on, all of you are friends. Agreed?"

Glenn and Edward agreed by clinking their glasses once more. The General was pleased. He smiled and called over the waitress.

"Another round for Edward and me," he said. "Glenn will break tradition and have a second martini tonight. No argument from you, Counselor."

Glenn knew this was one of those times you didn't say "no" to the General. "Submitted, Your Honor," he said. Glenn realized how long it had been since he'd uttered those words, words he said every day when he was a criminal lawyer slogging his way through the courts of the San Francisco Bay Area. *I don't miss it at all,* he assured himself. *Or do I?*

Glenn always thought of trial lawyers as rock stars entertaining the jury. He enjoyed the reality that for hours a day, a jury had their eyes on him, much the same way an audience had their eyes on Bruce Springsteen, Mick Jagger, or David Lee Roth. It took a strong ego to bear the judgment that went with the observations, but if one was good, like Bruce, Mick, and Diamond Dave, the good reviews far outweighed the bad. It wasn't all that different in criminal defense, where even after losing a case, lawyers received excellent reviews.

"You can only build with what you have," a judge once told Glenn after the jury returned a guilty verdict. "And most of the time you defense lawyers aren't given a whole lot to build with."

The judge was correct. Glenn, like every criminal defense lawyer, recognized he was in a profession where the very best of the lot nearly always lost. Glenn had a better-than-average acquittal rate, but still lost more than he won.

Who picks a job like that? Is that why I'm here?

Winning cases, especially tough ones, resulted in better offers for prosecutors, so the risk of losing went down. Glenn's rule of thumb had been to never try a case he didn't think he had a reasonable chance of winning at trial, but on occasion, an obstinate defendant insisted on a kamikaze mission. Those were the worst, because after conviction and lengthy sentences, those clients always forgot Glenn's entreaties to accept a good deal. His good friend and colleague Charlie advised Glenn to ignore these disgruntled clients, but one of Glenn's problems was that he couldn't.

If only every client had been like Johnny Brancini.

∾

The Deputy Director stared across his desk at the head of the FBI's organized crime unit. Both men looked as if they had just swallowed something very unpleasant. They were stocky, short-haired, middle-aged men in their early fifties, with weary eyes and dark suits. They had reached the highest levels of management in an agency where this took decades. However, it only took seconds for a career to be ruined, for a demotion to be carried out immediately, for an exile to the sub-offices in the Dakotas, Maine, or Alaska. The Deputy Director sipped from his official FBI mug. *Government office coffee really sucks,* he thought. *I'm being paid enough to bring in my own coffee maker and some decent beans.* The bad coffee only made a bad morning worse.

"Whose brilliant idea was it to send an agent with no background in facing violence and no actual work in the field?" he asked the unit head. "How did she manage to meet with the Embassy, and I didn't even know she was over there?"

The organized crime unit head looked down at his well-polished shoes and then at his boss.

"It was run up the chain through her immediate supervisor in New York, through the head of the office, and then through my deputy and myself. No one thought this was important enough to be brought to your attention. We know how busy you are. Special Agent O'Halloran was sent over purely to investigate, talk to the local authorities, find anyone who might be a resource. She was absolutely not to make any arrests, not to take part in any stakeouts, not to be anywhere near where a firearm might be discharged, surely not carry one. This is all in the written orders and memorialized in our meetings minutes. She is, or rather was, a researcher and investigator, not a field agent, personally and directly confronting criminals."

The Deputy Director considered what the unit chief had just said. He took another sip of his bad coffee, grimaced and promised not to drink any more.

"And how did Special Agent O'Halloran wind up working with this Thai police lieutenant, the one who reported her death to the Embassy? It was a most reluctant report as I understand it. Someone from the hotel called the Embassy when they saw that an American guest had been shot. This procedure would of course be known to a high ranking policeman responding to such a crime scene. He thus had no choice but to make his own call or it would appear suspicious. Just covering his tracks while hoping to cover it all up."

An uncomfortable silence followed, broken by the organized crime unit head.

"The police officer was referred by the Embassy. He's known as reliable, honest, smart, and efficient. Plus, he speaks excellent English. If I may be so bold, sir, the lieutenant may have had his own reasons, but keeping the lid on this now does benefit everyone. This operation was a complete failure. The hijacking has not been solved. The booze was brought to Thailand and sold, and the Mafia got the money. Our agent was shot dead on a public street while protected by two Thai police. A street she should have never been walking on if she knew a wanted Mafia gunman was running amok."

The Deputy Chief nodded. He looked at his mug and pushed it away.

"This lieutenant filed no report with his own department, and apparently some retired Thai military intelligence officer has prevailed upon the Ambassador to make certain the two Foreign Service Officers who showed up forget they were ever there."

"You think they will?" the organized crime man asked.

"Absolutely," the Deputy Director replied. "They have to deal with the same obstacles as us. They anger a superior the wrong way, there goes their career. I'd bet those two Embassy people dream of their next posting being Paris, Geneva, or London. I bet they don't want Cameroon or Paraguay any more than we want Minot, North Dakota, or Homer, Alaska."

"So, what are we going to do?' the unit chief asked.

"We're going to quietly take Special Agent O'Halloran off the books. There's no reason to keep paying someone who's dead. We'll create a record showing she resigned for personal reasons. Down the road, when everything has died down, we'll create a death certificate that no one will question. There will be no body, of course. The Thai cop saw to it that she was cremated earlier this morning our time. Don't ask me what he plans to do with the ashes."

The organized crime head thought for a moment.

"Our records show she's married. What about her husband?"

"We've worked that out," the Deputy Director said. "The husband will be told his wife came across some compelling evidence while overseas, and she will be in deep undercover for several months. He cannot have any direct contact, but we'll of course be happy to pass any messages back and forth. Our document people will be able to perfectly mimic Mary's writing style."

"How long can we pull the wool over his eyes?" the unit head asks.

The Deputy Director frowned in a way that made him look sad, not angry.

"A few months. The poor man has stage four cancer. He's getting by on painkillers."

"And his wife left him alone? If we knew, she would never have been sent. We have other experts on the Brooklyn Mob who could have gone, and they would have stuck to their role of investigate and research, no cowboy stuff."

"This is off the record, you understand because it's all based on unverified scuttlebutt given to me just this morning. From what I hear, their marriage was in the dead letter box before he was diagnosed. Maybe he was relieved to be left alone in peace for a while."

"Good," the organized crime head said. "That's all he's getting from now until the end. Anyone else who might be looking for Mary O'Halloran down the road we should be worried about?"

The Deputy Director shook his head.

"As you know from your own background checks, she was an only child and both parents are deceased. She listed her supervisor in New York as the backup contact after her husband. She's moved around quite a bit with the Bureau, eight offices in her fifteen years with us. That doesn't allow much time to develop deep relationships, especially when you're a cop and everyone is suspicious of being around you. So almost anyone she knows, anyone who might think of her, is with us, and I think you know what that means."

"I do," the organized crime chief replied. "With no report, and any trace of Special Agent O'Halloran disappearing, this means the Brooklyn Mob gets away with a hijacking, a few murders, smuggling, tax evasion, not to mention the likely murder of one of ours."

"You win some, you lose some," the Deputy director said. "Either way, it comes to an end."

"Oh yes," the Deputy Director said. "The Thai officer insisted upon working with an American lawyer who lives over there. No issues with him, but I see the late Special Agent did promise him a former client would be getting a pardon if he cooperated with her, which he did. I'm assuming he wants his man out, and I don't think we want any declarations about this showing up in court, do we?"

"Of course not," the organized crime head replied. "What do we do?"

"I'll call the governor and tell him to sign a pardon," the Deputy director said.

"If he balks?" the organized crime chief asked.

"Then I'll let him know what we have on him," the Deputy Director said.

"That takes care of that," the organized crime man said. "I have other things I need to discuss with you, but they can wait till next time. How about if we take a break and get out of this tomb for short while?"

"Love to," the Deputy Director said. "I'm dying for a good cup of coffee."

TWENTY-FIVE

SIX MONTHS LATER

Robert Starr gazed out at the Gulf of Thailand from the restaurant's second-floor veranda. The morning sun dappled the calm waters with white droplets. A gentle breeze held the perfect temperature, and Robert was exceptionally comfortable in his tropical-weight cotton khakis and white two-button shirt with blue piping around the collar.

Despite the name on the American passport, he was not Robert Starr. He was Tommy Turterello, aka The Turtle. Robert Starr was a creation of Baxter's forger. The face on the photo and on Turterello/Starr himself was the work of Baxter's plastic surgeon. Baxter's visa man took care of getting Starr a retirement visa.

Tommy lived in a condo unit Baxter owned in a well-guarded development. Tommy paid him a year's rent in advance. There was no reason for Baxter to be in contact with Tommy, but he called him every few weeks to check in on him.

"It's awfully nice of you, but it's not really necessary," Tommy told Baxter on more than one occasion.

"Hey, I just want to make sure that if I ever need a man of your talents, he's alive and available," Baxter would respond.

Not on your life, Tommy thought when this was raised. *The three of us came here as made men in the Mafia. Now we're all out of the game for three different reasons, but we're all out. We know Paulie ain't getting back in, I doubt Johnny's thinking of double-crossing the local cops, and when the lease ends, I'm taking off to where Baxter can't find me. Baxter's forger and visa guy ain't the only ones in this country, that's for sure.*

Robert aka Tommy met a woman that day. They were both in the new mall, checking out a stand promoting clear sunscreen, which seemed like a Nobel winning discovery to Tommy. The attractive Thai woman asked him if he had ever tried it, and he replied he had not. He asked her why she was interested.

"I didn't think Thai people got sunburned," he said.

The woman laughed.

"We can get burned, but it would take a very long time," she said. "Mostly it's because we don't want to get dark." Her English was excellent

"Wouldn't it be good to be dark in a place where the sun is always blazing?" he asked.

"Maybe to a farang, not to a Thai," she said.

Robert aka Tommy invited her to have coffee with him, and when they finished, they exchanged contact information. He asked her to dinner the following night, her last in Hua Hin. She mentioned she was enjoying a brief get away after recovering from a minor injury.

"Nothing serious, I hope," he told her. "You look fine right now."

"Thank you," the woman replied. "It was a torn meniscus in my knee that kept me out of action for a while. Too much jogging. Now I'm fully recovered and back to work next week."

Over dinner, she told Robert aka Tommy she worked in Bangkok in financial services. He said he was fortunate as a younger man to have known several of the key people in a few Silicon Valley startups, and a modest amount of investment allowed him to retire a few years ago and enjoy life. When the woman mentioned she planned another trip to Hua Hin the following month, he told her to call him right before she left Bangkok, and they'd see each other. She told him she would like that very much.

Robert aka Tommy walked her back to her hotel, near the restaurant. They discussed the merits of Hua Hin as they strolled.

"I love it here," he said.

"So do I," she replied. "See you next month."

Johnny Brancini sat at the bar at the NJA Club, nursing a diet coke. He had finished his late-lunch hamburger, which would tide him over until dinner with Fah later that night. He enjoyed sitting at the long teakwood bar with the mirror running the whole length of its wall. He didn't drink but did imbibe the fantastic storytelling of Ray the Bartender. The Lieutenant needed Fah to translate into Thai the written statement of an Englishman who witnessed a serious crime, and she wouldn't be home until after seven.

NJA Club was now his regular venue, and Ray, the Irish bartender, reminded him of many barkeeps he'd encountered in Brooklyn. For a man who never touched alcohol, Johnny spent a lot of time hanging out in bars and drinking club soda when he was with the Mafia, because Mafiosos have a preternatural tendency to be where the alcohol lies. None of the Brooklyn watering holes had a bartender quite like Ray.

"The wife is working with the police now, I hear," Ray said in the Irish lilt that had not diminished one bit in all his years in the Kingdom. Ray donated a bottle of top flight champagne to the little wedding party held at the NJA club after the Buddhist ceremony three months ago. Neither Johnny nor Fah drank, but they appreciated the gesture.

"The General and Sleepy Joe don't provide enough protection for you, Sonny?" Ray asked. He often referred to Johnny as "Sonny." Johnny did not understand why, nor did he care. Ray could call him whatever he liked so long as he kept the stories and the companionship flowing.

Ray could also joke about Johnny being in danger because everyone knew he wasn't. Having Sleepy Joe and the General as friends was certainly reassuring, and the Lieutenant had promised Johnny that he was not under investigation by the United States and never would be. The Lieutenant declared this a few weeks after the Thais closed their case with the deaths of Mary and Paulie, the defection of Johnny and the disappearance of Tommy, whom the Thais officially listed as "likely to have fled the country." The Lieutenant had joined Johnny and Fah for lunch on a mutual day off. Johnny was at first skeptical, telling the Lieutenant it seemed the murder of an FBI agent would be a reason to keep investigating, but the Lieutenant assured Johnny that on that point he was wrong.

"We get different results here," he explained.

Johnny refocused on the present. He answered Ray's crack about the General and Joe not being enough protection.

"You may think having the cops on top of our NJA friends is overkill, but if Cambodia invades, I'm in good shape."

"You're getting a sense of humor, Sonny," Ray said. "I must say, though, from the sound of it, a bit of our friend Glenn is rubbing off on you. That's the kind of thing he'd say."

"Glenn's the first normal friend I ever had, besides you, and it's a close case about you being normal." Ray made an angry face then relaxed it to show he was not really angry.

"Everyone here is good," Ray replied, "If someone isn't good, Wang or I kick them out."

"Like I once got kicked out," Johnny said.

"You kicked yourself out that time, but it's all worked out. We are a forgiving bunch around here. You picked a hell of a good place to land, Sonny."

And to think I didn't want to come here in the first place.

When Johnny saw Glenn and Sleepy Joe enter the NJA Club, he told Ray he'd see him later and went over to join his two friends. They told Johnny that Oliver would be dropping by as well and they were going to have dinner and then watch a movie or two over at Glenn's condo, and he was welcome to join them.

"I appreciate the offer, but Fah and I have to get up early tomorrow. We're going to look at a condo that might work for us. Not too far from here in fact." He didn't have to add that with Fah's salary from the Thai Royal Police and Johnny's consulting fees from the General and Oliver, the couple could afford a condo in one of Bangkok's better neighborhoods. The NJA Club was almost at the dividing point between Thong Lor and Ekamai, two neighborhoods within that category. That was also the area where Glenn lived.

The General discovered Johnny was a fountainhead of knowledge about hijackings, extortions, loansharking, and other criminal activities against which the General's security company clients needed protection, and he regularly paid for his advice on how to stop the bad guys.

Oliver joined the group. He clapped Johnny on the back before seating himself.

"Need to pick your brain about this case I have, one an overseas police department has asked me to consult upon. I see organized crime's fingerprints all over it, and I suspect a man of your experience can guide me in the right direction, help me figure out who and what I ought to be looking at. I'm getting government rates, mind you, so I can't be as generous as last time, but I'll make it worth your while."

Johnny and Oliver agreed to meet at Oliver's condo the next morning. Oliver would be leaving for his favored retreat on the beautiful island of Koh Phanang right after the meeting. Ten minutes later, they left together, Johnny going home to meet his wife, Oliver planning to call his favorite masseuse over for the evening. He clapped Glenn on the shoulder as he walked by him.

"Get yourself down to the island," he said. "This place will be here when you get back."

When Glenn and Sleepy Joe were alone, Glenn expressed his delight that everything had worked out so well for Johnny, and the unpleasant ordeal was over.

"I'm not the sensitive type," Sleepy Joe said, "but I still feel bad about that FBI lady. She didn't deserve to die like that, shot in the throat and the face on a public street. By a damn American Mafia gangster."

"I feel very bad as well," Glenn said, knowing his friend could not feel the strange blend of shock and sadness with relief, an emotion that can be experienced only by a man who learns of the death of a woman he did not want known he had slept with. "She made some serious mistakes. She made it personal when she insulted those mobsters at the docks and then she compounded the situation by going out on the street where any fool would realize they are an easy target. But she didn't deserve to die just because she made mistakes."

"Something's been bothering me," Joe said. "I recall you telling me the Lieutenant's instructions were that Mary was not to go anywhere when not accompanied by those two police guards, am I right?" Joe emphasized the words "go anywhere."

"The General told me that was what one of the guards claimed, but added the Lieutenant denied it," Glenn said. "The Lieutenant says his orders to her were to stay in her room, and she disobeyed. What were the two guards supposed to do? They had no legal right to detain her, so they did the next best thing and went with her. Nothing about this is in any report because there are none. Not by either country."

Sleepy Joe stroked the three day stubble on his bony chin.

"Good," he said. "If there were reports, we'd probably be in them."

Glenn and Sleepy Joe understood the Lieutenant wanted the episode off his plate forever. He was happy to see the crisis in Thailand end, content to allow America to prosecute their gangsters in the States.

"No concern to the Thais. The money would have gone to the insurance company that paid off the hijack victims," Joe noted.

"Well, even if the bad guy got away, probably with all the money, at least neither of us killed anyone this time." *At least I hope not.*

"Good point," Sleepy Joe said. "And on that note, I'm taking leave of the club tonight. There's a rugby match on Australian television. I'll just lie in bed smoking a joint and watching my sport. See you tomorrow, Glenn."

~

Sleepy Joe really did go to his room, the location of which was a secret known only to him. He remained less than five minutes, all he needed to gather what he wanted.

On the way to the BTS, Joe dropped the fancy Italian loafers inside the doorway of a store that had just closed. *Someone who needs shoes will find them tonight.*

He took the BTS Skytrain to the Nana station, where he made certain to exit on the side of Sukhumvit Road he wanted. He was on the other side of Sukhumvit Road from Soi Nana, so there were no bargirls calling out, only dangerous-looking freelancers who Joe knew carried disease, criminal intent, or both. They leaned against the buildings or lined the curbs and eyed any farang man foolish enough to approach. Three blocks up from where he exited he reached the object of his search.

"It was you that arranged to take them away, wasn't it?" Sleepy Joe asked the stocky middle-aged woman hovering over a table filled with displays of sunglasses. Even after eight at night, there is a market for sunglasses in a land where everyone could use a pair.

"*Chai,*" she replied, using the Thai word for "yes," one of the only words Joe understood,

"English, please," he said.

"They bad men. Hurt many people selling. Take money from all of us many time. Police no help us. You do. You not like bad people. I know. I think police always make trouble for farang, want money, don't help poor people.

"I follow you that time. You don't see me. I have feeling when you look at them and follow, I know how you thinking. I right, because I see you kill them. I no want you get in trouble. I help."

Sleepy Joe stared at the woman.

Who would have thought? Well, if I were still Aussie Special Forces, probably me.

"How did you get three bodies out of that street without anyone seeing? And what happened to the bodies?"

The woman smiled. Two upper gold teeth shined.

"You not have to know. I work here long time, know many people."

Sleepy Joe nodded. *Does it matter anymore?*

"For your troubles," he said, handing her the envelope he had stuffed in his pocket. It contained fifty of the newest thousand baht notes. The woman took the envelope, gave a wai, and the two stood there looking at each other in silence.

"I like those mirror sunglasses over there," Joe said, pointing to a pair. The woman moved them from the holder and handed that to Joe, who put the sunglasses in his pants pocket. Not another word was said. Joe turned around and walked away.

The Boss savored the thick and heavy smoke he drew from the seven inch Churchill cigar. He let it rest in his mouth a few seconds more before exhaling a cloud of smoke. He had just returned home from his monthly meeting with the crooked cop who fed him any information about law enforcement investigations that might impact the Boss's family. They met every month on the same date for morning Mass at a church near the Boss's home. They sat in a pew a few rows from the very rear and talked after the legitimate worshippers left. The priests and altar boys all knew the Boss and were careful to stay out of ear-length of his conversations. Before ending a meeting with this cop, the Boss always places a fat envelope between them.

The cop had access to even the most sensitive FBI reports. He assured the Boss there had been no reports by anyone after the night of the hijacking, and little was known other than the booze was stolen and three made men and two employees disappeared, including the unfortunate Bobby Giannelli.

"How sure can you be that nothing's gonna come of this stuff in Thailand?" the Boss had asked.

The cop answered in a slow and deliberate cadence.

"If there's not a single report, not a single word about it over a six-month period, we can safely assume none will ever be written. Police reports are considered reliable because they're written as close to the events as possible. No one writes them six months after a known event. You got off easy."

Easy? the Boss thought, weighing the cop's words as sat in his favorite reclining chair, his corpulent frame sinking into the plush leather. *I lost my right-hand man and consigliere, my top dealmaker, and my main tough guy. The clowns I got now are the best I could get my hands on, and they ain't like the old-school guys I just lost. I lost an insider who set up the hijack, and a close family friend also disappeared with him. The Santuccis lost three men and they think I was somehow mixed up with the hijack. Everyone figures it was Tommy's hijack, and since Tommy worked for me, the Santuccis can't be too happy with me. And I never saw a single penny from the booze.*

"Nothing's like it used to be," the cop said softly.

The Boss asked the cop if he learned anything new about Bobby Giannelli.

"Not much," the cop replied. "He wasn't supposed to work but filled in for someone who had an emergency. He drove the truck that was hijacked. After he left the warehouse, he was never seen again. We're sure the other guy in the truck with Giannelli was bent. The guy was at least forty grand in the hole over gambling, and the calls were getting nastier. He has lower-level mob guys in his family. We had him on a taped call to one a few months ago, offering to sell booze the day after a hijacking went down in Flatbush. Another cousin worked for that distributor. We think some beef broke out between this inside guy and Tommy's hijack crew, and your pal got caught in the crossfire. Sorry for your loss."

The Boss next inquired about how Santucci now saw things.

"Our informants tell us the old man is hopping mad," the cop explained. "The hijacking was done in your territory by your man. Tony Santucci knows that the day of the hijacking and disappearance of Bobby and the insider, three of his men disappeared. Low-level guys, but all were made men and made men can only be whacked on the orders of the head of their family, and Tony's approval would be needed here. Tony figures Tommy was behind his guys disappearing, and since you're the head of his family, he blames you, though he's got no proof. You're a big man, well connected, his equal, so it's unlikely he'll make a move against you on such weak facts. I'd still watch my back if I were you. One more screw-up and you can become an easy target."

The last question the Boss had asked was about Johnny. The cop said that the organized crime experts were divided on whether Johnny had become a rat.

"He's married to a woman who works for the cops, and no one's bothering him. Raises questions, but if you want my opinion, Johnny's no rat. If he was, by now, you and a bunch of others would have been arrested. I think that when the booze thing went sideways and Paulie was dead, and Tommy gone with the wind, Johnny decided it was time to bail and start a new life. I hear lots of guys go over to Thailand for that very reason. Sounds like Johnny got out before the shit hit the fan, and if he's married to a police employee, I'd say he's safe in a place like that. Especially if he's got some money with him."

The Boss couldn't stop thinking about Johnny after the bent cop left. Johnny was to be his successor, his most trusted business and personal adviser. If mob bosses could have real friends, the Boss thought Johnny was his. Things were bad and getting worse, but however much he missed him, the Boss knew Johnny made the right choice.

If I had the chance to get away clean, I would too.

On the other side of the United States, Freddie Trammel punched in for his shift at the parking garage on Stockton Street. His cousin took him to the DMV to take his road and written tests and let him practice on his old Honda Civic. Freddy had never scratched a single car of the thousands he had parked the last several months.

Freddie had no idea why the governor decided to pardon him. All he knew was that he was innocent and there must be someone up there looking out for him.

Six weeks after their dinner in Hua Hin, the woman called Tommy and said she'd be there in five days. She referred to him as Robert, like everyone else did these days.

Tommy felt a warm glow inside. As much as he enjoyed the safety and calmness of his existence, he often felt lonely. In Brooklyn he was never alone, and here he almost always was. Maybe not as much if things worked out right.

"First I'm going to Isan for a few days to check up on a house I'm having built for my parents," she explained. "I'll fly down after I'm done."

"Knee all fixed up?" he asked. She said it was fine.

She asked the man she knew as Robert how things were coming along for him.

"Still loving it, but it is a big change from what I'm used to. Change is hard. Even a change you're glad you made."

I can understand that, Dang thought.

ACKNOWLEDGMENTS

Bangkok Changes is the fourth book in the NJA series, and my first acknowledgment must go to those readers who inspire me to keep writing. Glenn and the rest of the NJA gang feel the same.

Barry Weissman read the final draft before it went to the proofreader. His eagle eye for errors and his wise suggestions improved the draft with an efficiency that would be the envy of any editor anywhere. He knows more about what goes into a good thriller than anyone else I've encountered.

Dawn Wooten completed the final proofreading and also provided sound editing advice in key scenes.

It goes without saying, I must again thank the Kingdom and people of Thailand, who never fail to provide this author with an endless string of intriguing tales and kindness.

Once again, a deep appreciation to my wife, Josie, for her understanding of the writer's obsessions and delusions.

ABOUT THE AUTHOR

Stephen Shaiken practiced criminal law for more than thirty-five years, the first four in Brooklyn, and the rest in San Francisco. He is a graduate of Queens College and Brooklyn Law School and earned a MA in Creative Writing from San Francisco State University before starting his legal studies. He and his wife, Josie, are residents of Tampa, Florida.

Stephen lived in Bangkok, Thailand, for several years and has authored four novels in the acclaimed NJA Club Series, best described as exotic noir thrillers. The four novels-*Bangkok Shadows, Bangkok Whispers, Bangkok Blues, and Bangkok Changes* -feature American expat lawyer Glenn Murray Cohen and his eclectic friends from Bangkok's mysterious NJA Club as they face intrigue and danger.

Stephen recently published *Queensborough Rock* - a different kind of novel, set in New York City in the late sixties and early seventies. The protagonist is a young rock and roll manager struggling to break out of the second-tier Queens rock scene into the glamor and stardom of Manhattan. The novel was loosely inspired by Stephen's brief career as a rock manager in 1970-71.

When he isn't writing, Stephen enjoys travel, gardening, yoga, guitar, and following politics and current events with a passion. He's a voracious reader of fiction and nonfiction in too many genres and subjects to list. Stephen and Josie just adopted a greyhound rescue dog named Ginger.

Stephen's Blog
http://www.stephenshaiken.com

Follow Stephen on Twitter
https://twitter.com/StephenShaiken

Sign up to receive Stephen's Newsletter
http://eepurl.com/dBomIX

ALSO BY STEPHEN SHAIKEN

NJA Club Novels

Bangkok Shadows - Book 1

Bangkok Whispers - Book 2

Bangkok Blues - Book 3

Bangkok Changes - Book 4

Bangkok Circles - Book 5

Standalone

Queensborough Rock

www.ingramcontent.com/pod-product-compliance
Lightning Source LLC
Chambersburg PA
CBHW060423180626
46817CB00007B/2639